A Valiant Quest for THE MISFIT MENAGERIE

A Valiant Quest for THE MISFIT MENAGERIE

Jacqueline Resnick

razОr
bill

An Imprint of Penguin Group (USA) Inc.

razOr
bill

A division of Penguin Young Readers Group
Published by the Penguin Group
Penguin Group (USA) Inc., 345 Hudson Street
New York, New York 10014, U.S.A.

USA / Canada / UK / Ireland / Australia / New Zealand / India / South Africa / China
Penguin Books Ltd, Registered Offices: 80 Strand, London WC2R 0RL, England
For more information about the Penguin Group visit penguin.com

Published simultaneously in Canada

Library of Congress Cataloging-in-Publication Data is available.

ISBN: 978-1-59514-590-1

Printed in the United States of America

1 3 5 7 9 10 8 6 4 2

This is a work of fiction. Names, characters, places, and incidents either are the product of the author's imagination or are used fictitiously, and any resemblance to actual persons, living or dead, businesses, companies, events, or locales is entirely coincidental.

**Misfit Menagerie novels
by Jacqueline Resnick:**

The Daring Escape of the Misfit Menagerie

A Valiant Quest for the Misfit Menagerie

*For my sister, Lauren, who dreamed
with me from the beginning.*

1

No More Cupboards

"No more burlap-sack beds," Bertie whispered. "No more early mornings in the Big Top or late nights scrubbing caravans."

Susan turned onto her back, pushing a strand of long blond hair off her face. She and Bertie were lying with the animals in a makeshift bed of leaves on the ground. Through a gap in the willow tree above them, she could see the sun starting to slink into the sky, sending fingers of light filtering through the branches. "No more dry oats for breakfast," she said. "Or lunch or dinner." It was their new favorite game: What We Won't Miss about the Circus. They'd been playing it ever since their escape two nights ago.

"No more fingernails in our faces," Bertie said triumphantly. He was leaning against Smalls, his head propped up against the bear's back. Wombat was curled up in his arm, his furry snout tucked under his hand.

"No more stinky hot cocoa breath," Susan shot back. She threaded her fingers through Rigby's long white tufts of fur. The dog's head was resting on her leg, his cold, wet nose pressed against her ankle. "I used to love hot cocoa," she added grudgingly. "But after watching your uncle chug it down by the urn-full for six months . . ." She shuddered. "I never want to see or smell it again."

Bertie wrinkled his freckled nose, making a sour face. "I never want to see or smell *him* again. Which reminds me"—his lips turned up in a smile—"no more cupboards to be locked up in."

"No more blisters or rope burn," Susan chimed in happily. She could feel the words fizzing out of her, like cola from a fountain. She held up a hand, raw from hours spent twirling on the aerial ropes. "No more never-ending practices."

Several strands of bright red hair slipped into Bertie's bright blue eyes as he looked over at Susan. "Honestly, I don't know what that kind of life *feels* like." For an instant, his face clouded over, and Susan wondered if he was thinking about the motor-car crash from years ago, the one that stole his memories and made him an orphan in one fell swoop.

"It feels incredible," she assured him. "And amazing and fantastic and . . ."

"Stupendous?" Wombat offered groggily, opening one eye. He yawned as, around him, the other animals began to wake as well.

"Like being home," Susan finished. "Well . . . almost." She reached into the waistband of her shimmery blue skirt and pulled out the letter she'd stuck there. It had started to crumple around the edges, and she smoothed it out now as she read it over once more. It was proof—real and tangible—that her parents wanted her, that they'd always wanted her.

For six months, Bertie's uncle Claude, the owner of the Most Magnificent Traveling Circus, had hidden her parents' letters from her, made her believe she'd been abandoned. But now she knew the truth: in a small farmhouse in the town of Mulberry, her parents were waiting for her. She closed her eyes, picturing her home: the fields of berries that glistened like rubies in the sun; the jewel-blue waves trailing clouds of foam into the sand; the way the house seemed to sparkle in the early morning light, as if shards of diamonds were trapped inside the stone. It was a treasure chest of a home, a place that made you feel rich, no matter how far from it you were. Something pulsed inside her chest. She wanted so badly to be there, to see her parents with her very own eyes and feel their arms wrapping around her.

"You must really miss it," Bertie said softly.

Susan opened her eyes to find Bertie's freckled face staring down at her. He'd sat up and was now tugging absently at his suspenders as the animals began to stand and stretch around him. "I do," she admitted. Above them, orange sunlight swept across the sky, and the woods were suddenly alive with sounds. Trees whispered and twigs cracked. The high whistle of a bird drifted in from a distance. "I miss waking up to *my* sounds, you know?"

Bertie stared at her, unblinking, and it hit her that he didn't—that until now, the only sounds he knew were the angry, muted ones of the circus: the roar of the crowd, and Claude's nasal whine, and the groaning of the caravans as they trundled through the night.

"My favorite is how I can hear the ocean from my bed," she told him. "Sometimes it sounds like it's talking just to me." She could feel tears pricking at her eyes, and she blinked hard, looking down.

"You're going to get back there," Bertie told her, his voice low and determined. "*We're* going to get you back there."

"After we find Tilda," Susan said firmly. She looked back up, meeting Bertie's eyes.

Tilda the Angora rabbit was part of the Misfit Menagerie,

as they'd come to be known, along with Smalls the sun bear, Rigby the Komondor dog, and Wombat the hairy-nosed wombat. At least she was until a few days ago—when Claude sold her off to make a quick buck. But last night, after the animals drifted off, Bertie told Susan he had a plan: now that they'd escaped from the circus, he was going to do whatever it took to reunite Tilda with the Menagerie, to make his new family whole again. "When Smalls came to the circus, he saved me," Bertie had said in a hushed voice as the animals slept soundly around them. "He changed my whole life. It's my turn to do the same for him."

Now, Bertie released his suspenders, breaking into a smile. "After we find Tilda," he agreed.

Behind Bertie, Wombat nodded furiously. "That's correct," he said as he launched into step one of Tilda's sixteen-step grooming process. "Our first matter of business is procuring Tilda from wherever she's being held captive!"

"Are you really grooming *again*, Wombat?" Rigby asked with a groan. He walked over to Smalls, several golden-hued leaves clinging stubbornly to his long strands of fur.

"It makes me feel like I'm communing with Tilda," Wombat huffed. He picked several specks of dirt out of his fur, step two in Tilda's grooming process. "This is what you do when you're separated from the love of your life, the peanut butter to your jelly, the stars to your moon, the web to your spider, the—"

"It's a great idea, Wombat," Smalls jumped in. He shot Rigby a warning look. The last thing they needed was to set Wombat off again. In the one day since they'd escaped from the circus, he'd been particularly temperamental, constantly swapping between bemoaning Tilda's absence and scolding Smalls and Rigby for not moving fast enough. "We're on a quest!" he kept shouting. "There's no time for dillydallying!" It had gotten even worse after the Lifers had taken off the night before to go look for Lord Jest—leaving them without the protection of two lions.

"Thank you, Smalls," Wombat said primly. He buffed his stubby tail up against a leaf. "As you're aware, we're on a most vital quest, and I know my love, Tilda, would want me to look my best on a quest." He paused, cocking his head. "Look at that, I'm a poet."

"And you didn't even know it," Rigby joked.

As Rigby and Wombat began listing words that rhymed with quest—*test, west, zest!*—Smalls rubbed absently at the yellow marking of a horseshoe on his chest, watching Bertie talk to Susan. They were both still wearing their outfits from the circus: Susan in her acrobat's uniform of a leotard and skirt, old ballet slippers on her feet, and Bertie in his threadbare white shirt and too-short brown pants, held up by a pair of red suspenders.

Smalls watched as Bertie broke into a smile; he listened as Wombat snorted and Rigby barked; he inhaled the sweet scent of autumn leaves swirling around him. All of a sudden, he felt something tingling inside him, a feeling he'd missed since being hauled off to the circus. *Excitement.*

It was the best kind: warm and bubbly, the kind that started at his ears and spread all the way down to his claws. The last time he'd felt it, he'd been at his old home at Mumford's Farm & Orchard, playing Capture the Clover with Wombat, Rigby, and Tilda.

Tilda. Smalls sat back on his haunches, feeling more determined than ever. Bertie and Susan were right: there was an Angora rabbit–sized hole in their midst, and they had to do whatever it took to fill it. To make their family whole. Then things could finally be right again.

"If only I was proficient in time travel," Wombat said wistfully, drawing Smalls out of his thoughts. "Then I could deliver us back to Mumford's, to before the circus and the escape, when we were all still together . . ."

"No!" The grunt burst right out of Smalls. "Then we would never have met Bertie." He looked over at the fiery-haired boy, who had pushed his baseball cap off his head to soak in the morning sun. A month ago, Smalls hadn't even known Bertie existed; now he couldn't imagine his life without him.

"Or Susan," Rigby added, his tail thumping against the ground.

"But don't worry, Wombat," Smalls said fiercely. "We're not going to let that whiny little girl who bought Tilda get away with it."

Smalls growled under his breath at the memory. That curly-haired girl had stomped into their caravan wearing a ridiculously poufy yellow dress and bought Tilda right out from under their noses. "We're going to get Tilda back," Smalls swore. "No matter what kind of testy, zesty quest it takes us on." He touched a paw to the four-leaf clover tucked behind his ear. Lucky clovers always used to flock to him, but so far he hadn't found a single new one in the woods. He would, though; he had to. Once he had his luck back, they would be sure to find Tilda. "I promise," he said, locking eyes with Wombat.

Bertie looked over at the sound of Smalls's grunts. "Sometimes I swear Smalls is *talking* to the other animals," he told Susan.

"Who knows?" Susan smiled. Flecks of green shone in her light brown eyes. "Maybe he is."

Bertie walked over to Smalls, scratching him absently

under his chin. "I bet you're thinking about your friends, aren't you?" he murmured. He'd been thinking about them a lot, too. Not just Tilda, but also Lord Jest. Every time he closed his eyes, he could hear it: the thundering crash as Lord Jest leapt in front of Claude's car. The elephant had stopped the car from hitting Bertie and Smalls, and now Bertie had no idea if he was okay . . . or even alive.

Bertie swallowed hard. The memory made him want to jump up and race all the way back to the circus grounds. But he couldn't. Because if Lord Jest was still there, then his uncle Claude would be too. The thought of facing his uncle again made Bertie feel like he'd just swallowed a live toad. The second Claude saw him, he'd probably lock him up in a cupboard for a whole year. And then Bertie would be of no help to anyone.

Bertie touched a hand to his pocket, trying to think of something—anything—else. He could feel the outline of the small wooden boy he'd found abandoned on the circus grounds. Yesterday, he'd noticed something new: a stamp on the underside of the boy's foot, two bright green *T*'s, connected at the top. He was itching to take the boy out now and examine those letters again. *TT*. What could they stand for? A litany of options ran through his head. Tiny Toy? Terrific Tim? Terrible Terry?

But Susan was sitting right next to him. What would she think if she saw he'd brought a doll along? Not that it was *really* a doll. It was a wooden figurine, which, when you thought about it, was a different thing entirely. Still, Bertie kept the wooden boy tucked safely inside his pocket.

He'd dreamed about the figurine again last night. In his dream, he was lying on a bed—a big, plush, downy bed, in his very own bedroom—making the boy gallop stiffly across his pillow. He'd come up with a voice for him too, and he'd been so busy pretending the boy was talking that he hadn't heard anyone enter the room. But suddenly he'd looked up, and there she was. His mom.

Her flame-red hair hung loosely over her shoulders and she was laughing as she watched him, a soft, happy laugh. "I didn't think your little guy should be alone," she said, holding out her hand. In her palm lay two new wooden figurines: a woman with flame-red hair and a man with bright blue eyes. "He needs his parents."

The next thing Bertie knew, he was waking with a jolt to find himself on the hard ground instead of a plush bed. As he lay there under the willow tree, running through that scene in his head again and again, he'd gotten the strangest feeling that it wasn't so much a dream as a memory.

"And then I'll jump off a cliff."

Bertie started a little at the sound of Susan's voice.

"Finally." Susan elbowed him playfully in the side. "I only had to threaten cliff-jumping to get your attention."

"Sorry," Bertie said. "I was just . . ." He trailed off. He wanted desperately to tell Susan about the wooden boy and the memories it had been drawing out of him drop by drop, like sap from a tree. But every time he tried, he wimped out. Those memories were all he had of his mom, and the idea of voicing them out loud, letting them loose in the world, terrified him. "I was just . . ."

"Daydreaming?" Susan offered.

Bertie blinked in surprise. "Remembering a dream, actually." He took a deep breath. Here went nothing.

In one fluid motion, he yanked the wooden boy out of his pocket. It had bright blue eyes painted onto it and a shock of painted red hair sticking out from beneath a tiny wooden baseball cap. He handed it to Susan. "I found him on the circus grounds before we left." He said it so fast that the words came out in a big jumble, one bumping into another. Susan gave him a strange look as she lifted the wooden boy up to the sunlight, examining it. "It's not a doll," Bertie added hastily. "It's a wooden figurine, which is really very different because—"

"He looks like a younger you," Susan interjected. She

didn't seem the least bit concerned about whether it was technically a doll or a figurine. She touched a finger to the boy's red hair. "Exactly like a younger you, actually."

"That's why I took him," Bertie admitted. "That and . . . he reminds me of my mom." He blinked in surprise. He'd said it. And hearing it out loud, in his own voice, had actually felt good. "I have this memory of her giving the same kind of figurine to me when I was younger. When I look at him, it's like the fog in my head clears a little, and I can remember things about her again. Just bits and pieces: her voice, her hair, the way she laughed. But it's more than I've had in a long time."

"Like a memory trigger," Susan said thoughtfully. "We did an experiment like that in school once. All different things can trigger memories: images, sounds, even smells."

"Well, what's not triggering a memory is this." Bertie reached over, turning the boy upside down so Susan could see the two green *T*'s stamped onto its foot. "I've been trying like crazy to figure out what it means."

Susan burst out laughing. "Every kid in America knows what that means!" She paused, her face darkening. "Well, every kid who didn't grow up with Claude *un*-Magnificence," she amended, crossing her eyes at the memory of Bertie's uncle. "It's the logo for Toddle's Toys."

Bertie plucked a blade of grass, wrapping it slowly around his finger. "Toddle's Toys," he repeated.

"Toddle's Toy Emporium is the biggest toy store in the country," Susan told him. "Probably even the world. I've never been, but kids at school used to talk about it all the time. It's this huge building, supposedly, and it's filled with every toy imaginable, tons you've never even heard of before . . ."

Susan kept talking, but Bertie had stopped listening. Because in his head several pieces were suddenly clicking into place, one after another.

Toddle's Toy Emporium. An image of a watery-eyed woman flashed through Bertie's mind. *That was it.* That was where she'd said she'd taken Tilda! He'd been struggling to remember ever since their escape. But he could swear he'd seen that name elsewhere too . . .

Everything had happened so quickly the night of their escape that he'd forgotten all about the check he'd taken out of Claude's cocoa urn, the one inscribed with the words *For the rabbit.* Bertie dug into his pocket. *Please still be there*, he begged silently.

At the very bottom, he felt it: a thin sheet of paper coated in lint and crumpled into a ball. His breath released in fast spurts as he smoothed it out on the grass. *For the rabbit,* someone had written along the bottom, just like he remembered. Typed in the top left corner of the check was a name: *The Toddles*. And beneath that name was an address: *Toddle's Toy Emporium, 1 Toddle Lane, Hoolyloo City.*

Click. The final piece of the puzzle fell into place.

Tilda was at Toddle's Toy Emporium, the very place where Bertie's wooden boy had come from.

And he had the address.

"I know where Tilda is!" he burst out. Nearby, Smalls, Rigby, and Wombat all bolted upright, almost as if they'd understood Bertie's words. "She's at Toddle's Toy Emporium," he continued. He held up the check for Susan to see. "The same place where the wooden boy came from." He paused, excitement zipping through him like a bolt of lightning. He would look for Tilda at Toddle's, but he would also look for that wooden boy—his memory trigger. Maybe it would help him remember something more about the past, about *his* home. A smile spread across his face. "It looks like we're going to the biggest toy store in the world."

2

Jumping Through Hoops

In the highest room of a tall stone house, Tilda was suffering through a game of dress-up with her new owner, Chrysanthemum. "You look *marvelous*," Chrysanthemum screeched as she yanked a frilly pink doll's dress over Tilda's head.

"I look like an oversized Barbie," Tilda grumbled. She knew all about Barbie dolls now. She also knew about Pretty Princess dolls and Kangaroo Pocket dolls and Chrysanthemum's personal favorite, I-Pee-Like-You dolls. Tilda twisted out of Chrysanthemum's grip, backing up into the fluffy purple blanket that dangled off the canopy bed. Across from her, Toddle's Toy Emporium rose on the other side of a large, arched window.

Chrysanthemum giggled. "You have the funniest squeak, Carnation."

"My. Name. Is. Tilda!" Tilda yelled. But it only made

Chrysanthemum laugh harder. On Tilda's first day living with Chrysanthemum, she'd renamed her Carnation, so they could both be named after flowers. "Like twins!!!" she'd squealed.

Tilda shook her head. "Why does no one seem to understand that I already *have* a name? A very pleasant one, if you ask me! Wombat would agree with me if he were here." A sad look flitted across her face. "Where are you now, Wombat?" she whispered. She glanced hopefully back out the window, as if at any second a hairy-nosed wombat might come crashing through it.

"Time to walk the runway," Chrysanthemum announced, patting the red sheet she'd rolled out across the purple-carpeted floor. "Just wait until Lauren Nicola sees you in this outfit," Chrysanthemum said, twirling down her makeshift runway. "Especially when I show her this." Chrysanthemum held a small, sparkly hoop in front of Tilda. "Jump!" she commanded.

Tilda rolled her eyes. "I thought I left the circus."

"Jump!" Chrysanthemum repeated, her voice leaping into a screechy whine. "We only have an hour before I leave for school!"

"If it will keep you quiet . . ." Tilda leapt through the hoop, landing smoothly on the other side.

"Again!" Chrysanthemum cheered, clapping her hands together.

Tilda let out a loud sigh as she jumped back through the hoop. As she landed on all fours, she looked longingly up at the window once more. "Please save me, Wombat," she whispered.

3

The Wombatopolis Theorem

The group had been walking for over an hour when Smalls, Wombat, Rigby, Susan, and Bertie found themselves facing a soaring oak tree with the initials *NJR* carved into its trunk. "Not again," Bertie groaned. This was the third time they'd ended up in front of this very tree. Bertie clenched his hands into fists at his side. They'd been following a wisp of gray smoke they'd seen curling into the sky, in the hope that it would lead them out of the woods, to wherever there might be a chimney. Instead, it had led them right back to where they'd started. "And now I can't even see the smoke anymore."

Susan tilted her head up, using her hand to shield her eyes from the sun. A single white cloud drifted lazily along in the sky, marring the otherwise spotless stretch of blue. "It's gone," she confirmed.

A few feet away, Smalls rubbed nervously at the horse-shoe on his chest. "Holy horseshoe," he muttered. "This is not good."

"This simply cannot be," Wombat balked. He furrowed his snout as he stared up at the tree. "According to the ancient Greek Wombatopolis Theorem, the sun should be leading us forward, not backward. And certainly not in circles!"

"Where did you learn this Wombatty theory anyway, Wombat?" Rigby asked, flopping down next to him with a yawn.

"Wombatopolis Theorem," Wombat corrected indignantly. "And it is simply part of my innate set of knowledge. It would be part of yours too if you were a wombat with an IQ of five thousand."

Rigby plucked a purple wildflower with his teeth and wove it into his fur. "Can your IQ of five thousand explain why we're right back where we started?"

Wombat glanced up at the blazing sun, which was making them all pant in spite of the cool autumn air. "It's obvious, isn't it? The sun must have risen incorrectly today." He shook his snout, looking frustrated.

Behind Wombat, Bertie was pacing in tight circles. "One Toddle Lane, Hoolyloo City," he murmured, as if the words could somehow make the Emporium magically appear. Instead, they just made him wince. His throat felt as dry and cracked as a piece of sandpaper.

"If only we could blink our eyes and be there," Susan sighed.

"Blinking Boy," Bertie said wistfully. "That's a hero I wouldn't mind being." Bertie had spent his whole life dreaming up hero counterparts for himself, alter egos that would allow him to escape his dreary, dismal life. When he'd run away from the circus, he'd felt like a true hero for the first time—no alter ego necessary. But here in the woods, homeless and lost, he felt very much like a plain, ten-year-old boy again. A hero wouldn't just *sit* here, he thought angrily. He would do something. He would fix this.

Susan let out a dry cough. "I would take Water Boy too," she said with a weak laugh.

Bertie straightened up. Susan was right. He could hear Smalls clearing his throat and Rigby barking hoarsely. They all needed water. Bertie paced faster. He might not be able to blink them to Hoolyloo, but he *could* do this.

A few years ago, back when he was traveling with the circus, Bertie had snuck out to follow Alfredo, one of the circus's old performers. Alfredo was known in performance circles as a Purveyor of Natural Wonders, and Bertie had been dying to follow him on one of his famous treks into the woods.

That day, Bertie had followed Alfredo down a long, steep hill. When they'd finally reached a tiny creek at the bottom, Alfredo had pumped his fists triumphantly into the air. "Just like I thought," he'd said. "Water always drains downward."

Now, Bertie turned slowly around, studying the leaf-speckled ground. Off to his right, the grass sloped downward the slightest bit. "That way!" he exclaimed.

Susan raised her eyebrows. "That way what?"

"See how the ground slopes downhill? I'm going to follow it until I find us some water," Bertie declared.

"Not alone you're not," Susan countered. She fixed Bertie with a steely gaze. "If you go, I go."

Bertie's dry, chapped lips curled up at the corners. "I know better than to say no to that look." Turning to Smalls, he lifted his hand in the air. It was a gesture he'd used countless times during their training sessions at the circus. "Stay," Bertie said firmly, using a command he was sure Smalls would recognize. Instantly, Smalls sat back on his haunches. "Good boy," Bertie beamed. "We'll be back soon."

The instant Susan and Bertie were out of sight, Smalls jumped back to his feet, making his four-leaf clover flap behind his ear. "If Bertie's getting water, then it's our job to find food," he told the others. He pawed thoughtfully at the ground. "And in honor of our mission, I've created a new game."

"Game?" Wombat spit out. "There's no time for games on a quest, Smalls. This very minute Tilda is probably waiting for me, perfectly coiffed!"

Smalls suppressed a groan. *He's hurting*, he reminded himself. Last night, Smalls had woken up to the sound of Wombat whispering Tilda's name in his sleep. "This game is part of our quest," he said gently. "We'll never make it to Tilda on empty stomachs."

Wombat let out a begrudging sigh. "All right, just make it *très rapide*." He stuck his snout in the air. "That means 'very fast' in French."

Rigby shook several strands of fur out of his eyes. "I'm ready," he panted. "What's the game?"

"I call it Food-and-Seek," Smalls announced. "The first one to find food in the woods wins! And extra points for honey," he added quickly. At the thought of his favorite food, a list unrolled in his mind.

Times I've Gone without Honey:
1. When it was offered to me by a hyena who wanted a bear claw in return.
2. When that pesky squirrel Lorenzo decided to make my honey dish his own personal toilet.
3. At the Most Magnificent Traveling Circus.

Smalls had no interest in adding a number four to that list.

"My burrowing skills will make me a perfect candidate for victory," Wombat said. "I bet I dig up a whole beehive." He cleared his throat. "In a *très rapide* fashion, of course."

Smalls nodded solemnly. "Of course. Okay, on three we disperse. Good luck, fellow players." He reached up to touch his four-leaf clover, which was slowly beginning to wilt behind his ear. "One. Two—"

"Trois!" Wombat cut in. With an excited grunt, he took off waddling through the woods.

Smalls gave Rigby a nod. "Three," he confirmed. Instantly, he and Rigby galloped off in different directions.

Smalls's eyes jumped expertly from bush to plant as he loped through the woods. The sun bore down on him, making his black fur feel lit with flames, but he willed himself to ignore it. He had a game to win. His legs pumped faster. His eyes doubled forward and backward, not wanting to miss a thing. But it wasn't until he scrambled up a tree for a better vantage point that he finally saw it.

His breath caught in his throat. Just a few yards away was a bush crowded with fat, pink berries. Smalls was back on the ground and in front of the bush in two seconds flat. A syrupy scent wafted off the berries. His stomach let out a hungry growl at its pungent sweetness.

But as Smalls stepped closer, he caught a whiff of another smell too, a darker, denser scent. It lingered among the leaves, as if under all those ripe, juicy berries, something was rotting. Smalls sniffed furiously at the air. One second the berries smelled sweet, and the next sour. Deep down inside him, something began to tingle—a gut feeling, the kind that told him when snow was on its way or a storm was brewing. This time, it was telling him he didn't want those berries.

Still, Smalls moved closer. He was so hungry, and the berries looked so delicious. Besides, if he brought some back, he would win the game! He stretched out his long pink tongue.

"Stop!" Wombat flung his small furry body between Smalls and the bush. "I forbid you to lay a tongue on those berries! Those are billyons, the most poisonous berries known to bear." He shuddered. "Just one bite and all your fur would have fallen out. And then every one of your claws and each of your eyeballs and—"

Smalls held up a paw to stop Wombat. "I get the picture," he said shakily, stepping away from the bush.

"Just wait until I tell Tilda that I saved your life!" Wombat said proudly. "She'll think me a hairy-nosed hero!"

Smalls looked over at his friend. His stomach was growling louder than ever. "Did you find anything better?" he asked hopefully. "Honeycomb, perhaps?"

"I saved your life, Smalls," Wombat sniffed. "I can't do *everything.*"

Smalls turned longingly back to the billyon berries. It took every ounce of his willpower not to tear into them, let their juicy sweetness pool inside him. "Let's just hope Rigby is having better luck than we are."

Rigby was deep inside a tangle of branches. They snagged and yanked at his long tufts of fur, but still he pushed forward. He chanted a pep talk to himself as he did. "I will find food. I will find food. I will . . ." He trailed off as an unusual smell caught his attention.

"Musky yet sweet . . . spicy yet pleasant . . ." He crouched down in front of a small spiky rock with an excited bark. "Coconut," he decided. "No, kiwi. No, an oversized nut!" He crept closer, sniffing wildly. "Yes, definitely some kind of—OW!"

Rigby let out a howl as his nose bumped up against the spiky rock. He leapt backward, pawing frantically at the spot where the spikes had stabbed his muzzle.

"Serves you right for thinking I was a nut."

Rigby froze. Slowly, his eyes traveled down to the ground. There, standing in the grass, was the spiky rock. Except it wasn't a rock. And it wasn't a nut. It was an animal.

Rigby let out a surprised yelp.

"What, you've never seen a hedgehog before?" the animal demanded. He plucked one of the long, sharp spikes off his back, holding it in front of him like a sword. "State your name and purpose!"

Rigby stared silently at the hedgehog, his muzzle trembling.

The hedgehog took a step toward Rigby, waving his quill-sword menacingly. "Declare yourself as friend or foe instantly, or I'll be forced to battle you!"

"I'm a friend!" Rigby croaked. "My name is Rigby."

Slowly, the hedgehog lowered his quill. "Why didn't you just say that in the first place?" He tucked the quill back in among the others. "Welcome to Maplehedge Woods, Rigby. I'm Alfie."

4

An IQ of Seven Thousand

A scream. At the sound, every strand of fur on Smalls's body stood on end. He would know that voice anywhere. Bertie was in trouble. Kicking up his paws, he took off racing toward the sound. Somewhere in the woods, Wombat and Rigby were still caught up in their game of Food-and-Seek, but eating was suddenly the last thing on Smalls's mind. He threw back his head, letting out an earth-shattering roar. "I'm coming, Bertie!"

Smalls's paws ate up the ground as his muscles clenched and released, instinct taking over. The memory of Bertie's scream looped through his mind again and again, urging him on. He leapt over a fallen tree and tore through a patch of bramble. He trampled through overgrown grass and plowed through a pile of fallen leaves. Under branches and over bushes, around a poison ivy patch and over a gaping, muddy hole. To his right, he caught a glimpse of what looked to be fruit, but he didn't even slow. Only when water rushed over his paws, dampening his fur, did he skid to a stop.

There, letting out a yell of joy as he splashed in a river with Susan, was Bertie. Smalls heard the growl of relief before he realized it was coming from him.

"Smalls!" Bertie broke into a huge smile when he spotted him. "Look what we found." He threw his arms up, spraying water through the air. "Drink up!"

Smalls yelped with excitement as he thrust his muzzle into the water. Cool and fresh, it tasted almost as good as honey. He was in the middle of a nice, long drink when the sound of Rigby's bark made him look up. A blur of white was racing toward him, like a mop head flying through the air. At his side was a furry wombat, his short legs working overtime to keep up with Rigby's long ones. "We heard your roar," Wombat panted. "We came as fast as we could."

The animals stumbled to a stop at the water's edge. At the sight of the river, Wombat's eyes widened. "You found H_2O," he cheered. He dunked his head into the river and began guzzling away.

"Well, look what *I* found," Rigby said proudly. He turned to the side, and for the first time, Smalls saw the tiny spiked animal standing on his back, his paws wrapped tightly around

Rigby's long fur. "I won the game!" Rigby said gleefully.

"No!" Smalls hollered. He leapt over to Rigby in a single stride. "That's not food, Rigby!"

Rigby shook out his fur, forcing the animal to hold on for dear life. "Of course it's not food," Rigby replied. "This is Alfie the hedgehog. I met him in the bushes."

"I stabbed him with my quills," Alfie offered. He had a wispy voice and beady black eyes that studied Smalls appraisingly.

Wombat lifted his head from the river. Water dripped down his snout, darkening his brown fur. "Yes, you've already informed us of that five times," he griped. "Now can you please stop blathering on about your quills and direct us to this patch of raspberries you claim to know so much about?"

"See?" Rigby snorted happily. "Alfie knows where we can find raspberries. Like I said: I won the game!"

"Who cares who won?" Wombat said impatiently. "What we require is food, so we can get on our way!" As Wombat continued to snort angrily, Susan and Bertie climbed out of the river and crouched down next to Rigby to get a better look at the hedgehog on his back.

"He's so cute," Susan cooed.

"He's like a spiky little hamster," Bertie added.

"Cute?" Alfie spat out. "Hamster? I carry over three

hundred weapons on my back and have dueled with almost every animal in Maplehedge Woods, thank you very much."

"And each of your quills is hollow inside," Wombat said, sounding exasperated. "I think that covers all we need to know about hedgehogs. Now can we please get going?"

"A hairy-nosed wombat who knows his hedgehog facts?" Alfie looked surprised. "I'm impressed."

Wombat's ears flickered appreciatively. "It is true I'm no ordinary hairy-nosed wombat," he acknowledged. "I have an IQ of seven thousand."

"It's seven thousand now?" Rigby asked. He stuck his snout into the river, jostling Alfie a little as he happily lapped up water.

"Of course it is," Wombat snapped. "I think I would know my own IQ. Especially considering that I know every word in the English language and most in French as well. In fact—" Suddenly he stopped short, clearing his throat. "We don't have time for this!" he scolded. "We need to eat so we can get moving again." He glanced up at the sky. "According to my precise metric calculations, we only have a few hours of sunlight left, and we still have no idea how to get to Hoolyloo City."

"You're going to Hoolyloo City?" Alfie's wispy voice dropped to a hushed whisper. "Why would you do *that*? Only the bravest of animals dare to venture into Hoolyloo."

Wombat whipped in Alfie's direction. "Are you indicating that you know where Hoolyloo is?"

"Of course I do. I've *been* to Hoolyloo." Alfie reached for his quill sword, rolling it between his paws. "And I barely lived to tell about it."

5

A World Record

In the highest room of the tall stone house behind Toddle's Toy Emporium, Tilda was suffering through one of Chrysanthemum's afternoon games. "Now remember, Carnation," Chrysanthemum instructed. "You have to swim your fastest when I drop you in the water. I'm going to time you, and then we're going to make the *Guinness Book of World Records*!" She smiled smugly. "Lauren Nicola and the other girls will *have* to notice me then."

Tilda stared in horror at the huge water-filled bathtub. "Uh uh," she said, backing away. "Absolutely not. The only thing I like less than getting muddy is getting wet!" She shuddered. "The way my fur gets so heavy and soppy and sticks to my body, it's . . . it's . . . revolting, as Wombat would say!"

"I know, Carnation," Chrysanthemum said, nodding

solemnly. "This is my best idea yet." She picked Tilda up, holding her over the white claw-footed bathtub.

"Let. Me. GO!" Tilda wiggled and squirmed, but Chrysanthemum held on tight. "Looks like someone's excited," she said cheerfully. "Okay, here we go." She dropped Tilda into the tub, sending water splattering everywhere.

"Ahhh!" Tilda sputtered, spitting out a stream of water. "Cold! Wet! Slimy!"

Chrysanthemum held up a watch. "Get ready and . . . swim!" she commanded.

Tilda eyed the other end of the bathtub, where freedom—and dryness—awaited her. "Just so you know, this is not for some record," she grumbled. She took off swimming, her tiny paws paddling like her life depended on it. "Awful!" she screeched as she scrambled out on the other side. Her fur was wet and flattened against her back, making her look like a scrawny, bedraggled mouse. "Happy?" she spat out. "I'm going to have to groom for hours to look like myself again."

Chrysanthemum applauded. "That was fun!"

Tilda glowered at her. "About as fun as being eaten by a lion."

"What's that you're squeaking about?" Chrysanthemum leaned down, petting Tilda's matted, wet fur. "Are you saying you want to go again?" She picked Tilda up, dangling her over the bathtub. "If you insist!"

"I do not!" Tilda squeaked. "I do *not* insist!"

"On three," Chrysanthemum continued, oblivious to the fury in Tilda's squeaks. "And this time, even faster. One, two, three!" She dropped Tilda into the tub with another splash. "Go!" she cheered. "Beat the world record!"

And Tilda was off, splashing angrily through the water once again.

6

A Wild, Overgrown Land

"There's a train that slithers through the woods twice a day like a giant gray snake," Alfie said. Around him, Susan, Bertie, and the animals were stuffing their mouths with raspberries from the patch he'd led them to. "It carries no passengers, only toys and toy parts. And it ends in Hoolyloo City. I learned to jump the train when I was just a baby hedgehog. Usually, I get off near my favorite blueberry bush, but one time I made the dire mistake of falling asleep. When I woke up, the train was pulling into Hoolyloo for the night."

"What did you do?" Rigby asked. He'd taken a break from eating and was now rubbing raspberry juice over his paws, admiring the way they became streaked with red.

"I did what any brave hedgehog would do. I had my precious gem with me, so I plucked a quill from my back, and with sword in paw, I embarked into the wilderness of the city." Alfie climbed onto a clump of raspberries, letting his tiny legs dangle off.

Smalls looked up from the pile of berries he'd been devouring. "What was it like?"

Alfie twirled his sword. "It was a wild, overgrown land, the kind of place that could eat a hedgehog alive." His eyes took on a distant glaze. "The first thing I encountered were mammoth hard-backed turtles in the strangest of colors. These turtles raced faster than wolves and roared as loud as thunder. And they were ruthless. They'd run you right over and never look back."

"I believe you're referring to motorcars," Wombat interjected, sending a thin line of juice trickling down his snout.

"No, they were definitely some kind of mutant turtle," Alfie insisted. "And there were trees with no leaves! They grew so tall they blocked the moon."

"Buildings, most likely," Wombat chimed in.

"And," Alfie went on, ignoring Wombat, "there were fallen stars everywhere! They were so bright, your eyes burned if you looked right at them. But worst of all were the gangs: cruel, thieving, lawless gangs. It was to one of these gangs that I lost my rare, precious gem. But don't fear." He thrust his sword into a nearby raspberry with a loud *hi-ya*! "I have spent two years studying with the sensei of hedgehogs, and soon I shall return to the city and win back what is rightfully mine!"

"Soon?" Wombat repeated. "How soon, precisely?"

Alfie cocked his head, studying the sky. "The sensei said that when the moon has completed two full cycles, I shall be ready."

"Or," Smalls said slowly, an idea taking shape in his head, "you *could* be ready now."

"That's right!" Rigby chimed in. "You could lead us into the big city."

Alfie twirled his sword through the air. "I don't know . . . a hedgehog in training must always listen to his sensei. It's a law of dueling."

Smalls made a strangled noise, trying not to laugh. "Of course," he said solemnly. "It's too bad, though. Because if you went now, you could return for your gem with your own gang in tow. Including"—he bared his fangs—"a bear."

Alfie studied Smalls's gleaming, razor-sharp fangs. "I suppose the moon *could* have completed two cycles already, without my realizing it . . ."

"Definitely," Smalls said.

"Absolutely," Wombat said.

"Sure," Rigby said.

"Plus," Wombat added, "you'd be assisting us greatly in our quest."

Alfie perked up instantly. "*Quest*? I didn't realize this was a quest! What kind? A duel to the death? A battle of the brains? A combat between comrades?"

"Nothing of the sort," Wombat reproached. "Our quest is an awe-inspiring, stupefying, valiant rescue!"

"Of a princess?" Alfie exhaled. "A beautiful, long-haired princess trapped in a tall tower?"

"Well, long-furred, to be accurate," Wombat said thoughtfully. "And in an emporium, not a tower."

"Valiant rescues are my specialty," Alfie said eagerly. "Once I rescued a baby chipmunk trapped in a tree, which everyone knows is practically the same thing as a princess in an emporium." He leapt down from the clump of raspberries, landing steadily on his paws. "That settles it," he declared, hoisting his sword into the air. He looked from Smalls to Wombat to Rigby. "Comrades, it's time we cross enemy lines, into Hoolyloo City!"

While the animals talked, Bertie and Susan lay sprawled out behind them, eating berry after berry. "I think I might explode," Susan groaned.

"Or turn into a raspberry," Bertie joked. He let out a long, contented sigh. He couldn't remember the last time he'd been this full. He felt like a squirrel storing away nuts for the winter—and he loved it. At the circus, everything had been rationed, regulated. He'd reach the end of a cup of dry oats, and he would know it would be hours until he could eat anything else. Never in all those years had he experienced what it was like to be truly and fully stuffed. Now he knew what he'd been missing out on.

Under his head, Bertie felt a soft rumbling in the grass. "Did you feel that?" he asked Susan.

"Feelmmm?" Susan replied through a mouthful of raspberry.

Bertie pressed his ear to the ground. The rumbling was still there, soft but steady. Every few seconds it grew just a little bit stronger, almost as if it were approaching them. "It feels almost like . . ." He was halfway through his sentence when he heard it, traveling through the earth until it reached his ears: the faintest sound of a steam whistle.

Bertie bolted upright. He'd heard that sound before. "It's a train!"

The raspberry Susan was holding slipped from her grip, tumbling to the grass. "Where?"

"I'm not sure." Bertie jumped to his feet, pulling Susan with him. "But we have to try to find it." He stuffed his pockets with berries as he spoke. "If we can get on it, it will have to take us to *some* sort of civilization. And then we're sure to find somebody who knows where Hoolyloo is!"

Over by the animals, Smalls perked up. "A train?" he murmured. He cocked his head, listening hard. Far in the distance, he could just make out the sound of a soft clanging, blowing toward them on the wind. "Bertie's right!" he blurted out. "There really is a train coming!"

"Of course there's a train coming." Alfie glowered at Smalls. "Weren't you listening to anything I said? It's the train to Hoolyloo!"

Smalls ran over to Bertie, grabbing one of his suspenders in his teeth. "Well then, we better go catch it."

7

A Running Jump

"To my left you'll find the spot where I escaped from the clutches of a coyote using only my quills," Alfie announced, walking backward as the group fought their way through a dense patch of woods, following the rumbling of the train. "And to my right is the bush where I had my very first duel, against a porcupine twice my size. I was triumphant, of course."

"How long until we reach the train tracks?" Wombat grumbled. Alfie had already showed them the tree where he had miraculously evaded a fox and the patch of dirt where he had gallantly speared a black widow spider.

"Just another couple minutes now," Alfie said vaguely. "Now, up ahead you'll see the creek where I bravely swam to safety from a rival gang of hedgehogs. And around this bend we have the—oh. We have the tracks."

"It's about time," Wombat muttered.

Smalls peered into the distance as the rumbling of the train grew louder. He'd heard all about trains before. There was a stop near their old home at Mumford's Farm & Orchard, and he used to listen to the visiting kids gush about their train ride: the plush velvet seats and the way the conductor walked up and down the aisle, collecting tickets. But he'd never actually *seen* a train before, and as this one shot toward them, long and gray and sleek, his jaw dropped open and his long pink tongue unfurled in surprise.

The train flew along the tracks, faster than any motorcar he'd ever seen. With every passing second, it seemed to grow larger. It let out a sharp whistle as a spiral of steam shot into the air. "Holy horseshoe," he said.

Behind Smalls, Bertie was steeling himself as he watched the train approach. Closer and closer it drew, and it wasn't slowing down. "We're going to have to jump on," he declared. He glanced nervously at Susan, worried she would refuse. But she nodded.

"Looks like it," she said gravely. "Which means we better start running. The question is, how do we tell the animals?"

"I've got that covered," Bertie said with a smile. "Smalls," he called out. "Run!" It was another one of the commands Bertie had used with Smalls during their circus training.

Finally, it could be put to *good* use. Smalls's eyes met his. In them he saw a flash of recognition—the same one he used to see before Smalls performed a trick flawlessly. Satisfied, Bertie grabbed Susan's hand, breaking into a sprint of his own. Immediately, he could hear Smalls and the other animals following behind them.

"We're going to need to do what's called a leap in ballet," Susan called out as the clanking of the train continued to grow louder. "Run as fast as you can and then do this." Letting go of Bertie's hand, she jumped gracefully into the air, her legs spreading out into a perfect split. "Got it?" she asked. She landed lightly on her feet and seamlessly resumed running.

Bertie swallowed hard. He wasn't an acrobat or a dancer like Susan; there was no way his body was moving like that. But there was no time to second guess their plan. Because suddenly the train was *there*, thundering toward them, a flash of silver and black.

Bertie looked back at Smalls, waving wildly to get his attention. "Jump!" he screamed over the hiss and roar of the train. He pointed behind them to a freight car with a broken door that hung open. "Jump on there!" He didn't have to time to wait and see if Smalls understood. He just had to trust him. He picked up his speed, racing alongside the train next to Susan. "Jump on three," he told her. Behind them, Smalls was grunting loudly, the deep sound rolling out around them.

"We need to jump on that car," he was telling the other animals, as they ran full speed next to the train.

"*Jump?*" Wombat croaked.

"Don't worry, it's as easy as a karate chop," Alfie assured him.

"On three, like Bertie said," Smalls called out. "One!" he began.

"Two!" Rigby chimed in.

"THREE!" Alfie finished, just as the broken freight car swung up next to them. All at once, everyone leapt into the air. Susan landed in the freight car first, sliding gracefully to the back. Smalls landed easily next to her, with Bertie, Alfie, and Rigby collapsing in a furry heap in front of him.

"We did it!" Bertie cheered, peeking out from under a patch of Rigby's fur.

No sooner had he uttered those words than, in quick succession, several things happened. First, the train hit a bump in the tracks, making it jolt heavily forward. Wombat, who had been in midair, loudly calculating the precise angle necessary for optimum landing, was suddenly thrown off course. Instead of landing smack in the middle of the freight car, as he'd predicted, he landed right on the edge, his back legs dangling off.

"Wombat!" Rigby howled, grabbing onto the scruff of Wombat's neck with his teeth. Immediately, Rigby began sliding forward, Wombat's weight dragging him out the door.

"Rigby!" Susan grabbed the back of Rigby's legs before he and Wombat could both tumble off the train. But she wasn't strong enough to stop them, and she too began to slide toward the edge, her skirt snagging on a loose floorboard.

"Susan!" Bertie reached for Susan's arm, trying desperately to pull her backward. But the weight of a ten-year-old boy was no match for a wombat, dog, and girl. The faster the train sped down the tracks, the closer the line slid toward the edge of the freight car. "Help!" Bertie screamed as Wombat's front paws slid off. Suddenly, Wombat was dangling in midair, connected to the train solely by Rigby's grip.

Smalls had been watching the scene unfold, frozen with fear. But that single word—a plea from Bertie—thawed him, and he leapt into motion. With a rip-roaring growl, he grabbed the back of Bertie's suspenders in his teeth and pulled with every ounce of bear strength he possessed.

Instantly, Bertie snapped backward, bringing Susan with

him. Rigby came next, and finally, with a disgruntled snort, Wombat flew into the car, landing in a heap on top of Rigby. For a moment, everyone was silent, breathing heavily.

Then Alfie, who'd been quivering quietly in the corner the whole time, leapt to his feet. "See?" he chirped, slashing his sword through the air. "As easy as a karate chop."

8

The Forgotten Car

Everywhere Smalls looked, there were broken toys. They were heaped into every corner and crevice of the freight car: torn stuffed animals stacked on top of limbless dolls, draped haphazardly over a pile of cracked trampolines. There were battered board games and splintered building blocks and torn Halloween costumes and a tall pyramid built entirely out of toy cans of food, all dented and bruised. Smalls pressed closer to Bertie. The whole thing gave him the eeriest feeling, like he was sitting in a graveyard of toys.

"The other freight cars carry new toys and unused toy parts," Alfie informed the animals. "But this one . . ." He paused, his gaze trailing from an eyeless rocking horse to a tin man who had lost both his hands. "This one is the Forgotten Car."

"The what?" Rigby asked. He trembled a little as he climbed into Susan's lap.

"It's where all the rejected, broken toys are tossed," Alfie explained.

"And apparently," Wombat added softly, "the rejected, forgotten animals."

"No," Smalls said forcefully. "We are neither of those things, not if we're all together. And when this train takes us to Tilda, we will be."

Wombat glanced out the broken door, where the sun was setting rapidly outside. "I wonder if my Tilda's thinking of me right now," he said sadly.

"I'm sure she is," Smalls replied. His eyes landed on a stuffed ladybug lying on the ground across from Wombat. One of its legs was torn, but it had seven perfect black dots on its back. At Mumford's they called all seven-spotted ladybugs Lady Luck. Smalls used to find them almost as often as he found four-leaf clovers. He touched a paw to the single clover behind his ear, making a silent wish on the toy. *Please return my luck to me, Lady Luck. Let it bring us to Tilda.*

Next to Smalls, Bertie leaned back against a broken dollhouse, listening to the soft grunts of the animals. "They seem uneasy," he said to Susan. He patted Smalls's back, watching as Wombat buried his snout under his paws.

"I wonder why," Susan said wryly. She lifted a mangled

toy butterfly between her fingers. "This place doesn't feel like a haunted house at *all*."

Bertie laughed. "I just hope it helps us get to Hoolyloo." A huge yawn wracked through him, and it hit him suddenly how tired he was. "And then to your home," he added with another yawn. He tried not to think about what would happen after that. His future felt blank, like a book with no words. But Susan's wasn't; that's what he had to focus on.

Susan cuddled into a pile of stuffed animals and dolls, with Rigby curled up in her lap. "I keep thinking about what it will be like," she said sleepily. "To be there again, to see my parents."

Bertie grabbed a stuffed penguin to use as a pillow. "Tell me more about it," he said, lying down on Smalls's back. Smalls twisted around to lick his cheek.

Susan closed her eyes. "We have space," she told him dreamily. "So much space. Our house is small, but it doesn't matter, because we have the ocean and the sand and the fields of crops. So many places to play and dance . . ." She trailed off, and for a second, Bertie thought she'd fallen asleep. But finally she spoke again. "It used to make me feel like there was a little slice of the world where I would always belong."

On the other side of the freight car, Wombat let out a sigh. "That's how Tilda made me feel too."

Soon, Susan's breathing began to deepen and slow, and before long Bertie could hear the sound of sleep all around him: Susan's long breaths and Rigby's soft pants and Wombat's snores and the hedgehog's whistle and of course Smalls's steady, even breathing, his chest rising and falling against him. Bertie snuggled deeper into the warmth of Smalls's fur, his thoughts growing fuzzy. He was just drifting off when a single thought rose in his mind, bright as a star. *I want that*, he thought. Then he fell fast asleep.

Bertie was dreaming of the wooden boy again. But in his dream, he wasn't wooden. He was a real, live boy: a walking, talking version of a young Bertie. "We're the same," the boy was saying. "I'm you and you're me. We're one and the same."

Bertie jolted awake, breathing hard. He blinked several times, letting his eyes adjust to the darkness. It was clear he'd slept into the night. The sunlight that had filtered into the train earlier was long gone, replaced by a thick, oily blackness. Slowly, shapes began to emerge from the darkness. Smalls, pressed up against him. Susan and Rigby, curled up together in a pile of toys. Wombat, with his head tucked beneath his paws. And the hedgehog, standing on top of a broken toy motorcar, watching him with beady eyes.

"You look like you're keeping watch." Bertie laughed under his breath. He was about to say something else, when he was interrupted by a strange noise. It was a soft jangling, coming from somewhere in the distance. Alfie grabbed his sword, wielding it in front of him. Bertie didn't notice; he was too busy holding his breath as he strained to hear more. The jangling rang out again, a little closer this time. It sounded almost like . . .

"Keys," Alfie whispered.

And mixed in, unmistakable: "Footsteps," Bertie gasped.

Someone was coming.

An Intruder

As the jangling of keys grew louder, Bertie piled several torn kites on top of himself and Smalls, trying to mask their hulking shapes. Smalls lifted his head. "What's going on?" he murmured groggily.

"Intruder," Alfie hissed, leaping down from atop the motorcar.

Wombat's eyes flew open. "Tilda?" he exclaimed. He looked from Bertie to Smalls to Alfie. "Oh," he said, his voice laced with disappointment.

The keys jangled again. This time, the sound was coming from right outside their freight car.

"Hide!" Bertie whispered. As Wombat leapt snout-first into a box of doll limbs and Bertie pulled a frayed peacock mask over his face, Susan and Rigby slept on in the pile of dolls and stuffed animals, blissfully unaware of the danger approaching.

Bertie heard the person before he saw her. A lilting, female voice, lifted in song. "Just me and the toys, just me and the toys, all day loooong. Nothing but toys, nothing but toys, to listen to my soooong."

The door to the train car flew open. In stomped a tall woman with a thick mass of black hair. She was wearing a pair of worn, blue overalls and had a cluster of keys hooked onto one of her belt loops. In one of her hands she held a small lantern. She slowed her pace as she crossed through the freight car. "My favorite car," she said cheerfully. "Don't have to take inventory here!" A beam from her lantern swung upward, illuminating her nametag. *I'm MARTHA*, Bertie read, peeking out from under a kite. *A Toddle's train conductor!*

Bertie blinked several times, sure he'd seen wrong. But as he squinted back up at the nametag, it remained the same— seven red block letters spelling out that magical word: *Toddle's*. As Bertie's eyes darted around the toy-strewn train car, an incredible thought dawned on him. If Martha was a Toddle's train conductor . . . then this train wasn't going to just *any* city; it was going to Hoolyloo! It must be delivering toys to Toddle's Toy Emporium!

Next to Bertie, Smalls looked up, the whites of his eyes glowing. Bertie silently begged him not to move. If they went unnoticed, they could ride this train straight to Tilda. But if

Martha discovered them . . . Bertie shuddered as he imagined being hand-delivered back to Claude. He held his breath, not moving a single muscle. He couldn't let that happen.

Meanwhile, on the other side of the freight car, Susan and Rigby continued to slumber on. It had been a long day, and wrapped cozily in their pile of abandoned toys, they slept the kind of deep, sound sleep that isn't easily disrupted. Tucked between a torn stuffed hippo and a stained Raggedy Anne doll, Susan smiled peacefully.

Next to Susan, Rigby looked just as content, his paws twitching under several stuffed animals. He could have been dreaming about anything—playing fetch, or chasing a squirrel, or bathing in a pool of rainbow paint—but whatever the dream was, it must have good, because his tail suddenly gave a single, strong thump. If Rigby had been just an inch or two further into the pile of toys, his tail might have landed soundlessly on the furry head of a teddy bear. But instead, it smacked right into the pyramid of canned food.

All at once, the pyramid shattered, dented toy cans of artichokes and peas raining to the ground. "Heavens me!" Martha shrieked as the cans scattered at her feet. Her hand flew to her chest as she whipped around, taking in the mess. Cans were everywhere: on top of toys and piled on the floor and caught in the cracks of the broken dollhouse. "How did *that* happen?" Her eyes followed a can of spaghetti. It was rolling steadily along the floor—right toward Rigby, who was still sleeping soundly despite the ruckus he'd caused. Bertie felt every muscle in Smalls's body tense up as Martha's eyes traveled closer and closer to Rigby . . .

"No!" Wombat whispered. Lifting a can with his teeth, he flung it at Martha with all his might. As it bounced heavily against her ankles, Wombat dove back down in his box, trying to hide.

"Ouch!" Martha spun around, lifting her lantern as she scanned the boxcar. "Who did that?" But instead of spotting Wombat, her gaze landed on Alfie, whose beady black eyes were peeking out from underneath a pile of deflated bath toys. "RODENT!" Martha hollered with an ear-piercing shriek.

Alfie leapt out in front of Martha, wielding his sword. "I am no such thing! I'm a sword-fighting hedgehog, and I command you to leave this instant. Or . . . or I will challenge you to a duel!"

Martha cringed at the sound of Alfie's wispy twitters. "RODENT!" she screamed again. Grabbing a can, she chucked it at Alfie. It smacked right into him, bowling him over.

"That's it!" Alfie yelled as he went skidding across the floor. "You and me! A duel to the death!"

"Out, out, out!" Martha screamed, ignoring Alfie's twitters.

Breathing heavily, she chased after him. "Off my train!" she yelled. With a look of determination on her face, she lifted her foot into a powerful kick.

"No!" Before Bertie even knew what he was doing, he had burst out of his hiding place, diving for the hedgehog. But it was too late. At that very second, Martha's foot connected with Alfie and he was tossed into the air.

"Help!" Alfie sliced his sword desperately through the air, but it did nothing to stop his upward arc. He went soaring straight out the freight car's broken door. "Heeelllppp!" he yelled again, his voice fading into the distance. A second later, there was a soft *plop*, and then nothing.

Bertie let out a strangled scream, making Martha whirl around to face him. She put a hand on her hip, marching over to him. "And you! A stowaway? No way. No how. Not on my train."

"But we're just trying to get to—" Bertie began.

"You could be trying to get to the other side of the rainbow, for all I care." She grabbed onto Bertie's suspenders, glowering at him. "You're not doing it on MY TRAIN!"

Bertie wriggled desperately, fighting and kicking with all his strength. All he could think about was Smalls: the way he talked to him with a single glance, the wetness of his tongue against his cheek. Tears sprung to Bertie's eyes as he scratched frantically at Martha's arms. He'd lost his family once; he couldn't let it happen again. "Smalls!" he called out, a tear sliding down to his chin.

Martha scowled at Bertie. "That's right, you *are* small, you little runt. A small, measly criminal." Holding tightly to his suspenders, she began dragging him toward the door.

"Bertie!" With a roar, Smalls leapt out from his hiding spot under the kites, knocking a cardboard box over in his haste. Mangled doll limbs spilled everywhere, sending Wombat tumbling out with them. "Take your hands off him," Smalls growled. He bounded toward Martha, baring his long, white fangs.

"HOLY CANNOLI!" Martha screamed. All the color drained from her face. "THERE'S A BEAR ON MY TRAIN!"

Smalls pounced on top of her, knocking Bertie out of her grip. "I think you mean holy horseshoe."

Bertie's suspenders snapped against his chest as he went staggering sideways. He reached out blindly for something to steady himself. His hand had just made contact with the eyeless rocking horse when, out of nowhere, a toy can of brussels sprouts rolled under his foot. Bertie wobbled. He teetered. He flailed his arms through the air. "No!" he cried. But there was nothing he could do. Like a churning windmill, he went spinning out the door.

Smalls didn't stop to think. He didn't stop to plan. It was deep, guttural instinct that made him kick his paws up and, with a wild leap, follow Bertie off the train.

Martha collapsed on a mostly beanless beanbag chair, breathing hard. "Well, I never . . ." she said shakily. Her teeth were chattering as she lifted her lantern, making the beam of light swing haphazardly through the train car. As luck would have it, a trembling Wombat had chosen that moment to tiptoe toward Rigby and Susan, who were still sleeping away in the pile of toys, oblivious to the tumult. The beam swung over him, illuminating every strand of fur on his body. "Another rodent!" Martha jumped to her feet, screaming once more. "A HUGE, GROSS RODENT!"

"Gross?" Wombat sputtered. "Grossly *intelligent*, perhaps."

Still screaming, Martha strode over to Wombat and grabbed him by the scruff of his neck. "Get out with the rest of them, you . . . you riffraff!" Then Wombat too was sent flying through the air—calling for Rigby as he went tumbling out the door.

And all along, Susan and Rigby slept on, completely unnoticed.

Gone

Bertie stared at the empty tracks, where the train had roared out of sight, taking Susan and Rigby with it. All around him, the animals were pulling themselves up, but Bertie heard none of their groans and moans; he barely felt the bruise blooming on his own shoulder. All he could think about was Susan and Rigby, sleeping peacefully away in an empty freight car. He should have called for them, woken them, done *something*. But it had all happened so fast. And now they were gone.

Susan was gone.

Those three little words stabbed at him like daggers. He sunk blindly into the grass. For most of his life, he'd managed just fine without a friend. But now that he had one—a real one—he couldn't imagine being without her.

A wet nose pressed against Bertie's bare ankle, where his

pant leg didn't quite meet his shoe. Bertie looked over to find Smalls sitting next to him. He patted the bear on his head. "Do you think they'll be okay, Smalls?"

Smalls leaned against Bertie's knee, making several leaves crunch beneath him. "They have to be," he replied.

Of course, all Bertie heard was a soft whine. "They have to be," he said to himself.

Lying next to Bertie, Smalls's heart felt heavy. He thought of Rigby waking up to find them all gone. Would he think they'd abandoned him? Would he be scared? Those questions had been looping through Smalls's head since the moment he'd followed Bertie off that train. At least Susan and Rigby were together, he reminded himself.

Smalls looked over at Bertie, who was blinking away tears. He wanted so badly to make him feel better, but he felt that barrier rising between them—a barrier that could only be broken down by words.

No, Smalls thought stubbornly. There had to be another way. Determined, he pawed at Bertie's pocket, the one he'd seen Bertie tuck that wooden boy into. At first Bertie didn't notice, but again and again Smalls pawed at it, until finally Bertie dumped its contents onto the ground: the wooden boy, a crumpled check, and a few leftover raspberries. "What is it, Smalls?" Bertie asked. "Do you want some raspberries?"

Smalls ignored the berries. Instead, he picked the wooden boy up in his mouth. Lifting his head, he stuck the boy's feet right in front of Bertie.

Bertie swatted at the feet of the wooden boy, which Smalls was sticking in his face. "I'm not in the mood to play right now," he told the bear with a sigh. But Smalls kept shoving the feet at him—so close that he was staring right at the two green *T*'s stamped on them. *TT. TT. TT.* Bertie blinked. Suddenly a thought dawned on him, a thought so glaringly obvious, he couldn't believe he hadn't thought of it immediately.

"If Martha doesn't find Susan and Rigby, then they'll be delivered to Toddle's Toy Emporium with the toys," he said slowly. A tiny seed of hope began to blossom inside him. "Which means we have to get to Hoolyloo City. With or without that train."

Smalls let out a pleased grunt. "My thoughts exactly."

Meanwhile, on the train to Hoolyloo, Susan and Rigby were still fast asleep. In Susan's dream, she was swimming in the ocean outside her parents' house, the waves tickling at her nose. She took a break from swimming to scratch it, but the tickling sensation just grew stronger and stronger and— "Achoo!"

Susan woke with a sneeze. Rigby was lying on top of her, his fur tickling her nose. She untangled herself from him, fighting back another sneeze. As she did, it all came rushing back to her. Jumping onto the train. Curling up in a pile of toys with Rigby. Talking sleepily with Bertie. And then . . . nothing. She must have fallen asleep.

It was pitch dark in the train, night spilling in through the open door. "Bertie?" she said, rubbing at her eyes. She was met only with silence.

She stood up, squinting into the darkness. The freight car was filled with vague shapes: an eyeless rocking horse, a splintered dollhouse, and toy cans, littered everywhere. "Bertie?" she repeated. "Smalls?" But the car remained still, not even a hedgehog stirring.

Susan's hands grew clammy. There was something eerie about the stillness. Even in the darkness she sensed it; it was *too* still. She pushed her way through the car, reaching desperately into boxes and underneath piles. But as her eyes adjusted to the darkness, not a single boy or animal appeared.

She raced over to Rigby, shaking him awake. Rigby was as deep a sleeper as she was, so it took a minute. But finally he leapt to all fours, sending the tall pile of dolls and stuffed animals crashing to the floor. "What is it?" he barked. "What happened?" Suddenly he snapped his snout shut, falling silent.

Lifting his nose into the air, he began sniffing wildly. "No," he whispered. "It's not possible."

Susan grabbed Rigby's back, gripping his fur between her fingers. "They're gone," she gasped. "All of them." She looked slowly around the freight car as three tiny words blasted through her head like trumpets. "We're all alone."

11

Sleep Is for Weaklings

"I'm tired," Alfie whined. Even using his sword as a walking stick, he was struggling to keep up with the others on his tiny legs. "Is it time for a break yet? Maybe a little snooze?" He yawned loudly, his pace slowing even more.

"Absolutely not," Wombat replied brusquely. He kept his eyes on the train tracks, following them like Bertie had suggested. The moonlight glinted off them: a shining, silver path to Hoolyloo City. "In matters of love and rabbit-napping, there's no time for snoozing."

Alfie replied with a yawn so huge it made every quill on his back quiver.

"We do have to sleep eventually, Wombat," Smalls said. He stuck close to Bertie as he glanced up at the sky, which was still dotted with stars. "Before the sun comes up."

"Especially the hedgehog who stood guard on the train . . ." Alfie trailed off, yawning again.

Smalls's heart went out to the tiny animal, who was half skipping, half jogging to keep up with them. "Here," he said, crouching down. "Climb on."

Alfie scurried up Smalls's nose, making himself comfortable in the patch of black fur on the top of his head. "Ahhh," he sighed. "Now this is the life. A comfy bed, a nice night breeze, a valiant quest . . ." Before he could finish his sentence, he was fast asleep.

Soon, Bertie began to yawn too. That clinched it. "It's time to stop," Smalls declared. "We all need sleep."

"Sleep is for weaklings," Wombat protested. "Especially when there's a beautiful Angora rabbit awaiting our arrival." He was in the middle of shooting Smalls a disdainful look when he was suddenly overcome with a massive yawn. He broke into a loud cough, trying to cover it up. "But if *you're* all too tired to go on, then I suppose I have no choice but to stop with you."

They wandered into the woods, Bertie sticking close to Smalls. Moonlight threaded through the branches, casting a golden glow on the dandelions sprouting up through the grass. It reminded Smalls of Mumford's, back when the four of them were still together, and he felt a sharp sting of longing. But before he had a chance to wallow in it, something bright suddenly flashed above him. His eyes flew upward.

It was a tiny, sparkling star, racing across the sky. "A shooting star," he breathed. The luckiest of lucky signs. Quickly, he made another wish in his mind: *Return my luck to me, star. Let it bring us back together.*

Clearing his throat, he hurried over to Wombat, who had stopped next to a line of bushes. "This looks good," Wombat said. "Comfortable and hidden." Smalls nodded his agreement. Fallen leaves had drifted under the bushes, blanketing the ground. Stifling a yawn, Wombat plopped down on an especially thick clump of leaves. "Night," he murmured. Then faster than you could say "Sleep is for weaklings," he was out.

Inside Chrysanthemum's locked bedroom, Tilda was pacing. "Get. Me. Out. Of. Here," she grumbled as she took her thirty-seventh and a half lap around the room. All five thousand strands of her silky white fur were stuffed into a frilly white princess dress meant for a doll, making it impossible for her to complete more than three steps of her sixteen-step grooming process. To make matters worse, a heavy bejeweled crown was fastened to her head, and tiny silk booties were crammed onto her paws. She looked like a caterpillar in a cocoon: ready to burst out at any moment.

Tilda lifted a paw, examining the shiny strands of fur peeking out of her booties. "Maybe if I grow my fur long enough, I could lower it out the window to climb down . . ." She let out a sharp laugh. "Right. As if anyone would ever do *that*."

While Tilda continued on to her thirty-eighth and a half lap, Chrysanthemum stared dismally up at the purple wall-papered ceiling above her bed, unable to sleep. "Sure, Lauren Nicola, I'll sit with you instead of Chrysanthemum," she mimicked in a high-pitched voice. "Oh, Lauren Nicola, you're soooo much funnier than Chrysanthemum." She screwed up her face, as if she'd just eaten something sour. "After Miss-Queen-of-the-School moved away, *I* should have become the most popular girl. But noooo, it had to be Lauren Nicola. If only my parents had sent me away to Millstone Academy, like I'd wanted. I bet I'd be popular *there*. But nooooo, Chrysanthemum Toddle is too fragile to be sent away to boarding school!" Grabbing a pillow, she hurled it against the wall, watching in satisfaction as it collided with a thump before flopping to the ground.

"Who needs school anyway," she muttered to herself. "Especially *public* school. I have my toys! Let's see Lauren

Nicola get a toy trunk like this." Dragging herself out of bed, she flipped on a lamp and went over to a massive white chest. It was emblazoned with gold stripes and had an elaborate gold lock on the front of it. Chrysanthemum reached for the long bronze key she always wore on a chain around her neck. "That's right, Lauren Nicola," she muttered. "I bet *you* don't have your very own key for your one-of-a-kind toy trunk."

Unlocking the trunk, she pulled out a small wooden dollhouse. "Carnation!" she snapped, making the word sound more like a command than Tilda's pretend name. "Come here!"

She sat down on the floor and set the dollhouse up in front of her. It was hand carved of a deep, rich wood, every detail completely lifelike: white shutters and a shingled roof and even a smattering of flowers along the front stoop. "You can be the bunny in the front yard," she told Tilda.

"Whatever you say, Queen Chrysanthemum," Tilda grumbled.

Chrysanthemum seemed to cheer up a little as she opened the top of the dollhouse, revealing two floors. There were several miniature rooms on each floor, filled with tiny furniture. In the corner bedroom, a wooden boy stood in front of his wooden dresser. He had a mess of painted red hair poking out from underneath a wooden baseball cap, bright blue eyes, and a smattering of freckles. One of the dresser drawers was open, and his tiny wooden hands rested on the pile of knitted sweaters inside.

Chrysanthemum sighed theatrically as she patted the boy on his head. "All right, all right, Sebastian. You can wear a different sweater today." The wooden boy had a brown sweater painted onto him, but Chrysanthemum took a blue knitted one out of the drawer and pulled it over his head. "Do you like the name Sebastian?" she asked Tilda. "I chose it myself. It's a noble name, don't you think? Like a prince!"

Tilda wrinkled up her nose. "Personally I prefer Wombat."

Ignoring Tilda's squeaks, Chrysanthemum walked Sebastian into the neighboring bedroom, where a wooden girl with a painted mop of curly brown hair sat on a purple bed. "Hello, Little Chrysanthemum," the real Chrysanthemum said.

She picked up the wooden girl, examining her. The doll was wearing a poufy purple dress and sparkly purple shoes, and there was a bronze key dangling from a chain around her neck. "My very own Chrysanthemum doll," she said proudly. "I bet Lauren Nicola doesn't have *her* own doll."

"Well, la di da," Tilda replied. With a sigh, she lay down, resting her head on her paws. Inside the dollhouse, the wooden boy stared out at her. Tilda looked from his bright blue eyes to his strawberry-red hair to his maze of freckles. "You could be a younger Bertie," she said sadly. A cloud seemed to pass over her face. "I wonder where Bertie is now. I wonder where they all are." She looked out the bedroom's open window, at the dark blue sky unspooling outside. There were no walls or floors or dollhouses out there—nothing but space, space, space. "Where are you, Wombat?" she wondered.

"Wom-who?"

Tilda blinked. A small bird had landed on the edge of the windowsill, the tips of her blue wings glistening in the moonlight. "Who's this wombadiddy you're blathering on about?"

"Wom*bat*," Tilda corrected. "And he's the hairy-nosed love of my life, if you must know." Her voice caught and she quickly cleared her throat. "And who are you?"

"I'm Kay," the bird chirped. "As in the letter." She glanced toward Chrysanthemum, who was busy laying out a meal of miniature food for the two dolls. "So you're C's newest toy, huh?"

"I'm not a toy," Tilda sniffed. "I'm Tilda, a long-furred, purebred Angora rabbit!"

"Hmmm." Kay took in her poufy princess dress and bejeweled crown. "You look like a toy to me, honey."

Tilda let out a loud groan, her fluffy ears flopping underneath her crown. "You're right," she moaned. "I'm a long-furred, purebred Angora *toy*. If only Wombat were here. He would know what to do."

"This Wombat," Kay said, cocking her head. "Is he actually a wombat?"

"Not just any wombat," Tilda said proudly. "A French-speaking, genius-IQ'd, hairy-nosed wombat."

Kay snapped her beak, looking impressed. "I've never met a wombat before. Bet C over there would love to get her hands on that one. A nice new toy for her collection."

"That will never happen," Tilda said furiously. "Wombat's coming and he's going to save me!"

Kay spread her blue wings, revealing a silver lining underneath. "Oh, sweetie," she said, shaking her head. "You've got a lot to learn." With that, she stepped off the windowsill, letting her wings carry her off toward the clouds.

"Wait!" Tilda called after her. "What do you mean by that?"

But the bird was already gone.

12

Battle of the Herds

There was only a hint of sun in the sky when Smalls woke the next morning. Bertie was cuddled against him, so close he could feel his tiny boy heart beating in time with his own bear one. Immediately, Smalls thought of Rigby and Susan, traveling all alone. It made him feel like one of the toys in the Forgotten Car: missing half his parts. Sadness knifed through him. Rigby would smell his way back to them; he had to believe that. He would ride the train to Toddle's and then he would find them. It would all be okay. They would all be together—

"Do you hear that?"

Alfie's wispy tweet cut into Smalls's thoughts.

With a yawn, Smalls carefully separated himself from Bertie and sat up. "Hear what?" he asked sleepily.

"Every morning, I do my listening exercises, just like my sensei taught me," Alfie said.

"And?" Smalls pressed. He yawned again. All he wanted to do was curl back up against Bertie and slip into another dreamless slumber, where their quest—and the gnawing hunger in his stomach—didn't exist.

"And this morning I heard something odd," Alfie continued, oblivious to Smalls's disinterest. "There!" He clasped his paws together. "I just heard it again!"

Smalls flicked his ears forward. "I don't hear anything."

"That's because you're doing it all wrong," Alfie explained. "You must close your eyes. Relax your muscles. Let your breathing soften. Only when you commune with the world around you will your senses be at their strongest."

With a sigh, Smalls closed his eyes. He let his muscles relax and his breathing soften. "This isn't going to—" he began. He was about to say "work" when a strange sound met his ears. A deep thrumming, like a hundred birds flapping their wings at once. "Running," he murmured. He kept his eyes closed, listening harder. A low, threatening growl mixed in with the fast-paced footsteps. It was a growl that said: *I am not your friend*. Smalls's eyes flew open. "A herd," he gasped.

"An angry one," Alfie added.

Nearby, Wombat sat up and stretched out his paws one by one. "Did someone say 'herd'?"

"Yes." Alfie reached for his quill sword, clasping it tightly between his paws. "From the sound of it, one is heading straight toward us."

Wombat looked unbothered as he launched into his new grooming ritual. "What kind of herd?" he asked. "A herd of buffalo? A herd of cows? A herd of mice?"

"Does it matter? An angry herd is an angry herd, no matter what form they take." Alfie's quills twitched proudly. "The sensei taught me that."

"That makes absolutely no sense," Wombat argued. "And I should know. I have an IQ of ten thousand."

As Wombat and Alfie continued to argue over the herd, Bertie stirred next to Smalls. Slowly, the boy's eyes fluttered open. "What's going on?" he asked with a yawn.

Before Smalls could give Bertie a reassuring lick, something stole his attention. It was another growl, drifting in on a breeze, this one so low and fierce that even Wombat leapt backward in fear.

"The herd," Alfie said with a gulp. "They're gaining on us."

"Those are no mice," Wombat said.

"There's only one thing to do then." Smalls jumped to his paws and turned to face the other animals. "We have to get away."

• • •

"Come on," Smalls urged. He circled back around the others, nudging them forward. The sound of the herd was growing less faint by the minute. Smalls knew that if he gave his legs free rein, he could outrun any herd. But none of the others would stand a chance of keeping up with him. As if on cue, Bertie's foot collided with a rock, sending him careening forward. Smalls leapt to his side, steadying him just in time.

"Giddy up!" Alfie yelled. He was standing on Wombat's back, clutching his pointy ears as if they were reins. "Faster, Wombat! We must elude the herd!"

"I'm striving to," Wombat wheezed. His paws were spinning wildly, his snout trembling from exertion. At that moment, Bertie tripped again, grabbing desperately at Smalls to stay upright.

"Everyone stop!" Smalls halted abruptly, signaling for the other animals to do the same. Bertie collapsed against him, breathing hard. Beads of sweat clung to his temples, and his forehead was bunched up in confusion. "Why in the world are we running?" he panted. His weak human ears were no match for the animals', and even as the herd continued to draw closer, he heard nothing at all.

"We aren't anymore," Smalls replied. He knew Bertie

couldn't understand him, but the others could. "We clearly can't outrun this herd. It's time for a Plan B."

"Allow me," Alfie insisted. "Plan B's are my specialty."

"Along with rescuing princesses?" Wombat asked dryly.

Ignoring Wombat, Alfie reached for his sword and raised it into the air. "Fellow animals, it appears it's time we arm ourselves for battle." He looked at Smalls with calculating eyes. "Fangs and claws," he declared, pointing his sword at him. "Those are your weapons. Don't be afraid to use them!"

Under any other circumstances, the sight of a three-inch-tall hedgehog giving him orders would have made Smalls laugh for hours. But he could feel the earth groaning as the herd continued to close the distance between them. "Got it," he told Alfie.

"And you." Alfie whirled around to face Wombat. "How's your throwing snout?"

"I have meticulous aim," Wombat assured him.

"Then you're to gather as many rocks as you can. Your job is to ward off the herd for as long as possible."

Wombat nodded. "Just wait until Tilda hears about my heroics," he said under his breath as he began to gather up rocks. "I'll be her wombat in shining armor!"

While the animals twittered and grunted, Bertie watched

them curiously. "First we're running a race, and now this?" he murmured. "What is going *on*?"

At the sound of Bertie's voice, Alfie and Smalls both whirled around to face him. "Now," Alfie mused. "What are we going to do with the boy?"

"What we're going to do is protect him," Smalls said. Without another word, he stood on his hind legs and lifted Bertie in his front paws.

"Whoa!" Bertie yelped. "What are you doing, Smalls?"

In response, Smalls raced toward the closest tree and began to climb, holding Bertie tightly in his grip. Bertie yelled in surprise as they left the ground.

"It's okay," Smalls promised, hoping Bertie would find reassurance in his grunts. "I'm bringing you to a safe place."

Bertie wrapped his arms tightly around Smalls. "I'm trusting you," he said.

Halfway up the tree, Smalls noticed a nice thick branch, obscured by an umbrella of leaves. *Perfect*, he thought. Carefully, he deposited Bertie in the crook of the branch, where he could lean back against the tree trunk.

Bertie's eyes flickered down to his legs, which were dangling loosely off the branch. *I'm Fearless Boy*, he told himself. *No height is too high for me, no feat too scary!* But even Fearless Boy had to wonder why Smalls had brought him up here. Bertie searched the bear's eyes. There was a strange look in them: serious, guarded. *He's protecting me*, Bertie realized. A shiver ran through him as he wondered what, exactly, he was being protected from.

Bertie leaned back against the tree trunk as Smalls bounded down to the ground. Now that he was wide awake, all his worries about Susan and Rigby came flooding back to him, one after another, like a dam breaking open. Hopefully Martha had never spotted them . . . but what if she had? What if she'd kicked them off the train miles later, sent them tumbling into the woods, alone and confused? They'd be hungry and thirsty and, worst of all, there would be no Smalls to protect them.

Bertie groaned. Worrying wasn't going to help anyone. He had to trust that Susan and Rigby would take care of each other. He pulled the wooden boy out of his pocket, trying to distract himself. He'd dreamed about it again while he was asleep, and he replayed the scene in his head now, letting it push back his fears. In the dream, he was a little boy again, eating breakfast with his parents as the smell of ripe bananas wafted up from his bowl.

"He wants a bowl too," he'd announced, pointing at the wooden boy propped up on the table next to him. "He likes bananas in his oatmeal, just like I do."

His parents had traded a knowing smile. "Well, of course he does," his mom had said.

Bertie closed his eyes, replaying the scene one more time. It felt like the dream he'd had under the willow tree, real somehow, like a memory digging its way up from his past . . .

GRRRR!

The sound of a growl from Smalls made Bertie's eyes snap back open. He pushed several leaves aside, peering out worriedly. But when he saw what was happening on the ground, he had to choke back a laugh. Smalls, Wombat, and the hedgehog were all lined up side by side, one acting stranger than the next. The hedgehog had one of his quills clutched in his tiny paws and was waving it through the air as he twittered wildly. Next to him, Wombat was standing guard over a pile of rocks, rolling his snout in circles, almost as if he were stretching it out. And then there was Smalls. He was extending and retracting his claws as he lifted his paws into the air one at time, like some kind of weird bear aerobics. "What are they *doing*?" Bertie wondered out loud.

He didn't have to wait long for an answer. As the herd of animals pounded closer, even Bertie's weak human ears could soon hear the approaching sounds.

Smalls grunted once, twice, three times. All at once, the animals surged forward—the hedgehog swinging his quill,

Wombat batting rocks with his snout, and Smalls flashing his fangs.

A battle.

The words popped into Bertie's mind. That was it! The animals were preparing for a battle.

He pushed several more leaves aside, trying to get a better look. The hedgehog was so small that a bunny could squash him, and Wombat looked about as scary as a kitten. Only Smalls was the least bit menacing. Bertie was suddenly clutched by a terrible fear. What if that wasn't enough to win against their incoming foe, whoever it was? Smalls was a bear, but like his name suggested, he was a small bear—not much taller than Bertie himself.

Bertie pulled himself up, balancing precariously on the branch. He knew Smalls had been trying to protect him by depositing him in the tree, but he refused to just sit by while the animals risked their lives! His eyes landed on a clump of acorns dangling from a nearby tree branch. Quickly he began to collect them. If he aimed well, he might be able hold back some of the approaching animals, or at the very least slow them down. Winding up his arm, Bertie took a practice shot, aiming for a tree trunk a few yards up. *Not bad*, he thought, as the acorn bounced sharply off his target. He rolled the acorns between his palms. He could do this.

Down below, the animals continued their advance. "Charge!" Alfie bellowed.

"No one ambushes the Misfits!" Wombat added.

"This is for Tilda and Rigby!" Smalls chimed in.

"They're coming," Bertie breathed.

High in the tree, standing tall above the world, he was the first to see the herd as they rounded the bend. A cloud of dirt rose into the air around them, but through it Bertie could make out three animals: a striped zebra and two lions, one sleek and tawny, the other huge and wild-maned. "It can't be," he murmured. But as they pounded closer, there was no doubt in his mind: it was.

Bertie leaned forward, forgetting all about heights and fears as he projected his voice down to the others. "Stop!" he screamed. "Those are no enemies. They're the Lifers!"

13

Dropping In

"Hold your fire!" Smalls skidded to a stop, nearly top-pling over in the process. *Lifers*, Bertie had said. Smalls peered into the distance. From his vantage point, all he could make out was a cloud of billowing dirt—the kind that came from a huge, thundering herd. Next to him, Wombat stopped short, making Alfie ram headfirst into his backside.

"What is it? What's wrong?" Alfie was panting heavily, his words tumbling out on gusts of air. "If you're thinking of backing down, Smalls, don't. We can take them. Little can still be mighty!" He slashed his sword through the air in big, fancy loops as if to demonstrate.

Smalls barely noticed. Because through the cloud of dirt, three faces suddenly emerged. A large lion, a smaller lioness, and a striped zebra. A warm, sticky feeling spread through

Smalls's stomach, as if he'd just gulped down mouthfuls of honey. "Hamlet!" he called out. "Juliet! Buck!"

Juliet recognized them first. Instantly, her nostrils flared. Her huge, yellow eyes widened. Kicking up her massive paws, she began to run even faster, heading straight toward them. She opened her mouth—to say hi, perhaps—but all Alfie saw were her wet, gleaming fangs.

"Oh no you don't!" he bellowed, his wispy voice nearly drowned out by the pounding of Juliet's paws. "This is war!" He leapt into action, his tiny legs spinning wildly as he ran at full speed toward Juliet. "Hiii-*ya*!" he screamed with a jab of his sword. "Don't worry, Smalls. I'll stop this lion with my famous swipe-jab-uppercut move!"

"Who is this creature, Smalls?" Juliet asked, eying Alfie disdainfully. She slid to a stop, sending dirt flying into the air. Most of it landed on top of Alfie, burying him up to his ears.

"That's Alfie," Wombat offered, coming over to join them. "Or, it was," he added, eying the pile of dirt where Alfie used to be.

"*Is*, thank you very much." Alfie shook the dirt off his quills as Hamlet and Buck came up behind Juliet. "Another lion?" Alfie gasped. "And a *zebra*? I . . . I . . ." He trailed off, his spiky jaw coming unhinged.

"Well, if it isn't our favorite Misfits," Hamlet said. His muzzle furrowed as he looked down at Alfie. "And . . . ?"

"Alfie," Alfie filled in. He snapped his jaw shut and straightened up to his full height of three and a quarter inches. "The sword-wielding, commander-in-chief, sensei-trained hedgehog."

Buck rolled his eyes. "Who brought the shrimp?" Ignoring Alfie's furious retorts, he turned to Wombat. "Looking good, Wombat." He ruffled his short striped mane. "Of course, not as good as me. I've been fending off the ladies left and right in these woods. Speaking of which . . ." He glanced around, as if expecting someone to pop out from behind the bushes at any moment. "Any luck finding your furrylicious bunny love?"

"We're working on it," Wombat replied. "We're on something of a quest."

"That's right," Alfie confirmed. He tossed his sword into the air, catching it behind his back. "We're going to rescue that princess—or, erm, rabbit."

"And the others?" Juliet asked.

Smalls grimaced. "We got separated from Susan and Rigby. But we're hoping they find their way to Tilda. And Bertie is up in that tree." He nodded toward the tall tree where the soles of Bertie's mismatched shoes were just barely visible.

"I carried him up there because, well . . . we sort of thought you were an angry herd," he said sheepishly.

He expected them to burst out laughing, but instead Juliet nodded. "That was our plan."

"See?" Alfie spat out. "They *are* an angry herd." He hoisted his sword into the air. "Ready your weapons, comrades!"

"We're not *actually* an angry herd," Juliet explained in exasperation. "We were just pretending to be. To stay safe."

"We've learned that no animal in his right mind will dare approach an angry herd," Buck said. He glanced at Alfie, who was now pressing his sword against his chest like a shield. "Unless, apparently, they're a hedgehog."

As the animals continued to talk, Bertie fidgeted up in the tree. He could hear a commotion down below—grunts and roars and the bray of a zebra—but no matter what direction he shifted on the branch, he couldn't seem to get a good look. "Smalls?" he called out. But his voice got lost amid the chaos of the animals' reunion.

Bertie looked down to the ground. It seemed very, very far away, the blades of grass just specks in the distance. He thought of Susan again. She could climb down this tree easily. "And so can Fearless Boy," he decided.

But Susan, unlike Bertie, was both an acrobat and a ballet dancer. She had calloused palms and flexible limbs. Bertie had neither of these, and as he began the long descent down, his hands slid and his legs cramped. "I'm Fearless Boy," he chanted. But he was struggling to hold on. And when his hand hit a slippery patch of moss, suddenly Fearless Boy was falling.

Down below, Juliet's eyes widened in horror as she watched the small boy come plummeting through the air, his limbs flailing. "Bertie!" she yelled.

Immediately, Smalls whipped around. He was running before he even laid eyes on Bertie. All he knew was he had to get to him. He made it to the tree in record time, the others on his heels.

"Heeelllppp!" Bertie yelled as he came crashing toward the ground. His baseball cap slipped off his head, tumbling down beside him.

"A bed!" Smalls dropped frantically to the ground and spread out his paws. "We need to make a bed for him to land on!"

Juliet flung herself onto the ground next to Smalls. Seconds later, Buck, Hamlet, and Wombat joined the pack, squishing in close until, from a distance, they looked like a furry patchwork quilt. It wasn't a moment too soon. With a muffled thud, Bertie landed sprawled out on top of them, one leg on Buck, another on Juliet, his stomach on Smalls, an arm on Wombat, and his head buried deep in Hamlet's mane.

Buck, who had squeezed his eyes shut in fear, opened them one at a time. Slowly, he looked from Bertie's head all the way down to his feet. "Well," he said, grunting under Bertie's weight. "How nice of you to drop in."

Susan worried the hem of her skirt between her hands. She'd searched the freight car high and low, but there was no sign of Bertie and the others. All she'd found were several strands of Smalls's black fur, snagged on the broken door. Susan leaned against Rigby, watching as the morning sunlight streaked the sky pink outside the train. There was no doubt in her mind: Bertie and the others would have never left them intentionally. Which meant that something must have happened. Susan shook her head in frustration. Her mom used to joke that she could sleep through a train crash. Maybe she finally had.

Next to her, Rigby let out a soft whine, and she reached over automatically to pet him. She had to believe the others were okay. Bertie would find some other way to lead them all to Toddle's. Then she and Rigby could meet them there.

Outside, the scenery was morphing from woods into towns. Susan couldn't help but feel a tiny dart of excitement as she watched the world spin past. Before joining the circus, she'd never left the limits of her tiny beachfront hometown. With the circus, she'd traveled nonstop, but during those countless hours of driving, she'd been trapped in a windowless cubby. As the caravans trundled along, she used to dream up names for the towns and cities she was sure they were passing. *Dancing Toe Village* and *Arabesque City* and *Pirouette Heights.*

But here on this train, she didn't have to make up names. Because through the broken door, she had a perfect view of every station they passed. Her eyes soaked up the tiny wooden platforms with signs for towns like *Kinwood* and *Holly Vines,* towns with bustling centers and sprawling fields and houses that reminded Susan of her own. She was starting to grow tired again, sleep making her eyelids heavy, but she fought to keep them open, not wanting to miss a single one. For that reason, it was through tired, heavy eyes that she first saw it.

It was a sign, hanging above another train station platform up ahead. It was just like the others: old, faded, dangling from rusted chains. But this one was different. Because the town name painted onto it was one Susan knew very, very well.

She inhaled sharply, squinting to make sure her tired eyes

weren't playing tricks on her. But there it hung, the town's name clear as day. *Mulberry.*

Susan's hand went automatically to the letter tucked into the waistband of her skirt, the one with the return address she'd first memorized when she was three years old.

Three Honeysuckle Lane, in the town of Mulberry.

Susan leapt to her feet, sending Rigby skidding across the floor.

They were about to pass her hometown.

14
Proper Dining

In the center of the Toddle family mansion was a vast dining room so gilded and ornate, it could have belonged in a castle. It had gold-trimmed windows and a marble-tiled floor and not one, but *thirteen* crystal chandeliers dangling from the ceiling. In the center of the room sat a huge silver table, polished to a gleam. This table held thirty-four chairs—which the Toddles loved to boast was four more than the mayor himself had at *his* dining table.

Whenever the Toddle family sat down for a meal together, Mr. Toddle would sit at one end, frowning as always; Mrs. Toddle would sit at the other end, her eyes as watery as ever; and Chrysanthemum would sit smack in the middle, in chair number seventeen. (The chairs were all numbered, of course, so guests never had to fear getting lost among them.)

The table was so large that Mr. and Mrs. Toddle had to

yell to be heard from one end to the other. On this particular morning, they were attempting to catch up over a plate of fried eggs and broccoli. Mr. Toddle was wearing his favorite silk bowtie, and his bald head shone under the light of the thirteen chandeliers. The lights reflected off Mrs. Toddle's green taffeta dress as well and made her narrow face seem even paler than usual. "How was your night, dear?" Mrs. Toddle shouted across the table between bites.

"You're taking a flight?" Mr. Toddle shouted back. "But to where, dear?"

"You'd like a pear? But we're having eggs!"

In the middle of the table, Chrysanthemum rolled her eyes. "Why don't you just sit closer together?" she yelled to her mom.

Her mom pressed a hand against her chest, looking aghast. "I've told you, Chrysanthemum. Parents *always* sit at the end of the table. It's what's proper!"

Chrysanthemum turned to her dad. "Maybe it's time we get a new table," she yelled over to him.

Her dad stroked his chin, his frown deepening. "But our dining table is the pride of the town, Chrysanthemum. Larger than even the mayor's table! And nicer, if I do say so myself . . . No, no, I refuse to get a new table!"

"What's that dear? You hear a moo in the stable?" Mrs.

Toddle furrowed her brow. "But we don't *have* a stable."

"We won't be able?" Mr. Toddle yelled back, looking befuddled. "Won't be able to what, dear?"

As her parents continued to shout, Chrysanthemum returned to her plate. "Parents," she muttered, picking around the broccoli as she ate her eggs. Soon, all that was left on her gold-rimmed plate were nine green, prickly stalks of broccoli.

"Chrysanthemum, honey," Mrs. Toddle called out. "What is it going to take for you to eat your vegetables this morning?"

Chrysanthemum fixed her mom with a piercing stare. "I want one Golden Egg for each piece of broccoli I eat," she announced. Golden Eggs were the newest toy invented by Toddle's Toy Emporium. They were made of pure eighteen-karat gold, and when exposed to heat, they hatched to reveal a piece of one-of-a-kind jewelry.

Mrs. Toddle's eyes widened. "Golden Eggs are our priciest toys, Chrysanthemum! We can't very well give you"— she paused, glancing at Chrysanthemum's plate—"nine of them!"

Chrysanthemum dropped her fork on the table with a loud clatter. "No Golden Eggs, no broccoli," she said, her voice rising shrilly with every word. "Do you want me to shriek, Mother?" She opened her mouth wide, clenching her hands into fists.

"No!" Mrs. Toddle burst out. "Please, Chrysanthemum, no shrieking. You can have your Golden Eggs."

Chrysanthemum snapped her mouth shut. She unclenched her fists. Looking pleased, she popped two broccoli spears into her mouth at once. "That's two Golden Eggs," she said smugly, sending bits of green tumbling down her chin.

On the other end of the table, Mr. Toddle's frown deepened even more. According to local lore, it had been seven full years since Mr. Toddle had so much as attempted a smile. "You can't just give in to her all the time, dear," he yelled to his wife.

"What's that?" Mrs. Toddle yelled back. "You're living in your prime? Yes, well, I suppose you are."

In chair number seventeen, Chrysanthemum chomped down on several more stalks of broccoli, swallowing loudly. "That's five," she counted. "Let's see how popular Lauren Nicola is after *I* give all the girls in our class Golden Eggs," she muttered to herself. She picked up four more pieces of broccoli and shoved them all into her mouth at once.

Mulberry

"**Y**ou did precisely *what?*" Wombat asked. The remaining Misfits and Lifers were all gathered around a small pond, eating acorns and drinking up the cool water. None of them seemed able to sit still after the excitement of Bertie's near-disastrous fall. Only Smalls remained motionless, letting Bertie rest against him. The boy had an embarrassed pink flush on his cheeks, but otherwise he seemed to have made it through the fall unscathed.

"We went back to the circus," Juliet repeated. "We had to. It was the only way to find out if Lord Jest was okay."

Smalls's stomach lurched uneasily. Ever since they'd escaped the circus, he'd been trying to stay focused on the future—saving Tilda and now reuniting with Susan and Rigby. But at the sound of Lord Jest's name, he was sent zooming back to the past. He could see those last few minutes of their escape so clearly: Claude driving his motorcar straight toward him and Bertie, and Lord Jest leaping in front of it—twelve tons of elephant stopping the car in its tracks. "How is he?" he asked, his throat raw.

"We don't know," Hamlet replied. "Because he wasn't there."

"The circus was gone?" Wombat asked.

"Not the circus," Buck said. His black-and-white mane bristled. "Just Lord Jest."

"It took us a few days, but we found the circus caravans not far from our last venue," Juliet explained. "They were parked in an empty lot, with big FOR SALE signs tacked onto each one of them."

"It was like some kind of circus ghost town," Buck chimed in. He kicked up an acorn, popping it into his mouth. "No people, no animals, no circus tent. Just silent, empty caravans."

"And Claude," Hamlet added.

Smalls and Wombat both sucked in a breath. Alfie, who was busy sharpening his quill sword on a rock, looked up. "Who's Claude?" He waved his sword excitedly. "Is he the circus sensei?"

"If that means boss, then sure," Hamlet replied. "Claude Magnificence was the head of the Most Magnificent Traveling Circus. He was everything: owner, ringmaster, trainer."

"More like torturer," Buck grumbled.

"Well, when we found him, he looked like none of those things," Juliet went on. "We spotted him through the window of his caravan and he looked . . . terrible. He was wearing his pajamas, which clearly hadn't been washed in days, judging by the cocoa stains on them, and his beard was a mess, tangled and filled with crumbs. And strangest of all, he was crying. Not just a few sniffles, either. I'm talking red-faced, snotty-nosed *sobbing*. He kept looking down at a photograph of Lord Jest when he was just a baby elephant, blubbering on about how he couldn't believe he was gone."

"Gone?" Smalls repeated. "Does that mean . . . ?" He trailed off, unable to finish the sentence.

"At first we thought so," Juliet said. "Buck started wailing immediately—"

"I wouldn't call it *wailing*," Buck cut in.

Juliet swished her long tail. "Okay, sniveling then. The point is, we were sure Lord Jest hadn't made it, that the impact of the motorcar had been too much for him. But then . . . then Claude said something peculiar."

"What was it?" Alfie burst out. All five animals' heads swiveled in Alfie's direction. He was standing on the tip of his paws, his quills trembling in anticipation. "What?" he said with a shrug. "Even a sensei-in-training likes a good story."

Smalls pawed anxiously at the horseshoe on his chest. "So what *did* Claude say?" he asked.

Buck lifted his gruff voice into a spot-on imitation of Claude's nasal whine. "You just walked away," he fake-sobbed. "After everything we've been through, Lord Jest, you just stood up and walked away! You didn't even look back!"

Hamlet gave a nod of approval, making his thick mane swish through the air. "Pretty accurate."

Juliet exchanged a look with Smalls. "If that's true, it means Lord Jest is out here somewhere," she said. "Free."

"And alone," Hamlet added.

"And possibly hurt," Buck finished.

"So now we're searching for him," Juliet concluded. "We haven't found anything yet, but Hamlet thinks he caught a whiff of elephant on a breeze from down south, so that's where we're heading."

Smalls thought of Lord Jest wandering around alone, hurt and lost. For most of the time he'd known him, they hadn't gotten along. But when it mattered most, Lord Jest had proved himself to be a true friend. "If only Rigby were here to help us sniff him out," Smalls said softly.

Suddenly he straightened up, jostling Bertie. *Rigby*. For a minute he'd gotten so caught up in the Lifers' story that he'd almost forgotten their mission at hand. But Bertie clearly hadn't. He kept looking longingly over his shoulder, as if he hoped to find Susan and Rigby waiting on the other side of the pond. "We really should get going," Bertie murmured, scratching Smalls under the chin.

"Bertie's right," Smalls said quickly. "We need to get on the road. But to do that, first we need to figure out where, exactly, we are."

Smalls swiveled around, studying the landscape surrounding them. In their race to escape the herd, they'd ended up in a new section of the woods. The trees were taller and denser here, and the air was eerily quiet, the din of civilization—and train tracks—nothing but a distant memory. "I think we might be lost," he said slowly.

"Nonsense," Wombat retorted. "We can't be lost." He lifted his snout to study the position of the sun. "We've simply gone due north, or, I mean, due south, or, erm, well, maybe it was southeast . . ." He trailed off, looked befuddled.

"According to the sensei of hedgehogs, one can never truly be lost," Alfie piped up. He tossed his sword into the air, then leapt up to catch it. "We simply have to let our inner compass lead the way."

"Well, unless your inner compass can give us directions to Hoolyloo City, I don't think that's going to work for us," Smalls said gently.

Juliet's head snapped up. "Hoolyloo City?" she asked with a shudder. "Why would you want to go *there*?"

"It's where we're hoping to find Tilda, Rigby, and Susan." Smalls sighed. "But now that we lost the train tracks, we have no idea how to get there."

"Well, it's your lucky day then." Juliet flicked her tail out, tapping the four-leaf clover tucked behind Smalls's ear. "Because we do."

Susan stood on a wooden platform, looking up at the old, worn sign hanging above it. MULBERRY, it said, the letters softly faded.

It had been a split-second decision. If she jumped off the train, she could finally return to her parents—and then they could help her get to Toddle's to find Bertie. She patted Rigby on the head. She wasn't sure she could have done it without him by her side. But now they were in Mulberry. Or, at least so she thought.

She looked around at the empty, closed-up train station and the dusty dirt road that branched off in several different directions. She kept trying to conjure up some memory—any memory—of this place, but each time she drew a blank. She'd never seen this station before in her life. And why would she have? Until the circus, she'd never once left her hometown, on a train or otherwise. Besides, this station looked like it hadn't been used in a long, long time.

She glanced down at Rigby. "Now what?" she asked. "How are we supposed to find my house?" She let out a weak laugh, shaking her head. Asking a dog for advice was never a good sign. "Think, Susan," she said out loud. She took a deep breath, inhaling the salty scent of ocean air. "What I need to do is figure out which one of these roads leads to the ocean. That will at least get us closer to my house."

At the word *ocean*, Rigby's ears perked up. He barked several times, making the fur on his snout rustle. His words were simple—"I can smell my way to the ocean!"—but Susan, of course, only heard a string of barks.

"What's wrong, Rigby? Are you hungry?"

Rigby barked out a no. Then he sniffed the air several times. "Got it," he sang out. Leaping down from the wooden platform, he trotted over to the very last road, the one that wound off to the right. He planted his paws firmly in the dusty ground. "This way to the ocean," he barked.

Susan twirled a strand of hair around her finger as she watched Rigby. He was standing on the very last path, looking so . . . resolute. With a bark, he tossed his head, almost as if he was gesturing for her to follow him.

Susan looked to her right. She looked to her left. No matter how hard she studied her surroundings, she recognized nothing at all. "I guess it couldn't hurt . . ." she murmured. She hopped down from the platform. "All right, Rigby. I'm following."

16

A Goodbye

The animals were up to something. Bertie was sure of it. First of all, none of them could sit still. Wombat was burrowing a hole and Buck kept twitching his striped tail and Smalls was walking in tight circles around all of them, pausing every so often to paw at the four-leaf clover behind his ear. Yes, Bertie decided. The animals were definitely up to something. The question was *what?*

Bertie watched as Smalls walked over to Juliet. He grunted several times, nudging her with his muzzle. Juliet ducked her head, swishing her tail against the ground. Nearby, Wombat waddled over to Buck, letting out a soft snort. Buck brayed loudly in response. As Bertie watched, Smalls moved from Juliet to Hamlet to Buck, nudging each of them with his muzzle. Grunts and growls and whinnies were exchanged, and a look of sorrow flashed across Smalls's face.

They're saying goodbye, Bertie realized.

Smalls let out a final grunt, his glance lingering on Juliet. Then he walked over to Bertie and gave him a lick on his cheek. By his feet, Alfie twittered louder than ever, and Bertie knew, deep down, that things were about to change.

In the tall stone house, Tilda was counting leaves. "Seventy-four, seventy-five, seventy-six." She watched as they spiraled past the window, flashes of gold and orange and deep, dark reds. "Rigby would know the exact colors," she said with a sigh. "And Wombat would know how to translate them to French. And Smalls would think of the perfect game to play with them." She paused, counting out several more leaves. "Seventy-seven, seventy-eight, seventy—oh who cares."

She slumped down on the ground. Her fur was a tangled mess, and there were several Cheerios caught in her ears. It had been a long time since she'd lifted a paw to groom, since she'd even uttered the words "sixteen-step grooming process." She was dirty and she didn't care, which was a very dangerous state for Tilda the Angora rabbit to be in.

"Going for the dreadlocked look, sugar pie?"

Tilda's eyes flew back to the window. Kay was perched on the ledge, her blue head cocked to the side as she studied Tilda's sullied fur.

"Maybe I am," Tilda said defensively. "What does it matter, anyway? *She's* the only who sees me these days." She gestured toward a framed photo of Chrysanthemum hanging on the wall.

Kay fluttered her blue wings, their silver lining winking. "Life can change at any minute, honey. The way I see it, you might as well have clean fur when it does." She looked like she might say something else, but at that moment, the sound of Chrysanthemum's stomping rang out on the stairwell. It was heavy, loud stomping: the kind that signaled trouble. "That's my cue," Kay chirped. She spread her wings and, in a flurry of blue and silver, glided away.

"If only I had wings," Tilda muttered. But she was stuck with paws. Which meant all she could do was wait as Chrysanthemum's stomping drew closer.

Chrysanthemum, as Tilda had come to learn, was a fiery little girl. She angered easily, she whined constantly, and she wielded her stomping foot like it was the most dangerous of weapons. The only thing Chrysanthemum wasn't was a crier. She chose shouts over tears every single time. So when Chrysanthemum stormed into her bedroom, collapsed on her bed, and burst into tears, Tilda's round black eyes shot wide open in surprise.

"That stupid Lauren Nicola," Chrysanthemum choked

out through her tears. "All I wanted was to sit at her lunch table, but noooo, Chrysanthemum Toddle isn't good enough to sit with Lauren Nicola." She spit out the name as if it tasted like rotten fish. "Even though I had Golden Eggs! I wish Miss-Queen-of-the-School would come back from her stupid, fancy new life and kick Lauren off her throne. At least *she* was nice to me!" She paused, sniffling. "I just don't understand what I did wrong, Tilda," she said softly.

At the sound of her real name, Tilda looked up so quickly that her dirty, Cheerio-crusted ears flopped into her face.

"What did I do to deserve to be so alone?" Chrysanthemum went on. Tears ran down her face, leaving tiny streaks behind.

Tilda blinked. "I've been wondering the very same thing," she said.

"At least I'm not alone here." Chrysanthemum pulled Tilda onto her lap. A single tear rolled down her cheek, landing silently in Tilda's downy fur. "Not anymore." She picked up a brush and began combing it absently through Tilda's fur. "We have each other now, right?"

Tilda leaned into Chrysanthemum, letting her brush out her fur. With each stroke, she could feel the dirt and tangles falling away, until she began to look more and more like the Tilda she really was. "Yes," she said softly. "I guess we do."

17

Pandemonium in the City

The smells hit Smalls first: smog and cement and perfume and steel and ivy and rubber and garbage and food— every type of food imaginable. Bread and meat and fruit and fish and bagels and cream and sugar and coffee and pizza and pastries and even foods Smalls had never smelled before, foods that smelled spicy and doughy, fragrant and sweet. The aromas crashed and collided in his nose, tempting and teasing him, making him hungry and nauseated and confused all at once.

Before he could even begin to digest the smells, he was met with the sounds. The voices struck him first, hundreds upon hundreds, a toppling tower of words. And the movement: motorcars roaring and footsteps pounding and doors doing everything doors did, slamming and opening and creaking and slamming again. There was honking and screaming and laughter and the clatter of dishes and the crunching of gravel, and it all blended together into a dull, melodious roar.

Smalls, Wombat, Alfie, and Bertie had reached the city of Hoolyloo.

"Look at the buildings," Wombat said in amazement. His tilted his snout up as he took in the structures soaring above them. But it was the streets that Smalls couldn't tear his eyes away from. Traffic lights blinked as throngs of people wove their way through lines of motorcars, fumes lingering among them like a layer of mist. Smalls had heard people talk about city life, had caught snippets and anecdotes from the city dwellers that used to visit Mumford's Farm & Orchard, but never had he seen it for himself.

"Like I said," Alfie said darkly. "It's a dangerous world in there."

Wombat looked up at Smalls. "It can't be worse than the circus, right?"

Smalls took a deep breath. Wombat was right. They'd faced tight ropes and fire sticks and Claude in the circus. How much worse could the city be? "Let's go find Tilda," he said.

"Let's go *save* Tilda," Wombat corrected.

"And recover my lost gem!" Alfie chimed in.

Smalls was about to take a step forward when something off to the side caught his eye. It was a tiny green stalk, poking out through a pile of leaves at the edge of the woods. He cocked his head, studying it. It was a bright, springy green, its petals glistening in the sun. *A clover.* Forgetting everything, he pushed his way toward it. He counted one petal, two petals . . . but the rest of the clover was obscured by leaves.

Carefully, he began pushing the leaves aside with his nose. His insides were tingling like they always did when he spotted a four-leaf clover—right before he plucked it with his teeth and tucked it behind his ear, filled with a newfound certainty that luck was on his side. Breathing fast, he pushed the final leaf aside, revealing . . . a three-leaf clover.

"No," he whispered. He sank back on his haunches, the tingling dying instantly. He'd been so sure his luck was finally returning, that things would finally go right for him again. But this clover wasn't lucky. It wasn't anything at all.

"What are you doing, Smalls?" Wombat asked.

"I'd just thought . . . I'd hoped . . . never mind." He looked back down at the three-leaf clover. How would they ever find Tilda and Rigby if he couldn't get his luck back? He cleared his throat, looking back up. Wombat, Alfie, and Bertie were all staring at him. "Let's go," he said, as cheerfully as he could manage. Smalls nudged Bertie forward, and one by one, the animals stepped into the city.

The concrete was hot against the pads of Smalls's paws, nothing like the squishy coolness of grass. Everywhere he looked, there was something or someone to run into: people and bicycles and motorcars and pigeons, so many pigeons. "Hello," Smalls said politely as a line of them waddled past. "Humph," he muttered when not one of them replied. "They must be hard of hearing."

He didn't have more time to ponder it, though, because suddenly he found himself sidestepping left to avoid a bicycle and then sidestepping right to avoid a person and then leaping up to avoid squashing a straggling pigeon. He landed on the edge of the sidewalk with a frightened yelp, yanking back his claws before they could be flattened by an oncoming motorcar. Smalls's chest heaved up and down. In his natural setting, Smalls was an active bear; he could bound up trees and catch a fly with a single dart of his tongue. But they'd been in the city two minutes and already all the starting and stopping was making him short of breath.

"I do believe we're creating a spectacle," Wombat said wanly, distracting Smalls from his own troubles.

Smalls followed his gaze. He'd been so busy avoiding collision that he hadn't noticed the chaos unfolding around them. But now everywhere he looked, he saw it: gaping jaws and widened eyes and the outraged screams and mangled shouts of terrified humans.

"A . . . a . . . bear!" a woman shrieked, fainting into the arms of a nearby man. The man himself wasn't faring much better. His face turned ghostly white as he scrambled to back away from Smalls with the woman in his grip. In the street, a car screeched loudly as it slammed to a stop, the driver's eyes glued to Smalls instead of the road.

Bertie wrapped a protective arm around Smalls as pandemonium mounted on every side of them. People were shouting and crying out as they scattered left and right, cutting off motorcars and bicycles in their haste, and making traffic halt in the street. "Someone call the zoo!" a woman yelled.

Panic clawed at Bertie's throat. "There will be no zoos on my watch," he hissed. "Or circuses." Down on the ground, Wombat pressed himself against Bertie's leg, trembling furiously. The hedgehog stood behind him, clutching a quill tightly between his paws. "We need to get you guys out of here," Bertie said. "Especially Smalls."

He spun around, searching for a place to hide. But all he saw were people, everywhere: heeled women and suited men, hunched grandparents and screaming toddlers, clumps of teenagers and lines of school children, and all of them, every single one, was staring at Smalls in horror. "Forget the zoo, call animal control," a man shouted.

Bertie's eyes landed on a concrete building a few doors down. It climbed upward, window stacking upon window, taller than any building he'd ever seen. "Perfect," he decided. Behind one of those many windows, on one of those many floors, there *had* to be a place to hide Smalls. All they needed to do was stay out of sight until night fell, then Smalls's black coat could blend into the darkness. "This way," Bertie said, herding the animals toward the building.

"Stop right there!" A man dove in front of Bertie, making him skid to a stop. A chill ran down Bertie's spine as he caught sight of the star-shaped badge clipped to the man's jacket. *Hoolyloo City Sheriff*, it read. The sheriff glared down at Bertie with soupy brown eyes. "Are you aware that it's against the law to travel with a wild beast, son? This bear must be transported out of city perimeters immediately!"

"But he's not wild," Bertie protested. He thought quickly. "Watch for yourself. Smalls, stand!" Immediately, Smalls lifted onto his hind legs, a trick he'd done countless times in the circus. "Smalls, down," Bertie commanded. Smalls dropped down, lying flat on the ground, like a bear-shaped rug.

"I don't care if he can do tricks," the sheriff sneered. "A

bear is a bear, and I want him out of my city!" His hand went to his belt, where a long, metal baton hung.

A thousand terrible thoughts boomed through Bertie's mind at once, like a display of fireworks gone wrong: Claude reaching for his sharp-edged stick; Lord Jest howling in pain; Bertie standing on the sidelines, watching it happen. "Run!" he screamed, pushing Smalls and Wombat toward the building. Alfie grabbed onto Wombat's tail, holding on tightly as they all pounded across the sidewalk, dodging people left and right. The sheriff was close on their heels, yelling for them to stop, but Bertie refused to listen. He lunged for the building's door, yanking it open.

"In!" he yelled, ushering the animals inside. They stepped into a lobby with gleaming marble floors and a huge display of flowers in the center. Up ahead, he caught sight of an elevator, its iron door sliding open to let a group of businessmen spill out. "Ours," he whispered fiercely. He locked eyes with Smalls. "Run," he said, pointing to the elevator. They took off at the same time, paws and legs kicking up as they dashed toward it. Wombat followed behind, Alfie holding tightly to his tail. All around them, the lobby was exploding into a frenzy, shrieks and hollers clogging the air, but Bertie ignored it all, keeping his eyes on the elevator. If they could just get inside and close that iron door, no one would be able to get to them. Bertie was panting hard by the time he reached the elevator. He waited for the animals to pile in before leaping in after them. Quickly, he whirled around, trying to wrench the iron door shut.

"Not so fast."

A hand shot through the crack in the door, giving Bertie a rough shove. As he stumbled backward, the sheriff stepped into the elevator and closed the iron door behind him. He smacked his metal baton against his palm with a loud *thwack*, his soupy eyes darting over to Smalls. "Well, well, well," he said. "Look what we've got here."

18

Fire in the Elevator

The sheriff pushed the button for the building's top floor, making the elevator shoot up with a lurch. They were moving, locked in. Smiling cruelly, the sheriff took a step toward Smalls, swinging his baton through the air. On the ground, Alfie was twittering away, jabbing at the Sheriff's ankles with his quill, but the man paid him no attention. Nor did he seemed bothered by Wombat's furious grunts. He only had eyes for Smalls.

"The mayor won't be able to say I can't catch criminals after this," he growled, pointing his baton at Smalls. "Get ready to surrender, bear. I'm taking you down!"

"I'd be careful if I were you," Bertie burst out. He threw his shoulders back, standing up tall. He had an idea, but it would only work if the sheriff didn't sense his fear. Placing a hand on Smalls's head, Bertie looked calmly up at the Sheriff.

"Remember how he did those tricks for me before? Well, he knows other commands too. Like bite. And attack." He smiled coolly. "And, of course, kill."

The sheriff's Adam's apple bobbed as he swallowed loudly. "Kill?" he squeaked. As if on command, Smalls dropped his jaw, revealing his jagged, razor-sharp teeth. Several beads of sweat sprang up on the sheriff's forehead.

"Oh yes," Bertie lied. He couldn't imagine Smalls killing a bug, much less a man, but the sheriff didn't know that. "That's his favorite. He can rip out a heart in three seconds flat." He glared up at the sheriff, who had started to sweat profusely. "And if you move that baton a single inch, I'll have him demonstrate it for you. Or, if you prefer, you could get off at the next floor instead."

The sheriff backed away from Smalls, gripping the baton so tightly, his knuckles turned white. "N-next f-floor," he stammered, jabbing at the button for floor thirteen. The elevator jolted to a stop, sending Alfie sliding into a wall.

"Wait!" Bertie jumped in front of the sheriff, blocking the iron door. "First tell me where we can hide until nightfall. Or . . . or I'll sic my bear on you!" He couldn't help but smile. Standing in the man's way, he felt bigger and stronger than he ever had, as if he'd just doubled in size.

The color drained from the sheriff's face, making him

look ghostly. "The stairwell in the back," he choked out, stumbling over his words. "No one uses the stairs in these tall buildings." He pressed his back into the iron door, a greenish tint creeping into his cheeks. "Now please, just let me out!"

"Sure," Bertie said, stepping aside. "But don't forget," he added cheerfully as the sheriff dove out of the elevator, sliding the iron door shut behind him. "If you come back for us, or tell anyone about us, all I have to do is say the command and . . . well, you know the rest."

Adrenaline surged through Bertie as the elevator rose to a stop on the building's very top floor. There was only one way he could think of to get Smalls to the stairwell without being noticed. He first had to clear the floor. He pushed the red emergency button on the elevator, locking it in place. "Stay," he whispered to the animals.

Sticking his head into the hallway, he cupped his hands around his mouth. *Here goes nothing*, he thought. At the top of his lungs, he shouted: "Fiiiiiire! Fire in the elevator! Save yourself! Take the stairs down!"

"Fire in the elevator?" A woman's high-pitched voice floated into the hallway. "Oh my, fire! FIRE! Everyone evacuate! Take the stairs!"

As people poured out of their offices, stampeding toward

the stairs, not a single person took notice of the small boy and three scruffy animals hiding in the elevator. The mass of legs flew down the hallway, their voices growing fainter and fainter as they pounded down the stairs. And then, just like that, there was silence.

Bertie could hear the *whoosh* of his own breath as he stepped into the deserted hallway. It was lined with offices, desk chairs askew and abandoned. Hanging on the walls were framed sketches of motorcars. Next to a large corner office was a steel sign: *Greenberg Automobiles*, it read in fancy, swooping letters. "Coast is clear," Bertie whispered. He ushered the animals out, then reached back into the elevator to release the lock button. Once the businessmen and women realized that there was no fire, they would all take the elevator back up—leaving the stairwell free for the animals to hide in. Bertie took a deep breath as he led the animals to safety. He'd done it; he'd saved them. He should have felt thrilled, elated even, but instead a soft pang reverberated through him. He just wished Susan could have been there to see it.

There was a small window in the stairwell, and Bertie and the animals had been staring at it for what felt like days, though it was really just several hours. Outside, the sun continued to sink in the sky as, behind the stairwell, the office work day marched on. Telephones rang, doors creaked open and slammed shut, and every once in a while someone would start yelling. But just like the sheriff had predicted, not a single person had opened the door to the white-walled stairwell.

Bertie stood up, going over to the window for the twelfth time since they'd stowed away in there. Outside, a web of lights tangled and stretched across the sky, windows glowing in every building. But it wasn't the lights he was looking at, or the way the buildings cast long, flickering shadows over everything. No, it was the stone wall in the distance, rising like a fortress behind the crowded city streets. In the middle of the wall was a door, and jutting high above that door were two huge, green, interconnected *T*'s—the same *T*'s that were stamped onto the wooden boy's foot.

"Toddle's Toy Emporium." Bertie touched a hand to his pocket. Somewhere behind that wall was everything they were looking for: Tilda and the wooden boy and, hopefully, Susan and Rigby. "And now I know how to get there," he said.

Behind him, Smalls stood up, rising onto his hind legs to peer out the window over Bertie. Night was settling in, draping everything in darkness. Soon, it would be easy for Smalls to slip into the shadows, melt into nothingness.

Out in the hallway, the elevator door rumbled open, and

voices filled the air as people piled in. "I'm so glad it's Friday," Smalls heard someone say. He dropped back down on all fours, nudging Bertie's arm with his nose. He wanted to be out there, making his way toward Tilda, not in here, cooped up in a stairwell. What if the train dropped Rigby and Susan off at Toddle's Toy Emporium, and they weren't there to greet them? He whinnied impatiently, giving Bertie another nudge.

"I know," Bertie said softly, scratching him under the chin. "But we can't go outside until we're sure it's safe, Smalls." He sighed, his gaze drifting back to the window. "I refuse to lose you too."

So they waited in the stairwell, time creeping by. Wombat was telling Alfie all about Tilda, but Smalls couldn't bring himself to join in. All he could do was count the seconds, moaning softly when they piled up into minutes. Finally, when so many minutes had accumulated that Smalls was sure they must have turned into hours, Bertie gave a sharp nod. Behind the door, the building was silent, and through the window Smalls could see that the sky had blackened.

"Here we go," Bertie whispered. Putting a hand on Smalls's head, he led the way down the stairs.

19

A Cacophony of Voices

They stuck to back streets and alleyways as they made their way toward the tall stone wall looming in the distance. The rough pavement scratched against the pads of Smalls's paws, but he ignored it, concentrating only on slinking through the shadows, letting the night swallow him up. Wombat and Alfie trotted behind him, nothing more than wavering shapes in the darkness. Both were uncharacteristically quiet. They had to be thinking the same thing Smalls was: this was their last shot. If they were spotted now, they might never reach Tilda and the others.

"If we keep sticking to back streets, we should be able to make it to Toddle's without Smalls being seen," Bertie said, stepping carefully over a pothole. He jumped a little as a glass bottle shattered just a few feet behind them. From a window in the distance, a throaty laugh rang out.

Smalls's stomach churned nervously. These were dark, discarded streets, streets no young boy should be walking down, and Bertie was there because of him. He slowed his pace, sticking close to the boy's side. *I'll protect him*, he thought fiercely. *No matter what, I'll take care of him.*

No sooner had the thought crossed his mind than he heard it: the whisper of voices. It started out faint, but with each step Smalls took, the sound intensified, until soon even Bertie's human ears could hear it. Chants, rising into the air and swirling together, a cacophony of voices. "What are they saying?" Bertie whispered.

Smalls flicked his ears back, struggling to distinguish the words. One by one, he picked them out. *Bear. Catch. The.* Every muscle in Smalls's body tensed. The crowd was chanting the same three words, over and over. *Catch the bear.*

Bertie made a choked sound. He looked over at Smalls, his bright eyes blackened by the darkness. "Someone must have spotted us on our way out," he said shakily. But Smalls knew what he really meant: Someone must have spotted *you*.

Smalls whirled around to face Wombat and Alfie. "We can't let them catch us," he breathed. "We'll never get to Tilda then. We need somewhere to hide until they pass."

Alfie bent his sword between his paws. "I know just the

place," he said slowly. "Humans would never think to look for us there. But I have to warn you: it isn't for the faint of heart. It's a dark, unscrupulous place, filled with creatures of the city's underworld—creatures willing to do anything to get what they want."

"Will it keep us away from *them*?" Wombat glanced over his shoulder at the dark, narrow streets behind them. Somewhere in the distance, the voices continued to build, spinning toward them like a storm.

Alfie nodded solemnly. "No one will find us there." Gesturing for the others to follow, he made a sharp turn, leading them down an alleyway even darker and narrower than those before it. At the end of the street sat a long row of dumpsters, each one brimming with garbage. "Prepare yourselves, friends, for the horrors of Sewer Alley. You might want to plug your noses," he added. "Because our fate awaits us on the other side of that trash."

"Step seven completed!" Tilda held out a freshly groomed paw, admiring the way its fur glistened like spun silk. "Now, step eight: smooth ears." She had just flattened down her ears with the pads of her paws when the door to the bedroom suddenly flung open.

Tilda froze in her place. In bustled Petunia, Chrysanthemum's nanny. Petunia was a thick lady, with thick legs and thick arms and thick hands that, at the moment, were pushing an empty cart. "Let's see," she sang out. "Which of you need to be cleaned today?" She rolled the cart over to the tangled toys at the foot of Chrysanthemum's dresser.

"You could certainly use some work." She wrinkled her nose as she lifted a stuffed penguin by its ear. The penguin had what appeared to be a blob of jelly matted into its back and a sticky residue on its paws. "Oh yes, you need a good scrubbing," Petunia declared, tossing the penguin into her cart.

Tilda's eyes widened. "*Scrubbing?*" She looked down at her meticulously groomed fur, a scandalized gasp escaping from the back of her throat. "Uh uh, no way," she whispered. "No one scrubs me but me!" She held stock-still, waiting until Petunia's back was to her. Then, with a flying leap, she dove under Chrysanthemum's bed. She zigzagged around dust bunnies and abandoned toys until she had her back pressed up against the wall, far out of Petunia's reach. She gave her tail a smug twitch. "Let's see you try to scrub me under here!"

20
Karate King

Smalls was halfway over the dumpster when he made the mistake of looking down. Underneath him, the bin was filled to the brim with spoiled food and soggy bags and rusted tins of moldy bread. The stench wafting off it was like nothing he'd ever smelled before: the worst kind of rotten, as if someone had mashed up a thousand decaying bugs into one deadly stew. His eyes darted from a browning banana peel to a scaly fish head to a piece of paper dripping with dark, gooey liquid . . . and was that a *tail* moving underneath it?

He scrambled the rest of the way, nudging a doubtful-looking Bertie along with him. He'd had to practically pull the boy up onto the dumpster by his suspenders, but as they landed on the other side, Bertie broke into a smile. "This is great," he whispered, quickly plugging up his nose. They were in a small alleyway lined with sewers. The dumpsters were behind them and on the other sides were the backs of three buildings, their curtains drawn tight. "No one in that mob would ever *think* to climb back here."

Smalls looked around as Wombat landed next to him with a disgusted snort. Alfie came next, sliding down the corner of the dumpster with his sword pointed straight ahead. "He's right, Alfie," Smalls whispered. "This is perfect."

Behind the dumpster, the thunder of voices intensified. The sound thickened the air, each word like a dart of poison. *Catch. The. Bear. Catch. The. Bear.*

"Not if we're back here, you won't," Bertie muttered. Smalls pressed his muzzle into the boy's side as the chants drew closer. Out of the corner of his eyes he could see Wombat burrowing furiously at the pavement, his snout set in concentration. Next to him, Alfie was turning in circles, sword at the ready, as if he expected someone to jump out of the shadows at any second. The noise rose to a crescendo. *Catch! The! Bear!*

Soon the voices were only inches away, swelling through the air and making the dumpsters rattle. "I see something," someone shouted. Smalls stopped breathing. Bertie's hand clamped down on his fur. There was a ruckus: feet shuffling, voices arguing, and then the noise suddenly veered left. "This way," a man called out, his voice floating back to them from down the block.

Smalls's ears perked up. The men were passing; they were turning left!

The footsteps faded sharply, the voices whistling into the distance. A minute later, there was silence.

Bertie waited a beat before turning to Smalls, his cheeks pink with excitement. "Brilliant!" he said, scratching Smalls under his chin. "This was the perfect hiding spot."

"Hey, thank the hedgehog!" Alfie protested. "The one here to face this alley's gang of huge, filthy, ferocious—"

"Talking about us, pipsqueak?"

Alfie froze midsentence as a dozen pairs of glowing red eyes peeked out from the sewers. All at once, twelve rats emerged, their tails swishing across the floor as they circled the animals. Smalls tensed, his claws extending automatically. Next to him, Bertie gulped loudly. His eyes darted wildly from one rat to the next as he scooped Wombat up in his arms. Smalls moved protectively in front of them.

"Well, well, well," the largest rat said in a gruff, crackling voice. He snapped his jaw, sending a line of drool trailing down his dark, matted fur. His eyes were trained on Alfie, as if Smalls and the others didn't exist. "Look who's returned at last."

"Hello, Grubs," Alfie said smoothly. "You're looking as, well"—he eyed a chewed-up hard candy stuck to one of the rat's ears—"grubby as ever."

"And you're looking as puny as ever," Grubs replied.

"What I lack in size, I make up for in swordsmanship," Alfie shot back.

"And friends," Smalls growled. He took a menacing step toward Grubs. He didn't like how that rat was eying Alfie—as if he planned on making him his next meal. There was no way Smalls was letting that happen. Grubs might be twice Alfie's size, but he was barely as large as one of Smalls's paws. "Well-endowed friends," Smalls added, flashing his claws at the rat. Immediately the other rats closed in around Grubs, jagged teeth flashing and red eyes glowing as they formed a rat barricade. Undeterred, Smalls took another step toward them. But Alfie waved him off.

"It's okay. This is my fight, Smalls." He brandished his sword, facing the line of rats. "I have come to battle you once and for all, Grubs."

"You *have*?" Smalls and Wombat both exclaimed. Smalls froze in place, looking from Alfie to the rats and back again.

Alfie shook out his spiky quills. "I have. This is it, comrades. This is *my* quest. Now." He spun to face the wall of rats, sword pointed forward. "Come and face me like a real rat, Grubs. One on one."

Grubs laughed, a deep, savage laugh. Pushing his way through his bodyguards, he smirked down at Alfie. "I think you're forgetting what happened the last time we fought one on one, squirt."

"That's where you're wrong," Alfie replied. "I remember it every single day. You stole my gem from me that day, Grubs, and now I'm here for a rematch."

"His gem," Smalls said softly. *Of course*. That's how Alfie knew of this place. It was where he'd lost his gem.

Grubs bared his long, sharp teeth. "You must be a glutton for punishment, half-pint. You can have your rematch if you want, but I should warn you that I'll beat you in ten seconds flat, just like I did two years ago." Behind him, the other rats tittered gleefully.

Alfie slashed his sword through the air in a series of complicated loops. "Two years ago, I did not have a sword. Two years ago I had not trained with the sensei of hedgehogs. Two years ago, I lost what was most important to me in the world. But now I'm here to change that." Alfie took a step toward Grubs. Fury flashed in his eyes as he pressed the tip of his sword against the rat's chest. "Prepare yourself, Grubs, for the fight of your life."

"This is gonna be goo-ood," one of the spectator rats hissed.

"Grab some snacks, Sludge," another one chimed in. "Looks like we got ourselves a show."

"Gotta love a good smackdown," Sludge said gleefully.

He darted into one of the dumpsters and dug out a rotten, slimy apple. Ignoring the flies swarming it, he tossed it down to the rats. Then he dove back in, emerging this time with a moldy roll, half a fish tail, and what had once been a head of cabbage, but was now so hardened and blackened it looked more like a chunk of coal.

"Score," one of the rats cheered, catching the blackened cabbage in his paws. As Sludge clawed his way down from the dumpster, the rats all settled themselves on the ground. "Team Grubs!" one of them called out.

Smalls crouched down as he watched Alfie, ready to pounce at any moment. But Alfie seemed unusually calm as he closed his eyes and lifted his sword to the sky. "I, Hedgehog Alfred the Third, give myself to the battle," he chanted. "I will allow the power of the fight to flow through me, to become one with me, to channel my inner soul. Only then will I stand victorious."

"Only then will he stand a *loser*," one of the rats snickered. "In every sense of the word."

"Nice one, Fester," Grubs said approvingly. "Now, if you're done reciting your poetry, Alfred, how about we attempt some fighting—"

He didn't get a chance to finish. Because suddenly Alfie leapt into the air, kicking a paw out as he did two full rotations.

He landed smoothly in front of Grubs, his paw colliding with his chest. Grubs let out a squeal as he went stumbling backward, landing in a heap on top of Fester and Sludge.

Smalls took a quick glance over his shoulder at Bertie. The boy had his back pressed up against one of the dumpsters, an astounded look on his face. His arms were wrapped protectively around Wombat, whose round eyes were bulging. Satisfied they were safely out of harm's way, Smalls turned his attention back to the fight.

"Well, well, well," Grubs sneered. He pulled himself back up, brushing flakes of cabbage off his fur. "Look who thinks he's the karate king. Two can play at that game." Baring his teeth, he lunged at Alfie.

Behind Smalls, Wombat let out a cry of outrage. "Stop!" he yelled. "This is barbaric! This is senseless! This is—go, Alfie!" Wombat snorted excitedly as Alfie quickly yanked his paws and head into his quills, so Grubs's teeth were met with nothing but sharp tips.

"Owwww!" Grubs howled. His paws flew to his face as pinpricks of blood sprang up on his pointy nose.

Alfie seized the opportunity. He leapt to his feet, sword in hand. Instantly he began to advance, jabbing his sword at Grubs. Grubs dropped his paws and lunged at him, but Alfie just twisted away, evading him. With a single flying leap, he was back in front of Grubs. "Ya! Ya! Ya!" he yelled, jabbing mercilessly at Grubs with his sword. "This is called a *remise*," he announced, continuing to jab without withdrawing his arm. Grubs tried to claw at him, but Alfie ducked his attack. "And this," he continued, "is called a *feint*."

He pretended to slash his sword at Grubs in an undercut. But as soon as Grubs began to block him, he drew his sword back and did a flip through the air, landing behind Grubs. Before the rat knew what was happening, Alfie was reaching for his back paws. In two swift moves, Alfie flipped him over and pinned him to the ground on his back. Jumping on top of him, he pressed his sword against the rat's heart. "Cunning move, isn't it?" he asked cheerfully.

"You really did train with a sensei," Wombat said in amazement.

"Of course I did," Alfie said. "Did you think I was joking this whole time?"

Smalls looked over his shoulder, exchanging a sheepish look with Wombat. "Maybe a little," he admitted.

"Dueling is no joke." Alfie pressed harder on his sword, eliciting a high-pitched squeal from Grubs.

"Help me!" Grubs wheezed.

Instantly, the eleven other rats were on their feet. Alfie gave them a withering stare as they approached. "Do you really think it's wise to fight me?" he asked coolly. "I know many more moves than the feint. There's the *parry* and the *fleche* and the *ballestra* and the *flunge* . . .

One by one, the rats backed away.

"Sludge!" Grubs begged. "Fester! Grimy! Germ!" But the rats hung their heads, refusing to meet his eyes.

Alfie nodded in satisfaction. "That's what I thought. Now"—he looked down at Grubs—"admit defeat once and for all."

"Never," Grubs choked out.

Alfie traced his sword up to the rat's neck. "I'll say it once more. Admit. Defeat." He applied pressure to his sword, making Grubs writhe on the ground.

"Okay!" Grubs gave in. His voice was strangled. "You win." He coughed, gasping for air. "I lose! Happy now?"

"I am."

At the sound of a wispy female voice, Alfie leapt down from Grubs, his quills trembling. A tiny hedgehog walked out from underneath a dumpster. She had wide black eyes and long quills that glistened in the moonlight. "Hello, Alfred," she said.

For a long minute, Alfie just stared at the pretty hedgehog. When he finally spoke, his voice was trembling. "Hello, Gem."

742 Days

Gem walked toward Alfie, her quills gleaming with every step. "It's been a long time, Alfred." Her voice was as wispy as Alfie's, but more musical, like a bell chiming the hour.

"Seven hundred and forty-two days," Alfie replied immediately.

"You remember," Gem said, sounding surprised.

"Of course I do." Alfie tapped his sword against the ground, filling the alley with a soft patter. Behind him, Grubs struggled to his feet, his wide, frightened eyes following the tapping sword as it moved up and down, up and down. "A sensei-in-training forgets nothing." He moved closer to Gem, until they were standing almost nose to nose. "I've spent over two years training, Gem, so I could come back and fight for you. So I could win you back."

Gem shook her head sadly. "That's what you never understood, Alfred. I can't be won. Just like I can't be lost. I *choose* where I want to be."

"But I lost you when Grubs defeated me," Alfie said softly, "742 days ago."

"No." Gem met Alfie's eyes. "You lost me when you walked away—742 days ago."

Alfie scrunched up his tiny face, looking confused. "So I never had to defeat Grubs?" He was tapping his sword even faster now, a nervous, frantic tapping, and Gem reached out, removing it gently from his grip.

"You never had to defeat anyone, Alfred," she said, sounding exasperated. "When will you learn that, you stubborn hog? All you had to do was ask."

Alfie was silent for a moment, staring at his sword gripped between Gem's delicate paws. "I see," he murmured finally. "Okay, then." With a determined nod, he straightened up to his full three and a quarter inches. He shook out his quills and took a slow, deep breath. When at last he spoke, his voice was soft, but sure. "Gem, would you do me the honor of returning to Maplehedge Woods by my side?"

"*Finally.*" Gem rolled her eyes. "I've only been waiting 742 days for you to ask."

Alfie's quills shivered with excitement. "Can I take that as a yes?"

Gem slid her paw into his. "You can take that as a definitely."

As Smalls watched the two hedgehogs reunite, a dull ache began to spread through him. Alfie and Gem looked so *whole* together. He wanted that too—for things to feel whole again, no pieces missing. He looked around him, at the matted clump of rats and the moldy bits of garbage scattered everywhere. Bertie and Wombat were huddled together against the dumpster, Bertie pinching his nose to ward off the smell. One thing was for sure; he wasn't going to find that feeling here.

He straightened up. The night sky was black, and the menacing voices were gone. The mob of men had passed; there was no longer a reason to hide. "I think it's time we get back on the road," he said to Wombat.

"My thoughts precisely," Wombat replied. He wiggled a little in Bertie's arms, and Bertie placed him gently on the ground.

"I guess this is goodbye then," Alfie said. Gem's paw was still in his as he bowed to the animals. "It's been an honor, comrades."

"Good luck, Alfie," Smalls said softly. It hit him that he

would miss the little sword-wielding hedgehog. But judging by the dreamy look on Alfie's face, he was pretty sure the feeling wouldn't be a shared one.

"Thank you." Alfie pulled Gem close to him. "But as the great sensei of hedgehogs would say, there is no such thing as luck. There is only perseverance."

Smalls blinked, his paw going automatically to the worn and wilted four-leaf clover tucked behind his ear. For most of his life, luck had just come to him, found him, like a magnet zooming toward its other half. Lately, he'd found himself wishing on every lucky sign, hoping to draw that luck back to him, will it to return. But maybe he'd been going about it all wrong. Maybe what he needed was to persevere—to make his own luck.

"I'd hug you," Alfie went on. "But"—he shook out his quills—"it wouldn't be very enjoyable." So instead he waved, and Gem waved, and then they were gone, slipping under the dumpsters and into the darkness.

It wasn't until after, the alleyway eerily quiet in their wake, that Smalls noticed a small, sharp quill lying abandoned on the ground. Alfie's sword. He smiled to himself. It looked like he wouldn't be needing it anymore. Taking a deep breath, Smalls turned to Wombat. "Time for us to persevere."

22

A Ghost in the Night

Susan closed her eyes, unable to trust her own vision. But when she opened them again, it was all still there, shining in the moonlight. The small thatched cottage. The red spider lilies spilling through the grass like paint. And the ocean, roaring and crashing, so close she could feel the salty air grazing her fingertips. Rigby barked at her feet. She reached down absently to pet him, unable to draw her eyes away from the house. It was tiny—a dollhouse, her mom used to joke—but it was home. She was home.

Her eyes flitted between the house's two front windows. They were both dark, not a single light burning inside. Susan scrunched up her forehead. Her parents' days had always run like clockwork, every hour designated and accounted for. She wasn't sure exactly what time it was, but judging by when the sun had set, it seemed too early for her parents to be sleeping—but also too late for them to be out. So why was the house so dark?

She made her way up the front stoop, feeling like a ghost in the night, a shadow of her old self. *Stop it*, she chided herself. She'd only been gone six months. She was still her. She would knock on the door and her mom would come running out and gather Susan up in her arms. Rigby padded up the stairs beside Susan. It made her glad that she wasn't there alone. Taking a deep breath, she lifted a callused, blistered hand and knocked on the door.

Nothing.

Inside, no one stirred, no lights turned on, no voices murmured.

She tried again, louder this time, and longer.

But still the door remained shut. The house remained quiet. Rigby sniffed the air, then whined loudly. If there was someone inside, they couldn't miss that sound. But still nothing happened. Susan pulled at the front door. It didn't budge. "Locked," she affirmed. "Looks like we're going to have to break in. You wait here." Gesturing for Rigby to stay, she jogged to the back of the house, to the kitchen's low window. Behind her the ocean swelled and surged, the sound wrapping around her like an old, familiar lullaby.

For as long as Susan could remember, the lock on the

kitchen window had been broken. She yanked at the window, and with a groan, it cracked open. At least one thing hadn't changed while she was gone. She pushed the window up the rest of the way and used the strength she'd gained at the circus to hoist herself up.

She landed lightly inside, the kitchen's cracked blue tiles hard beneath her feet. She reached for the light switch, her fingers finding it automatically. The overhead bulb flickered on slowly, sending a thin beam of light stretching across the kitchen. It was exactly how she remembered it: the shiny red counter, the old wooden table with her initials carved in the corner, the three mismatched chairs tucked into the table in order of size. Her mom's yellow mug sat next to the sink, that morning's teabag still in it.

"Mom?" she called out. "Dad?" There was no answer as she crossed through the house, turning lights on as she went. Her dad's favorite blanket was strewn messily across the couch, and her mom's slippers were discarded by the bookshelf—strangely untidy for them, as if they'd only popped into the kitchen to make some tea. "Mom?" she called again. "Dad?" Still nothing.

She opened the front door and Rigby came bounding inside. He followed at Susan's heels as she ran up the stairs, taking them two at a time. "Mom? Dad?" She flung open their bedroom door.

Total darkness.

Frowning, she turned on the lamp. Her parents' bed was made up like always, and a book lay open on the night table, one of the mysteries her mom loved to read. Everything looked as it should. Except that her parents weren't there.

Susan bit back tears. There were only two more rooms in the house: the tiny bathroom, which she found empty, and her bedroom. She turned the lamp on in her room, blinking in the soft light. A tarp had been draped over her bed and dresser, and it didn't take her long to see why. "The walls," she breathed. They'd been painted a deep, shimmering blue, the color of the ocean in the early evening, when the sunlight was beginning to wane.

She spun around, letting the walls envelop her, like she was far out in the ocean, an island unto herself. It was what she'd wanted for her birthday: to bring the outside in, to be able to reach out from her bed and touch the waves. Her eyes fell on the wall behind her bed. Someone had used white paint to create the crest of a crashing wave. She tried to think back, to remember what day it was exactly. In the circus it was easy to lose track, one awful day bleeding into the next. But as she counted backward, it hit her suddenly that it was Friday, September 20, which meant her birthday was in less than a week.

"This is their gift," she realized. She walked over to the wall, touching her finger to the wave. It squished a little to the touch. She pulled her finger away. A smudge of paint was on its tip. For the first time, she noticed the bucket of paint in the corner. Two paintbrushes stuck out of it. Rigby tentatively dipped a paw inside, barking excitedly when the shimmery blue paint clung to his fur. Her parents had been here, painting, *recently*. She listened hard, but the house remained still and silent, not even a floorboard creaking.

So where were they now?

23

Toddle's Toy Emporium

In the city of Hoolyloo, a boy, a bear, and a wombat stood in front of a tall stone wall. The wall stretched to their right and their left before looping forward in an enormous, perfect circle. In the distance, a green building rose behind it, its white shingled roof giving it a snowcapped look.

In the center of the wall was a huge stone door with an iron handle. Two interconnected green *T*'s rose above it. Bertie tugged on the handle, but the door refused to budge. He tried again and again, but it was futile. The door was locked and bolted, sealed up tight. Bertie shook his head. "We're finally here, and now we can't get in."

Tears welled in Wombat's big brown eyes. "That," he whispered, "is what's called irony."

Bertie pressed his forehead against the stone. It was rough but cool to the touch, and his tired eyes began to drift shut.

Between the Lifers and the sheriff and the hedgehog's wild antics in the alley, it had been a long, long day. Bertie smiled briefly at the memory of the hedgehog's happy twitters as a second hedgehog appeared from beneath the dumpsters. When the two prickly animals had disappeared together, Bertie had gotten the strangest sense that the hedgehog had found what he'd come for. He would have to remember to tell the story to Susan.

The thought of Susan made Bertie's face crumple. His only chance of finding her, Rigby, and Tilda was behind this fence. They *had* to get into Toddle's.

At his feet, Wombat let out several snorts, each one more frantic than the last. Bertie opened one eye, looking down at the small animal. "You okay, Wombat?" he asked softly. This time, Wombat didn't snort. Instead, he lifted his strong burrower's paws and began to dig.

Bertie had never seen Wombat dig with a purpose before, and he watched in amazement as a wall of dirt flew up behind him, his legs moving so fast they were almost a blur. Soon, a hole had begun to form under the stone door, just wide enough for a sun bear to squeeze through. Bertie straightened up as he realized what Wombat was doing: He was trying to dig them into Toddle's!

Wombat continued to burrow, inching deeper and deeper

into his hole, until even his stubby tail was out of sight. Bertie could hear him panting as he sent mounds of dirt flying into the air. Behind them, the city was dark and still, like a sleeping beast. Bertie could almost feel it heaving with each breath, just waiting to be woken. "Come on, Wombat," he begged. He felt restless, something unnamable bubbling up inside him. Nearby, Smalls was shifting nervously from paw to paw and soon Bertie found himself joining in, moving in sync with the bear.

Finally, Wombat reemerged, his snout dusty and his paws black. Bertie kneeled down, peering into the hole he'd dug. It was long and twisty, but he could see light filtering in from the other side. He broke into a smile. Wombat had done it! He'd dug them a tunnel. Carefully, Bertie wriggled his way inside. He wanted to go first to make sure it was safe for Smalls. Wombat could easily go unnoticed or ignored on the other side, mistaken for a rodent of some sort. But there was no way Bertie was letting Smalls enter until he was sure there were no bear traps awaiting him.

As he crawled, dirt clung to his clothes and flicked into his face, but he kept pushing forward, his eyes glued to the light. Soon he could make out whole spirals of it, flickering across blades of grass. Lanterns, he determined as he emerged on the other side. They lined either side of a long, narrow road, blowing softly in the night breeze. Bertie brushed the dirt off his hands as he followed the road with his eyes. It led to the green brick building he'd seen from the other side of the wall. *Toddle's Toy Emporium*, the sign in front read. His stomach went fluttery, as if he'd just swallowed a hundred moths. They were finally here.

The building was beautiful, a deep green the color of a jungle, with a white lace trim and a white shingled roof. It was huge too. It twisted and turned and fanned out, the kind of building with never-ending hallways and tucked-away rooms, the kind of building you could get lost in. In the distance behind it, toward the back of the fence, Bertie could make out a stone house with a tall turret and, off to the side, a small yellow cottage.

"Come on, Smalls," Bertie called into the tunnel. He gave a soft whistle. A minute later, Smalls squeezed his way out of the hole, grunting as his eyes landed on the building ahead. Wombat shot out behind him. With an impatient snort, he took off for the Emporium at his fastest waddle. Bertie looked over at Smalls. "I guess that's our cue." They hurried after Wombat, Smalls sticking close to Bertie's side.

There were several unusual contraptions dotting the Emporium's lawn, and Bertie studied them curiously as they neared the building. There was a tall silver coil that sprinkled bits of candy into the air. There was a boy built entirely of copper, waving a rainbow of balloons in his copper hands. And nestled in a tall oak tree, there was a life-sized version of the wooden dollhouse Bertie had found at the circus—the one that had been home to his wooden boy.

Bertie stopped so suddenly that Smalls bumped into him. A memory was rushing at him, so strong it knocked the breath right out of him.

He was lying beneath a tree, its leafy branches sweeping over him. His mom was lying next to him, and in between them was a small wooden house, the roof opened to reveal two floors filled with perfect, miniature rooms. The top corner room was a boy's bedroom, complete with a collection of tiny wooden baseball caps hanging from hooks on the wall and a miniature leather baseball glove discarded on the bed. There was a redheaded wooden boy in the room, a tiny baseball bat clutched in his hands. "BAM!" Bertie said, making the boy swing the bat.

"And it's outta here!" his mom cheered. "The crowd goes wild as the ball reaches the trees . . ." Bertie and his mom both looked up, following the trajectory of the imaginary ball. The leaves rustled above them, as if they too could feel it. "If only we could have a house like this up in the tree," Bertie said. "Like a real tree house!"

His mom looked over at him. Her red hair spilled into her

face, and her freckles caught specks of sunlight. "*Yes,*" *she said, breaking into a smile.* "*Wouldn't that be nice?*"

The memory was gone as quickly as it had begun, and Bertie was left staring up at the tree house, feeling like he'd been hollowed out. He leaned against Smalls, waiting for his breathing to return to normal. Up ahead, Wombat snorted anxiously as he paced in front of the Emporium, pausing every few seconds to nose at the door. Bertie took a shaky breath. These new memories and dreams meant something— were *telling* him something. They had to be. And there was only one way to find out what it was. "Come on," he said to Smalls. "Let's help Wombat find a way in."

Bertie pulled on the front door of Toddle's Toy Emporium for what felt like the hundredth time, but still it wouldn't open. With a sigh, he sagged against the door. That memory from the tree house had left him feeling more spent than ever. All he wanted to do was climb into a soft bed and sleep for days.

In the back of the building, Wombat was snorting up a storm. A grunt followed from Smalls, soft but urgent. Peeling himself off the door, Bertie headed around back. "We have to keep quiet," he whispered to the animals, as he stifled a yawn. "We don't want anyone to hear . . ." He trailed off when he saw what Smalls and Wombat were standing in front of. It was a small, child-sized door in the back of the Emporium. It stood slightly ajar, as if someone had forgotten to pull it shut behind them. Wombat had his snout in the crack, nudging at it. With a soft creak, it popped open the rest of the way.

Behind the door was a big room, filled to the brim with colorful plastic balls. Wombat pushed his way in, snorting sharply. Bertie followed hesitantly. His feet sunk into the pool of balls, the plastic cool against his bare ankles. He took another step, and another, until he was wading out chest deep. Next to him, Wombat was swimming through the sea of plastic balls, his head bobbing above the curves of color. Smalls walked behind Wombat, nudging him up with his muzzle every time he started to sink.

A wild impulse stole through Bertie, chasing away his exhaustion. Without stopping to think, he sunk beneath the balls, letting the colors swallow him up. Underneath, the whole world changed: sounds became muffled and colors became brighter, and rainbows seemed to fracture and split around him. When he finally sprang back to the surface, he was smiling. Just then, something hit him squarely in the forehead.

He looked down. A blue plastic ball dropped softly in front of him. Seconds later another ball came at him, this time bouncing off his shoulder. Bertie's eyes landed on Smalls. He had a yellow ball in his mouth and a mischievous glint in his eyes. Slowly, Smalls stretched out his long tongue and, while Bertie watched, flung the ball right at him. Bertie burst out laughing.

"Finally," Smalls said as Bertie's laughter rang through the air. It had been too long since he'd heard that laugh. He grunted happily, winging another ball at Bertie. This time Bertie fired back, laughing louder with each ball he pelted.

"*Some* of us have a job to do," Wombat chided, climbing out of the pool of balls. He stuck his snout in the air, sniffing several times. "Tilda?" he called out. "Are you here, *mon amour?*"

Smalls wanted to shout high and low for Tilda too. But first he needed to hear Bertie laugh one more time. Gathering up three balls, he tossed them into the air and juggled them with his long, graceful tongue.

"Looks like the circus was good for one thing," Bertie said, watching him admiringly.

"Circus?" Smalls repeated disdainfully between juggles. "I've been doing this since I was a cub! You should have seen the kernels of popcorn I used to juggle." As if to prove his point, he added two more balls to the mix, his tongue working overtime.

Bertie didn't know what Smalls's grunts meant, but he loved the look in his eyes as he juggled: determined, proud. He tossed Smalls another ball and the bear flicked out his tongue, incorporating it effortlessly.

"Go, Smalls!" Bertie cheered, and Smalls let out such a proud grunt in response that Bertie couldn't help but burst into laughter once more.

By the time they left the ball room, Bertie had all but forgotten his exhaustion. And as they crossed through a hallway, following the sound of Wombat's snorts, any final traces of it melted away. Because Bertie suddenly found himself standing inside the main room of Toddle's Toy Emporium. And everywhere, *everywhere* he looked—up and down and left and right and forward and backward—he saw one thing and one thing only. Toys.

24

Sweet Nothings

Standing in the entrance to Toddle's Toy Emporium, Bertie was reminded of a film he'd once seen. It had been soon after he'd gone to live with his uncle. The circus performers had set up a secret screening in the Big Top, and the smell of popcorn and cinnamon buns pouring out from the tent had been impossible to resist. Risking his uncle's wrath, Bertie had snuck over. He'd gone for the food, but it was the screen that drew him in.

On it, an actress was walking through a wooded area when she came across a horse, rearing and wild. As her hands flew to her mouth in surprise, the scene went fuzzy around the edges, blackness rolling in until eventually the only thing you could see was the horse—all sleek fur and flashing hooves, a slice of life in the center of the darkness. That was how Bertie felt as he stood inside the Emporium, like the rest of the world was blackening around him, the edges rolling in until all that was left was toys. He could feel his own hand flying to his mouth as he switched on a lamp and looked around.

The toys were everywhere: in every nook and cranny and shelf and cubby, hanging from every wall and crammed into every corner. Board games, stiff and unopened and stacked to the ceiling. Kites, bright and patterned and hanging from the walls. Dolls of every shape and size, in boxes and cradles and strollers and cribs. Pogo sticks, Frisbees, trucks, tea sets, tricycles, Barbies, jack-in-the-boxes, puzzles, stickers, Legos, even tiny winged planes, zooming and looping through the air. There were games to play, balls to throw, things to build, art to make, and, of course, winding through it all: stuffed animals. There were shelves and shelves of them, fur glossy and eyes shiny and stuffing plump, lizards and tigers and bears and monkeys and kittens and mice, spilling off the shelves and onto the squishy rubber floor, standing on tables and piled in bins, palm-sized all the way to life-sized, more stuffed animals than Bertie had thought existed in the entire world, and they were all right here, in a single building.

Bertie's head felt heavy with it all, colors spinning and swirling around him. He wished so badly that Susan was there with him. He had a huge toy store all to himself; it was like a genie had plucked one of his dreams and made it come true. But without Susan, it just wasn't the same. *Soon*, he told himself. If Susan and Rigby had managed to stay on the train, they had to be arriving soon.

Immediately, Smalls and Wombat ran off, going in opposite directions. Bertie hoped that if Tilda was somewhere nearby, they would be able to smell her. He planned to go search for her too—he knew there was no better time than when the store was closed—but for a minute he allowed himself to just stand there, taking it all in. He was in the middle of a slow sweep of the store when his eyes landed on the life-sized toy tree in the back.

It was carved entirely of wood and reached all the way up to the ceiling, its wooden branches curling and arching, laden with delicate wooden leaves. It reminded Bertie instantly of the wooden dollhouse. Every detail was captured perfectly: the roughness of the bark, the dewy green of the leaves, the wooden birds perched on its branches. At the foot of the trunk was a tiny door, just large enough to fit a child. It had four words inscribed across it: *Here, you may escape.*

Bertie walked over to the tree, unable to stop himself from climbing through its door. It was dark inside—the walls painted midnight black—but up at the top, where the trunk branched out into limbs, there were dozens of tiny, round globes floating through the air, light spilling out of every one of them. Catching that light on their gossamer wings were butterflies: hundreds of tiny, vibrant butterflies. Instantly, they began fluttering down to him, whirring loudly as they alighted on his shoulders and his hair, their wings velvet-soft.

Bertie watched as a purple-spotted butterfly landed on his hand. He knew it wasn't real, knew the whirring must be coming from a mechanical engine somewhere deep inside it. But it *felt* real, all of it, as if he'd stumbled into a field filled with butterflies, where the stars were so bright he could reach out and touch them. He leaned his head back against the tree trunk as a teal butterfly landed on his knee. His exhaustion was flooding back, turning his limbs to jelly and making his eyelids grow heavier by the second.

Groggily, he climbed up the stairs to the landing at the top. "I'll just lie here for a moment," he murmured, curling up on the soft, thick rug. "Then I'll go check on Smalls and Wombat and look for Tilda . . ." A moment later, he was fast asleep.

At the same time, Smalls was in the Emporium's vast main room, sniffing wildly at the air. He'd been smelling for Tilda, but instead a sweet, sugary scent wafted toward him, making his nose tingle with excitement. He followed it through a winding row of shelves, all the way to a set of stairs. More smells rushed up at him, syrupy and mouthwatering. Sniffing wildly, he bounded down the stairs.

"Holy horseshoe," he said. He was in a room full of candy. The floor was built of Twizzlers, the walls made of peppermint tiles. Oversized lollipops created a winding path through the room, guiding the way through buckets filled with candy and chocolate. On the back wall, brightly colored M&M's spelled out the words *Sweet Nothings*. Smalls's mouth watered. His big, empty stomach grumbled. He'd start his search for Tilda in a minute. First, it was time to eat.

He rose onto his hind legs. With his big paws, he scooped up gummy candies and toffee candies and caramel candies, gooey candies and hard candies and milky candies. He sucked them down one after another, letting them gather in his stomach, filling up every inch of emptiness. He was in the middle of a mouthful of candied peanut butter and maple syrup chunks when he suddenly caught a whiff of something familiar.

Sweet and tangy . . . fresh and oaky . . . balmy and fragrant. He knew that smell better than any other in the world. His eyes flew to a tower in the corner. It was built entirely of jars—jars featuring a bee on the label. Smalls couldn't read the words, but he didn't need them to tell him what his nose already knew. Every one of those jars was filled with honey.

He reached the tower within seconds. The jar on the top twisted open easily in his strong paws. Smalls's tongue darted out, sinking into the thick, sticky goodness. *Holy honey*, he thought.

While Smalls was busy devouring honey, Wombat was in a different wing of the Emporium, remaining all business. He didn't stop to admire the shelf of Angora rabbit stuffed animals; he didn't hop onto one of the red train cars rolling along an elaborate wooden track; he didn't utter a single fact about the collection of dinosaur fossils on display. He did one thing and one thing only, and that was call for Tilda.

"Tilda? Tilda, my love?" he repeated over and over as he went from room to room. He wove his way through bins of glistening marbles; he walked across a life-sized chess board; he jumped over boxes of jacks and rows of dominos. He turned left through a row of globes and right past a display of brightly colored crayons. Soon he found himself in yet another wing, passing several locked-up rooms. *Warning: Inventions–in–Progress!*, a brightly lit sign read. Wombat walked right past it, banging his snout against the locked doors, calling out for Tilda. But no matter how many corners he turned or how many stairs he took, no Angora rabbit answered his calls.

Soon his voice was raw and his paws were dragging. Still,

he pushed on. "*Mon amour?*" he called out hoarsely, turning into yet another room. "Are you here?"

"Keep it down," a voice answered. It was a female voice, clear and high. "Some of us are trying to catch some beauty *Z*'s!"

Wombat blinked, looking around for the first time. He was in the Emporium's Reading Room, a carpeted space piled high with pillows and lined with floor-to-ceiling book-shelves. There was a window seat in the corner, and dangling on the other side of the window was a three-story birdhouse. Standing on its deck, her head cocked in irritation, was a beautiful blue-winged bird.

"My apologies," Wombat said quickly. "I didn't realize I was disturbing anyone."

"Humph." The bird studied him for a second, cocking her beak. "What kind of animal are you?"

Wombat lifted his snout. "I'm a wombat of the rare hairy-nosed variety."

"A *what*?" the bird replied.

Wombat sighed. "A hairy-nosed wombat."

"No way." The bird let out a low whistle. "So you really came. She said you would, but I had my doubts. No offense to you, sweetie. It's just that prince charmings are a dying breed these days."

"Prince charming?" Wombat's fur bristled with pride. "I suppose that does suit me—wait." He looked up sharply. "Who said I'd come?"

The bird flapped her wings, exposing their shimmery silver lining. "Tilda, of course."

Wombat teetered unsteadily on his paws. "You've seen Tilda?" He whirled around, looking high and low. "Tilda, my love? I've come for you!"

The bird flinched. "No need to shout, honey. She's not going to hear you in here."

Wombat's snout quivered. "Where is she then?"

"The highest room of the Toddle family house." The bird pointed her wing at a tall stone house in the back of the Toddle compound, where a tiny pinprick of light shone in the window of its turret. "That's your girl's new home. Or prison, depending on how you see it."

Wombat kept his eyes trained on the turret. For once in his life, he was at a complete and utter loss for words. So he did what any self-respecting wombat would do and stole some from Smalls. "Well, holy horseshoe," he said.

25

Invisible Boy

Bertie woke to the sound of footsteps. "Smalls?" he murmured. He patted the ground next to him without opening his eyes. But seconds passed, and no sun bear cuddled up to him. Nearby, the footsteps grew louder. Two footsteps, Bertie realized, not four. *Human footsteps.*

He bolted upright, suddenly wide awake. The memory of last night came flooding back to him. He'd only meant to lie down in the wooden tree for a minute, but he must have fallen asleep. Moving quietly, Bertie crept down the stairs and peeked out the door of the tree. The footsteps belonged to a woman. She was wearing a blue-and-white-striped uniform shirt and a nametag that read: *MARIE, Certified Toy Specialist!* Sunlight poured in through the store's windows as the woman eyed the lamp Bertie had turned on last night.

"Someone must have forgotten to turn this off." She

shrugged and began moving through the store, flipping light switches and straightening shelves. "I hate working Saturdays," she mumbled. "Always the busiest day of the week." She stopped behind a long blue counter and pushed several buttons on the cash register. She was opening the store, Bertie realized. He ducked back into the tree, his heart pounding. He just hoped Smalls and Wombat knew to hide.

Footsteps. Smalls heard footsteps above him. And not Bertie's, either. Heavier, denser footsteps. He leapt to his paws. His fur was sticky with honey, and several empty jars were scattered around him. A few feet away, Wombat was fast asleep, his head resting on an empty jar of yogurt-covered pretzels. "Wombat," he hissed, nudging him awake. Last night, they'd stayed up for hours brainstorming ways to save Tilda from the turret she was trapped in. At some point, they must have both drifted off. "Wombat," he said again, nudging him harder.

"Tilda?" Wombat's head snapped up, his eyes popping open. "Oh. It's just you."

"Me and someone else," Smalls said. He gestured to the ceiling, where the footsteps were working their way across the main room of the store.

Wombat flicked his ears, listening hard. "Not Tilda," he said with a sigh.

"No, but someone we probably don't want to see us," Smalls pointed out. "Not if we want to find Tilda—and Rigby and Susan too."

That got Wombat to his feet. As he stretched out his paws, Smalls gathered up the empty jars, burying them in the bottom of a large tub of jellybeans. He clumsily rearranged the honey tower, hoping no one would notice that it stood a little shorter than yesterday. At the last minute, he snatched another jar in his teeth. A bear couldn't be expected to skip breakfast, after all. "Follow me," he whispered to Wombat. Padding softly across the floor, he took off to find a place to hide.

It didn't take long for the store to fill up with people. Bertie looked nervously around as he slipped out of the tree. But he quickly discovered there was no need to worry. In the midst of all those kids—climbing and running and playing and yelling—no one so much as batted an eye at the sight of a small, red-haired boy emerging from the tree.

Bertie stretched his arms overhead as he stood there in the bright light. Kids streamed past him as if he wasn't even there, as if he could be anyone. It reminded him of how he used to long to be Invisible Boy, a hero who could turn invisible at will. "It looks like I finally got my wish," Bertie said. And in a toy store, of all places.

Immediately, he began to scan the crowd, hoping for a glimpse of Susan's blue skirt and long blond hair. The room was packed with kids their age; everywhere he looked, he saw flaxen blond hair and g olden blond hair and strawberry blond hair. But there was no acrobat's uniform in sight. There was no Susan.

Bertie spun slowly around, studying the store. It looked as huge from the inside as it had from the outside: rooms unfolding into more rooms, stairwells shooting up and up. If Susan was here, she wouldn't have known to wait for him in the main room. Knowing her, she would have hidden Rigby outside and would now be traipsing from floor to floor, searching high and low for him. She could anywhere. And so could Tilda.

Bertie's cheeks puffed up in a smile. It looked like it was time to explore Toddle's Toy Emporium.

26

A Stuffed Piglet

Smalls was going stir-crazy. He'd never been very good at standing still, and for the past hour he hadn't so much as moved a muscle. It was working, though. Standing in the back of Toddle's Stuffed Jungle, between a life-sized tiger and a giraffe whose head scraped the ceiling, Smalls and Wombat had barely been glanced at. The problem was, Smalls wasn't sure how much longer he could take it.

Smalls sniffed discreetly at the air. If Rigby and Susan had managed to stay on the train, they could be arriving at Toddle's at any minute. Smalls might not have Rigby's impeccable sense of smell, but any bear worth his fur could easily sniff out a dog in an otherwise human crowd. He inhaled slowly, searching for a hint of Komondor fur or dog breath lingering amid the rubbery scent of toys and the perfumed scent of humans. But he caught nothing. Smalls's stomach churned uneasily. *It doesn't mean they won't come*, he told himself.

"Mom, look!" A girl with dark brown pigtails knelt in front of Wombat, ruffling his short, bristly fur. "This piglet stuffed animal looks so real!"

The girl's mom stopped next to her. "I don't think that's a piglet, honey. It looks more like a beaver to me."

"No, no." The girl's dad came over to join them. He had shaggy hair that was just as dark as his daughter's. "It's a wombat, honey. Most likely a hairy-nosed one, judging by his snout."

A pleased snort escaped Wombat.

"He makes noises!" the girl squealed. She squeezed Wombat's stomach, trying to make him snort again. "And he's warm too, like a real animal! Can I get him?" She looked beseechingly up at her parents. "Puh-leeeaaazze? I won't ask for anything else this trip, I swear!"

"How much is it?" her mom asked. She crouched on the ground, studying Wombat. "I don't see a price tag . . ."

Smalls stiffened. Of course there was no price tag. Wombat wasn't for sale! A terrible scenario suddenly flashed through his mind. The girl's mom getting the manager. The manager coming up with a price. And the girl walking out with Wombat tucked under her arm.

Or just as bad—the manager realizing why, exactly, Wombat *didn't* have a price tag.

"It doesn't matter," the girl's dad said. "Because you're not getting it, Hannah. You have enough stuffed animals! We're here for a jewelry-making kit, remember?"

Hannah sighed. "I know . . ." She gave Wombat a final longing pat before following after her parents.

Smalls blew out a sigh of relief as the family disappeared from sight. "That was close," he whispered.

"Too close," Wombat murmured out of the side of his mouth. "Which is why we need to construct a method to save Tilda pronto."

Thanks to the bird Wombat met last night, they knew where Tilda was now. But even after hours of brainstorming, they still hadn't come up with a fail-proof way to save her. Smalls knew that the longer they stayed in the store without acting, the more they risked being discovered. They needed a plan. One that would help them get Tilda back—and distract him from worrying about Rigby and Susan in the process. "If only Alfie were here," he sighed. "I bet he'd know a way to use his quill sword to get to Tilda."

"Or his karate kick," Wombat agreed.

Smalls was quiet for a moment, trying to channel the brave little hedgehog. Slowly, a list began to form in his mind:

What Alfie Would Do:
1. Use a mouse hole to sneak unseen into the Toddles'
house.
2. Unlock Tilda's turret prison with a sharp quill.
3. Duel courageously with the poufy-dressed girl hold-
ing Tilda captive.

It was a great plan, if you were a prickly, three-inch-tall, sensei-trained hedgehog. But those were Alfie's strengths, not Smalls's. "That's it," Smalls said suddenly. "Alfie would tell us to use our *own* strengths to come up with a plan! And I know exactly what my strength is." He flicked his ears forward happily. "I'm going to make a list."

"Of *course* you are," Wombat said. Out of the corner of his vision, Smalls caught Wombat rolling his eyes, but he chose to ignore it. His lists never failed him.

"Ways to Rescue Tilda," he began. "One. Climb up the side of the stone house."

"And slip and perish before we can rescue her?" Wombat gasped. "No, much too risky. Two," he said. "Propel boulders at her window in the turret."

"And get caught breaking a window?" Smalls countered.

"Valid point," Wombat admitted. They were both quiet for a minute, thinking.

"We could have that bird you met fly up to her window," Smalls offered.

"Or better yet," Wombat said slowly. "*I* could fly up to her window!" He looked up at the ceiling, where a toy hot air balloon hovered above them. It had a basket just large enough to fit a hairy-nosed wombat.

"That's brilliant!" Smalls exclaimed. It came out a little louder than he'd meant it to, and he quickly clamped his mouth shut. He looked around, worried someone might have heard his grunts, but between the patter of footsteps and the cheers of kids and the yells of parents and the rattle of toys, it was clear no one had noticed. Still, he lowered his voice back to a whisper. "And to think my next suggestion was for you to blend in as a stuffed piglet," he joked.

Wombat looked over at him, his round eyes lighting up. "That might actually be quite useful once I'm inside." A little boy ran past them, and Wombat automatically fell silent. He waited until the boy was gone to speak again. "It looks like we've found our plan."

"See?" Smalls said smugly. "I knew a list would help."

Bertie had been searching the Emporium for over an hour. He'd been through every aisle of the main floor and every inch of the candy room. He'd been up and down stairwell after stairwell. He'd passed a trampoline the size of a small pool and racks of dress-up clothes. He'd seen nooks filled with tea sets and toy barns and entire play kitchens. But no matter where he looked, he found no Susan, no Rigby, and no Tilda.

He let out a frustrated sigh as he headed back to the Stuffed Jungle to check on Smalls and Wombat. Before he'd started exploring that morning, he'd helped the animals get settled in a hiding spot there. Now, as Bertie wove through the aisles of teddy bears and penguins and stuffed snakes, even he had a hard time picking out the bear and wombat nestled between a huge stuffed tiger and an even larger stuffed giraffe. He broke into a relieved smile. They were still safe there, at least for now.

He gave Smalls a tiny wave before hurrying across the store once more. "Susan?" he called out tentatively. And then louder: "Susan? SUSAN?"

An elderly woman with a basket full of toys looked his way, but no Susan answered his calls. Bertie could think of only one other option. Squaring his shoulders, he marched over to the customer support desk in the corner of the room. The desk sat on a raised, swiveling platform and had the word HELP plastered across it, made up of dozens of twinkle lights. The tall, bespectacled man behind the desk looked a little queasy as the platform spun him around and around. "What can I do for ya?" he asked. His nametag said *HARRY, Certified Toy Specialist!* He adjusted his blue-and-white-striped bowtie before waving Bertie up.

The store began to cycle around Bertie the instant he climbed onto the platform. Toys winked in the corner of his vision, and the crowd blurred into a single, moving mass. He pressed his hands against the desk to steady himself. "I, um, I'm looking for a new toy," he told Harry. His voice was higher than usual as the lie spilled out of him. "I was told it was coming in on the next train shipment, so I was just wondering if you could, well, tell me when that would be?"

"Let's see . . ." Harry drummed his fingers against the desktop, looking thoughtful. "We are expecting a big shipment of toys, but the train makes several stops at our other factories along the way, so I can't say for sure when it will arrive. Maybe today, maybe tomorrow. Could even be the next day, if the factories move slowly."

Bertie's shoulders sagged. What if it really took *days*? He took a deep breath. He would just have to find a way to stay at Toddle's until the train got there.

He looked back up at Harry. He had one last question for him. "Also, can you tell me if Toddle's has some kind of petting zoo or pet store?"

"Not as far as I know," Harry said with a laugh. "Unless you're talking about the Stuffed Jungle, of course."

Bertie's heart sank. The check for Tilda had been written by the Toddle family! She had to be here somewhere. "There are no animals at all?" he pressed. "Because I heard there was a circus animal here now." Bertie arranged his face into a mask of innocence. "An Angora rabbit?"

Harry shook his head, making his bowtie jostle. "A rabbit? Where did you hear—oh!" He snapped his fingers. "You must be talking about the Toddles' new pet. Sorry, son, the rabbit doesn't live at the toy store." He pointed out the window, toward the huge stone house on the other side of Toddle compound. "That rabbit's living the royal life with the Toddles' own daughter."

27

Bertie Rots

Bertie collapsed in a beanbag chair, his thoughts spinning wildly. Getting to the Emporium had been difficult enough. How was he going to get into the Toddles' *house* now? The house might be in the same fenced-in compound as the Emporium, but there was at least half a mile of distance between them. If he even started walking toward the house in broad daylight, someone from the Emporium would surely stop him before he got very far.

In broad daylight. Of course! What he had to do was wait for nightfall, when the store closed up and all the employees went home. He'd been able to sneak into the Emporium at night; it was his best bet for the Toddles' house too.

Bertie stood up, a fresh burst of energy rushing through him. Hopefully Susan and Rigby would arrive soon. Then he and Susan could find a way into the Toddles' house together.

The thought gave him a happy, buzzing feeling as he hurried again toward the Stuffed Jungle to check on Smalls and Wombat. Fortunately, they were right where he'd left them, standing stock-still between the stuffed tiger and giraffe. He fought the urge to plop down at Smalls's paws and tell him everything he'd just learned. He knew the less attention drawn to the animals right now, the better.

He gave them a tiny smile before slipping away. As he paused in the middle of the store, it hit him that he now had an entire day to fill. And he knew exactly what to do with it.

He touched a hand to his pocket with a smile. He could finally research the wooden boy. Bertie thought of how excited Susan would be if he learned something new about the figurine—maybe even remembered something abo ut his past—by the time she arrived. It was the perfect way to pass his time.

But as Bertie took off through the store, searching for any signs of the wooden toy, his attention kept jumping. For most of his life, he'd had no toys and hardly any opportunities to play. Now, everywhere he looked, he saw both. He couldn't help it; each toy seemed shinier than the last. They drew him to them like he was a puppet on strings.

First it was the train set winding through the main room. His uncle had never let him have a train set; he'd laughed in his face the one time Bertie had asked, spitting a chewed-up fingernail at him for good measure. But here was a massive, elaborate set, complete with bridges and stations, and it was just sitting out in the open, waiting to be played with.

After that it was the motorcars: a small racetrack of miniature cars with real wheels and windows that rolled down. Bertie couldn't resist sliding into one, letting his hands grip the steering wheel.

"Wanna race?"

Bertie looked over sharply. A boy was sitting in the motorcar next to his, smiling expectantly. He had wildly curly hair and skin the color of a coconut husk.

"Me?" Bertie blushed as his voice squeaked slightly. He couldn't remember the last time he'd spoken to a boy his age—*really* spoken to him, not just served him cola at the circus's concession stand. He wasn't sure he even knew how.

The boy laughed. "Who else?"

Bertie glanced around. Here on the racetrack, with kids all around him and parents off in the distance, he could easily be one of them. An image of the wooden boy flashed through his mind. He cleared his throat. "I shouldn't," he said, his voice coming out firmer this time. "I need to go look for . . . a toy."

"It will only take a minute," the boy prodded. "Can't your toy wait one minute?"

Bertie looked longingly at the finish line, where a tall, skinny boy had just swept in for a win. "I guess it could," he gave in.

"All right!" the boy cheered. "Last one to the finish line is a rotten egg! I'm Chris," he added.

Bertie gave him a tentative smile. "Bertie."

Chris smiled back. "Get ready to lose, Bertie."

"I wouldn't count on it. I don't rot easily," Bertie shot back. He blinked. Had that really just come out of his mouth?

Next to him, Chris was laughing. "I don't know," he said, waving a hand in front of his nose. "I think I smell something already."

"Then it must be coming from you," Bertie replied cheerfully.

"We'll see about that. On three?"

Bertie nodded, planting his feet on the pedals. There was no motor in this car, only your feet to propel you forward.

"One," Chris counted. "Two. THREE!"

And they were off, Bertie pedaling as fast his legs would take him. Beads of sweat sprouted on his forehead and his breath tightened in his chest, but he just pedaled harder. Next to him Chris let out a holler, so he tried it too, throwing back his head with a "*Whooooo*!" It felt so good exploding out of him—no one to shush him or punish him—that he found himself doing it once more. "Whooooo!" He was inching ahead of Chris now, pedaling furiously. He was going to win. He could feel it.

That's when he saw it out of the corner of his vision: a wooden dollhouse, swinging through the air.

Bertie looked over sharply, his throat constricting. A young boy in a bright green sweater was swinging the dollhouse between his hands. Even from a distance, Bertie could tell it looked almost exactly like the one he'd found abandoned on the circus grounds—the one his wooden boy had come from. Up ahead, Chris reached the finish line with a shout of "Bertie rots!" but Bertie barely heard him. He had to find out where the boy had gotten that dollhouse.

"Got to go," he said hastily. He took off before Chris could respond. He practically raced over to the little boy. "Where did you get that house?" he asked breathlessly.

"This?" The boy held up the dollhouse. It had a copper-colored roof and red shutters. "It was in some room upstairs." He twisted around. "Hey, Mom!" he bellowed. "Where did we get this?"

A woman in a pink sweater even brighter than the boy's green one walked over. She was carrying a carved wooden airplane. It had a globe painted on its side, with the word "worldwide" emblazoned beneath it. Bertie's eyes widened when he saw the wooden figurine sitting in the pilot's seat. It was a red-haired wooden boy—just like his. "It was in the Fine Woods room," she said. "On the third floor. So was this airplane." She smiled at Bertie, revealing a silver cap on one of her back teeth. "Aren't they like little pieces of artwork?"

Bertie probably would have agreed if he had been there, but he was already halfway to the stairs.

28

A Pockmarked Thought

Rigby stared at the bucket of paint. The bucket of paint stared back at Rigby. "I shouldn't," he said. He took a step backward, his eyes still on the bucket. The blue paint shimmered and winked inside, like a pool of tears. "But look at that color . . ." He took a step forward. "No!" He took a step back. "Though . . ." He took a step forward again.

Rigby glanced over at Susan's sleeping form on the bed. "Maybe just a tiny bit . . ." Quickly he thrust a paw into the bucket. His tail began to thump as the paint coated his fur. He glanced over at Susan. Still sleeping. "Just a tiny bit more . . ."

He dipped his paw further into the bucket. Then he pulled it out and gave it a good shake. Specks of paint flung onto the wall, landing in a crooked spiral. Rigby cocked his head, studying the shape. "Once more," he said.

And then he was dipping and flinging, dipping and

flinging, his tail thumping wildly as a design took shape before him.

Susan opened her eyes. A familiar ceiling swam into view—the same spider web of cracks she'd woken up to every morning for nine and a half years. She sat up abruptly, remembering. She was home.

Rigby stood at the foot of her bed, staring up at her. His tail wagged furiously as she climbed to the floor. "What in the world did you do?" she murmured as she took in his paint-stained paws. Rigby's tail wagged even faster, drumming out a beat against the floor. Rising gracefully onto all fours, he trotted over to the far wall.

Susan's jaw dropped. There on the wall was a painting of some sort: thick dots of paint splattered in a wild, textured pattern. At first glance it looked haphazard, messy even. But the longer she looked at it, the more her eyes went loose around the corners, and suddenly an image began to emerge. The vague outlines of four animals: a dog, a rabbit, a bear, and a hairy-nosed wombat.

"Did you do this, Rigby?" Susan breathed.

Rigby's tail beat faster than ever.

Susan crouched down, taking his face in her hands. "Do you have any idea what this looks like, buddy?"

Rigby looked her right in the eye and let out an indignant bark, as if to say, *obviously*.

Susan laughed as she stood up, stretching her arms over her head. The silence of the house seemed to yawn around her. "They're still not here, are they, Rigby?" she asked softly. Rigby's tail stopped wagging as he looked up at her with wide, mournful eyes. Susan couldn't help but smile as he let out a soft whine. Sometimes she could swear that dog understood her.

Rigby followed her as she headed into the hallway. Sunlight poured in through the windows, washing the floors in light. She used to love to curl up at the top of the steps, where the pool of sunlight was always the warmest. *My little kitten*, her mom called her. Susan swallowed hard, refusing to let a single tear find its way into her eyes. She had no time for wallowing. Her parents didn't just vanish into thin air. No one did. They had to be *somewhere*; she just had to find them.

"What do you think, Rigby?" she asked, trying to break up the silence. "Could they be visiting Aunt Monica?" The last time Susan's parents could afford to visit her aunt was during a crop bonanza back when Susan was six. "Maybe they finally went again," Susan mused aloud. Rigby cocked his head as he followed her down the stairs. "I know, it doesn't sound right to me either," she said with a sigh.

As Susan walked into the living room, a thought crept into her mind. It was an ugly thought, pockmarked and misshapen, the kind of thought that festered slowly, waiting for just the right moment to lash out.

What if something was wrong?

She staggered backward so fast she slammed into a wall, sending shivers of pain down her spine. The full weight of it hit her all at once: her parents were really gone, she had no idea where they were. They could be hurt, in trouble . . . or worse. She felt cold all over, the way she used to when she was twirling on her rope at the circus, the wind a tunnel around her. Goosebumps lifted on her arms and tears pricked at her eyes against her will. She sagged onto the floor and buried her head in her hands.

Not a minute later, something soft and warm pressed against her leg. She peeked through her fingers. Rigby was leaning against her, his worried eyes looking out at her through thick tufts of fur. He began to lick her hand, slowly at first, then more urgently, like he was on a mission. The tiniest of half-smiles broke through her tears.

"I'm glad you're here, Rigby," she said, pulling him onto her lap. He responded with a massive, slobbery lick on her cheek. Leaning her head back against the wall, she scratched absently at Rigby's back. "Maybe everything's fine," she said softly. "Maybe they had a simple, logical reason for leaving. Which means there has to be a simple, logical answer around here somewhere. Some kind of clue as to where they went . . ."

She wiped away her tears and stood back up. She felt more determined than ever. If her parents were findable, she would find them. But as she began to root around downstairs, looking for some kind of clue, her stomach let out a hungry grumble. Down by her feet, Rigby's let out one to match.

"We should find some breakfast, huh?" she said to Rigby. She went into the kitchen, pulling open the cabinets and eying her parents' array of canned foods. "Let's see, we've got canned beets and canned oatmeal and canned spaghetti—"

Rigby interrupted with a loud bark.

"What?" She glanced over her shoulder at him. "You don't want cold spaghetti for breakfast, do you?"

Rigby barked again, his tail thumping against a cracked floor tile.

"Okay . . ." With a shrug, Susan grabbed the can out of the cupboard. "Cold spaghetti it is." She'd just dumped it into a bowl for Rigby when something caught her eye behind the table. A newspaper had been abandoned on the floor. It lay open, face up, almost as if it had slipped out of someone's hands mid-reading. Susan kept her eyes on it as she handed Rigby his spaghetti. If there was one thing her parents believed in, it was cleanliness: a place for everything, and everything in its place. A newspaper on the floor was definitely *not* in its place.

She picked the paper up. It was stiff in her hands, barely read. At the circus, she would have been thrilled to find an abandoned newspaper, would already be imagining a thousand different scenes to paint on its pages. But painting was the last thing on her mind as she stared down at the article the paper was open to—the last article her parents must have read.

THE END OF AN ERA, the headline blared. And underneath: THE MOST MAGNIFICENT TRAVELING CIRCUS SHUTTERS ITS DOORS!

Susan put a hand on the counter, steadying herself. She could barely breathe as she skimmed through the article.

After a fire blazed through the Big Top last week during the Most Magnificent Traveling Circus's one-ring show, the century-old circus was forced to park its caravans for good. "It was just horrific," Mary Toddle, the owner of the renowned Toddle's Toy Emporium was quoted as saying. "Twice I took my daughter to the Most Magnificent Circus, and twice we saw fire and chaos instead of magic and wonders! Mark my words: This circus is done for!"

It turns out Mrs. Toddle was right. Although the proprietor of the circus, Claude Magnificence, was unable to be reached for comment, signs have been tacked up on every one of his caravans, announcing an auction of all supplies this Saturday in the town of Truburg.

The article continued with a description of the circus's final fiery performance, but Susan had stopped reading. Because something had suddenly dawned on her. She collapsed in a chair at the table, relief rushing through her. It all made sense now: the half-drunk mug on the kitchen counter, the blanket strewn across the couch, that feeling of hastiness throughout the house, as if her parents had left in a rush. It was because they had.

Her parents had gone to Truburg. They'd gone to find her.

29

Suspicious Behavior

A checkerboard of glossy red shelves filled the Fine Woods room. Each and every shelf was overflowing with wooden toys: wooden turtles you could pull on a string, wooden nutcrackers whose jaws snapped loudly, wooden motorcars whose wheels spun around and around. In the center of the room, the shelves were wider and taller than the others. Crammed onto them, covering every inch of space, were the wooden dollhouses. Bertie couldn't help but touch them, run his fingers over the grainy bricks and painted shutters and tiny windows. He lifted the top off one house, peering into it. There was a family living inside: three identical brown-eyed girls, two parents, one dog, and a little boy.

Bertie pulled out the boy. It looked exactly like the one he'd found: painted wisps of red hair escaping from beneath a wooden baseball cap, a smattering of freckles covering his nose and bright blue eyes so much like Bertie's own. The only difference was the outfit. This one was painted into khakis and a spotless white shirt, a striped tie painted around his neck. Bertie wrapped the boy in his palm as he peeked into the next house. This one held a smaller family, just a dad and a son. Bertie pulled the son out. Again, the same boy looked back at him, wearing a green T-shirt and shorts this time.

He looked in the next house, and the next, and the next still. In every one, the members of the families looked different and the setup of the rooms varied, but the boy inside was exactly the same. Red hair, blue eyes, dark freckles; there wasn't a single house without him. Soon Bertie had a whole stack of the wooden boys in his hands, their outfits the only thing that set them apart.

"You're not allowed to just buy the wooden boys, you know," a girl said behind him.

Bertie's first thought was *Susan*.

But of course the voice was all wrong, higher-pitched and whinier than Susan's. Bertie spun around to find himself facing a girl his age. She was wearing a poufy purple dress and had a headful of brown curls. Her curls sprung wildly every which way, boinging into her face and against her shoulders, making it look like a living creature had taken residence on her head. She wore a pinched expression, as if she was trying very hard not to go to the bathroom. She seemed vaguely familiar to Bertie, though he had no idea why. He didn't have friends who wore poufy dresses. In fact, until Susan, he didn't have any friends at all. Maybe he'd served her at the circus once; he could never keep track of the hundreds of kids grabbing for cola at every single show. "I was just looking at them," he said defensively.

"I don't know." The girl crossed her arms against her chest. "You could be conducting what my dad calls *suspicious behavior*."

Bertie glared at the girl. She held her head up absurdly high, as if she were balancing an invisible crown up there. The smug look on her face was enough to make Bertie want to scream.

"Whatever you say, your highness," he muttered under his breath. He dropped the wooden boys back into their homes. He would wait to look at them until she left, he decided.

"No, no, no," the girl said, her voice rising shrilly. "You're putting them in all wrong!" She grabbed the remaining figurines out of his hand. With an exasperated sigh, she began placing them back inside the houses in the exact order he'd found them.

"How do you know where they go?" he asked.

"I know everything about this place," she said impatiently as she swapped two wooden boys into their correct houses. "I'm Chrysa—" She stopped short, her hand lingering over a blue cottage. "Chryssy," she finished slowly. "Yes . . . Chryssy. And I, uh, live near here, so I visit a lot." She looked up at Bertie with a snooty expression. "I'm kind of like a Toddle's Toy Emporium expert."

"Oh, really? Then how many floating globes are inside the hollow tree?" He'd counted them earlier today, when he'd slipped back into the tree for a moment alone.

"Forty-three," Chryssy replied easily.

Bertie took a step back in surprise. "That's right."

Chryssy rolled her eyes. "Of course it is. What I bet you don't know is that there's a secret door in the back of that landing."

"There is not," Bertie argued. He'd slept on that landing last night, and he hadn't noticed a single door.

"Is too." Chryssy tossed her hair, making her curls bounce wildly through the air. "If you knock three times in the back right corner, a door will open up. There's a slide behind it that leads all the way down to the candy room."

"How do you know that?" Bertie demanded.

"I told you, I visit a lot." She looked down, suddenly

very focused on her sparkly purple shoes. "I wasn't kidding that I know everything about this place. Like, did you know that everything in this room is made right here at Toddle's Toy Emporium? In fact, fifty-three percent of all Toddle's Toys are made in Toddle's own Development Center. That's over half," she added pointedly.

"I know what fifty-three percent means," Bertie said testily. This girl was getting on his last nerve. She was acting like she *owned* the place. But . . . if what she said was true, that meant someone in this very building had carved the wooden boys. "Where?" he asked suddenly. "If you know so much about this place, then where are these wooden houses made?"

Chryssy picked at her nails, looking bored. "Development Room 33Z. But shoppers aren't allowed there. My—I mean Mr. and Mrs. Toddle keep those rooms locked up tight."

"So you're saying there's no way for me to know if you're telling the truth? That sounds like a pretty convenient excuse to me." Bertie turned to leave. He'd had enough of this girl and her holier-than-thou attitude.

"Wait!" Chryssy grabbed his arm. She had a surprisingly strong grip for such a prissy-looking girl. "If you really want to see the woodshop, I'll take you there." She looked furtively around, lowering her voice. "But we're going to have to be really sneaky." She pursed her lips, making her face look more pinched than ever. "Do you think you'll be able to handle that?"

Bertie wanted to shake her off, tell her to find someone else to talk to like a little kid. But knowing the woodshop was within reach was giving him a scratchy, itchy feeling. He had to know more about those wooden figurines. He threw back his shoulders, meeting her fierce gaze. "Just call me Sneaky Boy," he said.

30

Plan Rescue Princess

"Freeze!" Smalls hissed. He and Wombat were attempting to work their way toward the boxes of hot air balloons, but it was slow going. Every time a person walked by, they had to freeze in place, pretending to be stuffed animals.

"*I'm* going to get the stuffed lizard," a lanky girl said. She tossed her little brother a smug look as she headed straight toward Smalls.

"But I want the lizard," her brother complained. "Remember? I told you that on the drive over!"

"Really?" The girl gave him an overly innocent smile. "I must have been sleeping when you said that." She stopped only inches away from Smalls, reaching for one of the lizards in the pile to his left.

"Your eyes were open," her brother argued. He hurried

over, bumping into Smalls as he glared at his sister. Smalls held completely still, not daring to breathe.

"So?" The girl hugged the stuffed lizard to her. "Sometimes people sleep with their eyes open."

Her little brother's face went red with fury. "Fine, I don't care! I'm getting a lizard too!" He bent down next to Smalls, rooting through the pile of lizards until he found the biggest one there. Smalls allowed himself a quick gulp of air as the boy shouted, "And mine's bigger than yours!"

The siblings continued to bicker as they headed toward the register. Only when they were out of sight did Smalls and Wombat start inching forward again. "*That* is why it's a miracle that only one hairy-nosed wombat is born per litter," Wombat whispered with a shudder. "Can you imagine having a sibling? I so prefer being independent."

"Yes," Smalls said dryly, twisting around to watch as Wombat followed closely on his heels, attempting to hide in Smalls's shadow. "Independent is exactly what I'd call you."

"Well it's hard not to be when you have an IQ of thirteen thousand." Wombat edged even closer to Smalls, accidentally bumping into his stumpy tail. "You really need to watch where you're going, Smalls," he lectured.

Smalls stifled a groan. He knew Wombat was just being

grumpy because he missed Tilda, but he wasn't sure how much more of his lecturing he could take. He took a big step forward. The sooner they got on with their plan to save Tilda, the better.

But Wombat had stopped moving. "Look!" he said. He pointed his snout at a low window a few feet away. It was tucked behind a tall shelf of craft supplies, and it was wide open. Behind it sat a line of bushes, just thick enough to conceal a bear. "Grab the hot air balloon," Wombat whispered. "My IQ of fourteen thousand has just given me a brilliant idea!"

"Sneak out the window into the bushes?" Smalls offered.

"Humph." Wombat snorted, looking miffed. "I was going to say *exit secretly into the shrubbery*, but I suppose you got the gist."

Smalls waited until the coast was clear to snatch one of the hot air balloon boxes with his teeth. He felt a stab of guilt, but he promised himself they'd return it as soon as they were done. Besides, saving Tilda—and reverting Wombat back to his old self—was worth more than any toy.

"Time to commence Plan Rescue Princess," Wombat declared.

Smalls shot him an exasperated look. "What happened to *Tilda?*"

"You always use code names on a rescue mission, Smalls," Wombat preached. "We can't just go around using Tilda's real name willy-nilly! What if someone were to hear? Our whole plan could be thwarted!"

Smalls could think of about a hundred different reasons why that was completely ridiculous—one being that humans only heard a series of snorts and grunts when they talked. But he kept his muzzle clamped shut. Squeezing behind the shelf, he gave Wombat a boost, helping him out the window. *This better work*, he thought as he climbed out after him.

Clay Master Pro

Chryssy led Bertie down a long, narrow corridor. Framed newspaper articles and advertisements lined the wall, each one featuring another toy Bertie had never heard of.

Introducing the Spangaphone! Why talk when you can spangle?

Toddle's Build-a-Monster takes holiday sales by storm!

Jump to new heights with Turbo-Jump 5000, the latest in bouncy technology!

Bertie couldn't take them in fast enough. How had he missed so many toys? It made him feel like he'd been floating in a black hole these past five years. The black hole of Claude.

Toddle's reaches record sales with the groundbreaking Crybaby Carrie!

Keep your kids laughing with Fart-Along Princess!

"Come onnn," Chryssy whined, pulling impatiently on his arm. "These are all boring old toys. The good stuff is behind these doors . . ." Her eyes lit up as she stopped in front of a room labeled 33E. The door was plastered with signs. **BEWARE! WARNING! DANGER! DO NOT GO ANY FURTHER!** Strange, muffled noises floated out of the room, thuds and clangs and what sounded like water churning.

Bertie eyed the signs doubtfully. "This is the woodshop?"

Chryssy waved a hand dismissively through the air. "We'll get to that. This is even better." Her eyes flitted through the hallway. "Keep watch," she demanded.

"The signs say . . ." Bertie began. But Chryssy had already pulled a bobby pin out of her hair and was using it to jimmy open the lock. It made a satisfying *click* as the door eased open.

"Where did you learn to do that?" Bertie asked, impressed in spite of himself.

"Lots of practice." She slipped inside the room, gesturing for him to follow. Bertie glanced over his shoulder. The corridor was empty. "Hurry," Chryssy urged. The sounds in the room were clearer now, soft booms mixed with the thuds and clangs, and definitely some kind of churning. Bertie couldn't resist. With a final glance over his shoulder, he ducked inside, pulling the door shut behind him.

The room wasn't very large, but it had a ceiling that seemed to stretch up and up. In the center of the room stood the strangest machine Bertie had ever seen. It was a hulking beast made of shiny silver, tubes sticking out of it in every direction. Some of the tubes were thin and some were as thick as trees. Some were short and some were so long they wound around the entire room. And each one was doing something different.

Thick bursts of steam rose out of one. Strange clanging sounds rang out from another. Pinwheels of ashy flakes spun down from a third. And all along, echoing in the very center of the machine, was a soft, steady boom, like the beating of a heart.

"This," Chryssy announced smugly, "is the Clay Master Pro." She ran a hand over a wide silver tube that was eliciting the churning sound Bertie had heard. It reminded Bertie of pressing a shell to his ear and hearing the ocean trapped inside. "It's a brand-new invention, still in testing phases. I was the first kid in the world to know about it. And one day I plan on being the first kid in the whole world to own it." She stuck her nose in the air. "Doesn't that make you wish you were me?"

"Then I'd be a girl," Bertie said flatly. What was *wrong* with her? At the circus, Bertie would have come up with a nasty nickname for her in two seconds flat. I-Still-Drink-from-a-Bottle Chryssy, maybe, or better yet: My-Head's-Too-Big-for-My-Crown Chryssy. But right now, the silver machine was beckoning to him, drumming out a heartbeat: *Ba-boom-ba-boom-ba-boom.* A spiral of something that looked like foam catapulted into the air. Bertie pushed the nasty nicknames to the back of his head. "So what does it do?"

For the first time since he met her, Chryssy broke into a real smile. "Watch." At the foot of the machine was a big silver lever. Crouching down, she used all her weight to pull it back. A loud gurgling noise erupted inside the machine. One by one, every one of its tubes began to spit out bubbles.

These weren't ordinary bubbles. They were bubbles like none Bertie had ever seen before: thick and creamy, opaque yet iridescent. The bubbles were colorful too: green and red and purple and blue, no two the exact same shade. Bertie had never seen colors that vivid before. They looked like they belonged in a painting—like they shouldn't be real.

"What are they?" he asked. His voice was filled with awe.

"Clay bubbles," Chryssy said proudly. "Invented right here at Toddle's Toy Emporium. Watch. In less than sixty seconds, they will mix together to form a sculpture that's so lifelike you won't believe it."

The bubbles began to gather in the center of the room.

As they bumped and collided, they melted together, until a mass of colors was swirling through the air: a glistening, dripping tornado. "What kind of sculpture?" Bertie asked.

Chryssy shrugged. Above her, the tornado was thickening, smoothing out. "Could be anything. The machine is programmed to make two thousand three hundred and twenty-one different sculptures."

Slowly, a shape began to emerge from the swirling mass of color: a single, high arch stretching across the room. As the clay settled, the colors intensified and separated, molding themselves into seven single bands, one clinging to the next: red, orange, yellow, green, blue, indigo, and violet. The colors were shimmering, gossamer, the reddest of reds and the bluest of blues. "A rainbow!" Bertie said.

A cloud of fog burst out from one of the tubes. For a second, the room was icy cold, as if a frost had settled over them. But as the fog evaporated, the room warmed. Bertie looked up to see that the clay had dried. The rainbow was hard and solid, rising all the way to the ceiling.

Chryssy planted a foot on one end of the rainbow. The clay held strong, neither bending nor crumbling. Her smile broadened as she began to climb. Bertie sucked in a breath. The rainbow looked frighteningly real, as if someone had snatched it right out of the sky. But here Chryssy was, *walking* on it. "What are you waiting for?" she called down. She was already high above him, her voice tinny and distant. "Are you scared?"

"Of course not," Bertie retorted. "I'm not a baby." He put one foot on the rainbow, then the other. It felt firm and solid beneath his feet. He began to climb, following after Chryssy. In the back of his mind, warning flags were waving, fighting for his attention: There were things to do, people and animals to look for. But standing on the rainbow, it all felt so far away, as if it belonged to another boy, another life. For the first time in as long as he could remember, he felt like a regular kid, just playing with a new toy.

Wanting to hold on to that feeling, he began to climb. Faster and faster, higher and higher, until he stood at the apex of the rainbow, looking down over the room. *Just once,* he promised himself. Afterward, he'd go back to being the Bertie he really was. Dropping down on his butt, he pulled his knees to his chest. "Timberrrr!" he shouted. Then he slid down the rainbow, all the way to the other side.

A Glass Box

Bertie kept his promise. After one slide down the rainbow, he stood up, dusting tiny bits of colored clay off his pants. "We have to go," he told Chryssy when she slid down after him.

"Already?" She was smiling again, and it made her look like a different person entirely. "We just got here!" She carefully dusted clay off her own dress. "That's the kink they're still working out," she told him. "The clay gets you dirty."

"You promised to show me the woodshop," Bertie said, ignoring her comment. The rainbow gleamed temptingly above him, but he wrapped his hand around the wooden boy in his pocket, refusing to look up. "Come on," he pressed. "I want to go before someone figures out we're here."

"Okay, okay," Chryssy whined. The pinched expression

was back on her face, any trace of a smile long gone. "You don't have to be pushy about it."

Bertie gritted his teeth as he followed her back into the corridor. "How far?" he asked.

Chryssy signaled for him to be quiet. Without bothering to see if he was following, she took off jogging. The corridor twisted and turned and twisted again, and still they kept going. Finally, they came to a stop in front of the very last doorway in the hallway. 33Z. This one was simpler than the others they'd passed, no **STAY OUT!** or **DANGER: EXPLOSIVES!** signs in sight. Just a single plaque, swinging from the handle. **Stanley's Workshop**, it said.

"Stan is Toddle's resident woodworker," Chryssy informed him. "Practically every piece of wood in this building was carved by him. Even the wooden tree in the main room." Once again she pulled a bobby pin out of her hair and used it to jimmy open the lock. "Luckily, Saturdays are his day off."

"How do you *know* all this stuff?" Bertie asked. For a second, Chryssy looked almost sad. She turned away, slipping into the room without answering.

Compared to the rest of Toddle's Toy Emporium, the woodshop was plain and bare. The only furniture was a long table lined with whittling knives. A blank chalkboard hung on the wall next to a single cabinet, which was bolted up tight. Along the back wall a huge collection of wood was lined up, sorted by size and color.

Bertie walked over to the table. Along with the whittling knives, it had the usual desk supplies on it: a spool of tape, a pair of scissors, several pens. There was also a small square of wood, half of which had been whittled away so that the form of a boy had begun to emerge. Bertie picked it up, running his hand absently over its rough edges. He'd been hoping to find something that would trigger more memories, but there was practically nothing here. Just an old room and a half-formed boy that reminded him of nothing more than the figurines he'd already found.

Frustrated, Bertie brought the chunk of wood closer, studying the tiny, precise knife marks. He waited for something to hit him, some memory or sense of meaning, but nothing came.

A noise from the hallway shook him out of his thoughts. "Hide!" Chryssy hissed. They both dove under the table at the same time, their knees clanging together. Seconds later, a slight, gray-haired man ambled into the room. He was humming under his breath, a light, cheerful tune, as he carried something over to the cabinet. Reaching up, he removed a key from the top of the cabinet to unlock it.

Bertie held his breath as he peeked out from behind the table's leg. Chryssy tried to pull him back, but he ignored her. His eyes were glued to the cabinet. There was an array of woodwork inside: figures and furniture and a few tiny motorcars and trains. Some, like the wooden boy the man slid inside now, looked freshly carved. But others were worn down with age, like they'd been sitting in that cabinet for a long, long time.

In the center of the cabinet, a small glass box held a single figurine. The man tapped the top of the box three times, fast, like it was some kind of ritual. Bertie shifted, trying to get a better view, but the sun was burning brightly through the window, casting a glare on the glass. No matter which way Bertie turned, he couldn't make out what was inside.

Chryssy grabbed one of his suspenders, shooting him a furious look. *Sorry*, he mouthed, freezing in place. On the other side of the table, the man locked the cabinet back up and placed the key on top of it. Still humming under his breath, he headed out of the room, leaving the door hanging wide open.

"We have to get out of here," Chryssy whispered the second he was out of sight. "Stan must have come in on his day off!"

Bertie eyed the key jutting off the top of the cabinet. It

would only take him a minute to get it down . . .

"Now!" Chryssy said urgently. "The only reason he would leave the door open is if he's coming back!"

Still Bertie lingered. He kept thinking about that figure in the glass box. What was so special it needed its own box?

Chryssy grabbed one of his suspenders, snapping it against his chest. "Let's go!" she ordered.

"Ow," Bertie grumbled, glowering at her.

"It will hurt a lot more the second time," she said. She glanced anxiously at the doorway. "I'll help you get back in tomorrow, okay? At noon, during Stan's lunch break. But we have to get out of here now, before we get in serious trouble with my—uh, the Toddles."

Bertie met Chryssy's eyes. "Promise me," he said evenly. The last thing he wanted was to spend another minute with this suspender-snapping, hoity-toity, know-it-all royal highness, but if it meant finding out what was in that glass box, it would be worth it.

"I promise." She grabbed his suspender again, yanking him toward the door. "Tomorrow at noon," she repeated. "I'll meet you in Fine Woods."

33

Brussels Sprouts

The Toddles were having chili for dinner. Chili and a big, steaming plate of brussels sprouts. Everyone in the Toddle household knew just how much Chrysanthemum hated brussels sprouts. She'd thrown many a fit over being forced to consume even half a brussels sprout, and her parents had famously built her an entire backyard swing set as a prize for eating a plateful. So it was with pure trepidation that Mr. and Mrs. Toddle watched Chrysanthemum sit down at the table.

"Chef Mary made chili today," Mrs. Toddle announced in an overly cheerful voice.

"What's that, dear?" Mr. Toddle called out, cupping his hand around his ear at the other end of the table. He was frowning, like usual. "There's dairy in the lily bouquet?"

"No, no, dear, chili! I'm telling Chrysanthemum about the chili!"

"You're chilly, dear? Then turn the heat up, why don't you?"

In chair seventeen, Chrysanthemum ignored her parents as she dug into her chili. Every few bites, she would repeat a single sentence to herself, as if it were some sort of chant. "I, Chrysanthemum-Chryssy Toddle, have plans tomorrow."

It had been a long time since Chrysanthemum had plans that didn't involve chores or school. If her parents had looked closely—had looked at all, really—they might have noticed that there was an unusual flush to their daughter's usually pale, pinched cheeks. But they didn't, of course. Instead they yelled across the table at each other, mistaking "miss" for "fish" and "mortgage" for "garbage," until Mrs. Toddle was shouting, "Why in the world would you fish in the garbage, dear?" It was only when Chrysanthemum asked to be excused that they both stopped yelling and looked over at her.

"Well now, Chrysanthemum," Mrs. Toddle said nervously. "You still need to eat your brussels sprouts."

"Did you tell her to eat her brussels sprouts?" Mr. Toddle shouted.

"Yes, dear, shush," Mrs. Toddle called back.

"Mush?" A wrinkle formed between Mr. Toddle's thick eyebrows. "They're brussels sprouts, not mush!"

Mrs. Toddle leaned forward in her chair, her watery eyes flitting from Chrysanthemum to the vegetables. "Just eat five, Chrysanthemum. Then you can be excused."

"Tell her we'll buy her a Sprouting Tree," Mr. Toddle yelled.

Mrs. Toddle looked over at her husband. "Why would she want a stinging bee?" she yelled back.

"I said a tree, not a *knee*!"

"A key?" Mrs. Toddle looked confused. "A key to what?"

"She's a nut? That's not a very nice thing to say about our daughter!"

Mrs. Toddle turned back to her daughter's place at the table, ready to insist that she'd said no such thing. But when her eyes fell upon Chrysanthemum's seat, her jaw fell slack instead. "Um, dear," Mrs. Toddle said slowly. "Where did all her brussels sprouts go?"

Mr. Toddle followed his wife's gaze. Chrysanthemum's chair was empty, and sitting on her placemat was a gold-rimmed plate that had once held eight brussels sprouts.

"She ate them," Mrs. Toddle said in amazement.

"She didn't ask for a toy," Mr. Toddle said in wonderment.

They stared at each other across the long table. "Do you think she's sick?" Mrs. Toddle asked.

"Yes," Mr. Toddle agreed. "That was very quick."

34

A Pair of Pelicans

Smalls sat back on his haunches, panting lightly. For the past several hours, he and Wombat had been hiding behind the bushes, out of earshot of the store's customers, as they struggled to put together the hot air balloon toy. Without a single opposable thumb between them, nothing had gone as planned. Smalls had hoped to open the box carefully, delicately, so they could return the toy to the store when they were done. But after almost an hour of tugging at it with his clunky paws, he had finally lost his patience and gone at it with his teeth. He'd gotten the toy out all right, but now the box lay in tattered pieces at his paws. Smalls had felt terrible, but Wombat had been too wound up by the prospect of seeing Tilda to be bothered.

"How many animals does it take to open a box?" he'd asked, his voice unusually high-pitched. "One—as long as it's a bear!" He'd then let out a very un-Wombat-like titter as Smalls dumped the contents of the box onto the ground.

Smalls had expected the toy to pop out in one spiffy piece, but much to his dismay, fifteen different parts had tumbled out, looking more like a motorcar collision than any type of balloon. Smalls had thought about finding Bertie to help them, but the boy was somewhere inside the store and Smalls knew he couldn't risk going back in there to look. So instead, he and Wombat had tackled it together. It had taken them an hour and a half of studying the instruction diagram and tinkering with every single part, but finally it had begun to resemble a hot air balloon.

Smalls blew out a sigh of relief as Wombat clicked the last part into place. "The moment of truth arrives," Wombat said. He pulled at a string with his teeth, and the balloon inflated instantly, a bright pink sphere the color of bubblegum bursting into the air. Smalls placed a paw on the balloon's basket, tethering it to the ground.

"Now, how many hairy-nosed wombats does it take to put together a toy?" Wombat asked gleefully. "One—as long as he has an IQ of twenty thousand!"

"It's up to twenty thousand now?" Smalls asked.

"You're right," Wombat said thoughtfully. "That's probably not accurate. It's closer to twenty-one thousand."

Smalls forced himself to keep his muzzle shut. "Why don't you climb in?" he suggested, nodding toward the basket. Behind it, the sun was just beginning to set in the sky, casting shadows across the long yard that stretched between the Emporium and the Toddles' house.

"Right. Climb in." Wombat eyed the basket cautiously. It was more than large enough for a stuffed animal or a doll, but a hairy-nosed wombat was going to be a tight fit. Wombat bounced a little on his paws. "I'm a knight in shining fur," he murmured to himself. Squeezing his eyes shut, he leapt into the basket.

"Do you remember our plan?" Smalls asked. He found himself wishing that Rigby were there to crack a calming joke, but he forced the thought to the back of his mind. Hopefully, Susan and Rigby would show up soon. Until then, he needed to focus on saving Tilda.

"Of course," Wombat replied huffily. "Some might say I have a photographic memory." He paused, burrowing lightly against the floor of the basket.

"DST," Smalls reminded him anyway, dropping several pebbles into the basket.

"It's called an acronym," Wombat informed him. "And as I said, I remember it." He pointed his snout in the air. "There's a reason Tilda calls me a hairy-nosed genius."

Smalls took a deep breath. "Here goes nothing," he said. He let go of the basket, sending it spiraling upward.

"I'm a wombat charming," Wombat whispered frantically as the balloon picked up speed. He peered down, his snout trembling at the sight of the ground becoming smaller and smaller. "Now what was that acronym? DRV? No, that can't be it. LSQ? No, not that either. DST!" A look of relief crossed his face. "It's just like I said: I have a photographic memory. Now, let's see . . . *D*. Duck in the basket."

Quickly, Wombat ducked beneath the rim, so no one could see the wombat riding in a hot air balloon. "*S*. Stay close to the wall." Using the tiny lever inside the basket, he steered the balloon toward the tall house, until he was only inches from the stone wall. "*T*. Toss pebbles through Tilda's window." Carefully, he gathered the pebbles up in his mouth.

The rest of the plan was simple. Wombat was to stay out of sight while floating up to the window of the turret, which was presently wide open. He would then use the pebbles to catch Tilda's attention. Once she saw him, she would immediately hop up onto the windowsill and leap into Wombat's waiting paws, at which point they would fly away together into the sunset.

It was a good plan, a solid plan. "As Alfie would say, as easy as a karate chop," Wombat assured himself. And it would have been. If the plan didn't have one tiny, little glitch. With his head tucked underneath the rim, Wombat couldn't see a thing that was happening outside the basket.

"Don't fear, my fair maiden," he whispered. "Your furry knight is on his way!"

Wombat was correct; he was on his way. But so, unfortunately, was someone else. Two someone elses, to be exact. Several yards away, a pair of pelicans were flying straight toward his balloon, too caught up in their conversation to notice.

"And then he said that I was the prettiest pelican he'd ever seen!" the bird on the left was saying.

"He didn't!" the bird on the right squealed.

"He did. And then he said that maybe we should, you know, go for a swoop together sometime."

"I'm dying here, Roberta! *Dying!*"

"And I'm not even done, Sally. Are you ready for this?"

Sally nodded her beak eagerly.

"*Then* he said, 'What about next Saturday?'"

They both let out loud shrieks of joy.

In his basket, Wombat cocked an ear. "Did someone just perish?" he muttered. He shook his head. "No distractions, Wombat," he lectured himself. "You have a quest to focus on!"

Meanwhile, the pelicans continued to fly closer and closer, still not noticing the balloon lifting directly into their path.

"You have a real date!" Sally squealed.

"I think he might take me to Pelican Point," Roberta said, snapping her long orange beak.

"Ooh la la!" Sally screeched.

"I'll have to fluff my feathers," Roberta said breathlessly.

"And buff your beak," Sally added eagerly.

"And—" But Roberta never got a chance to finish that thought.

Because suddenly the hot air balloon was right in front of them.

"Ahhh!" Roberta shrieked as her long, sharp beak punctured one side of the balloon.

"Oh my!" Sally shrieked as her long, sharp beak punctured the other side of the balloon.

"Holy horseshoe!" Wombat shrieked, spitting the pebbles out of his mouth as air leaked from both sides of the balloon. He began to spiral downward at an alarmingly fast speed. Wombat's eyes widened with fear. "I am formally requesting a rescue!" he squeaked, his voice high-pitched and strangled. But the balloon continued to plummet down, swooping left and right and upside down, like a dandelion puff tossed on the wind. Wombat dug his claws into the basket, hanging on for dear life.

"Is there a *mouse* in that basket?" Roberta asked incredulously.

"Is there a *piglet* in that basket?" Sally asked wonderingly.

"I'm a hairy-nosed wombat!" Wombat choked out.

Those were the last words he uttered before he hit the ground with a resounding, earth-quaking *thud*.

35

Two Blurry Shapes

Tilda's ears twitched. "What was that?" she murmured as a faint thud reverberated outside Chrysanthemum's bedroom window. She hopped closer. Outside, two pelicans were squawking frantically, their words a jumbled garble of *Oh my!* and *Did you!* and *Was that?*

"Was *what?*" Tilda muttered. "I can't see anything from this room!" She narrowed her eyes at Chrysanthemum, who was busy brushing black paint onto a large white T-shirt. "It's—it's abominable!" Tilda dropped her head, looking crestfallen. "Abominable . . . Wombat loves that word."

"Don't look so glum, sugar plum." At the sound of Kay's chirp, Tilda looked up with a start. The bird had landed on the windowsill, her clawed feet dangling off the edge. "Do I have news for you," she went on. "Boy oh boy, honey, you're going to love this."

From the other side of the room, Chrysanthemum let out a groan. "Why are there so many birds out tonight? It's throwing off my painting rhythm!" She went over to the window, waving a hand at Kay. "Shoo, little birdie. Go on!"

"What is it, Kay?" Tilda asked hurriedly. "What am I going to love?"

But Chrysanthemum had already nudged Kay off the windowsill. She slammed the window shut, nodding in satisfaction at the silence that followed. On the other side of the window, Kay fluttered in the air, her beak opening and closing. She was saying something—something that looked important—but inside her silent, sealed room, Tilda couldn't hear a word.

Smalls turned in a nervous circle behind the bushes. He couldn't see anything from this hiding spot! Just a minute ago, he'd watched as two sharp-beaked pelicans rammed right into Wombat's hot air balloon, sending him crashing to the ground. There had been a thud—and then nothing. Smalls strained his neck, trying to peer through the bushes. But they were too thick; it was useless. He touched a paw nervously to his four-leaf clover. If he went out to find Wombat, he risked being spotted. But if he didn't . . . He shivered. He had no choice. He had to make sure Wombat was okay.

He tried to stay in the shadows as he edged his way across the Toddles' vast, rolling lawn. The pelicans had flown off, leaving a heavy silence in the air. Smalls was careful not to utter a single grunt, but his heart was thudding so loudly he was sure it could be heard for miles. All he wanted was to be with his friends again, the four of them together, the way it was supposed to be. But with every passing day, that task seemed to grow more and more impossible. It reminded Smalls of the first time he'd juggled fire sticks. No matter how hard he'd chased after them, he knew eventually one was going to drop.

A few yards off, Smalls spotted a swatch of bright pink fabric lying in a mangled heap on the ground. His breath caught in his throat. Forgetting about the shadows, he galloped toward it. It was the hot air balloon. Its basket had splintered, scattering pieces everywhere. Lying in the center of them was the limp, punctured form of the deflated balloon—with a distinctly Wombat-shaped lump protruding beneath it.

"Wombat?" Smalls breathed.

From underneath the balloon came a low groan.

"Wombat!" Smalls lifted the fabric in his teeth, revealing a pile of leaves and a very dirty, very buried Wombat.

"I'm alive!" Wombat sobbed, dragging himself to his

paws. He shook the dirt off his fur. "Breathing! Standing! In one piece!" He threw himself at Smalls.

Smalls gathered him in his front paws, giving him a long, tight squeeze. "I was so worried," he whispered.

Wombat let out a strangled cough. "I can't breathe, Smalls!"

"Oh. Sorry." Smalls placed his friend back on the ground.

Wombat shook out his fur, clearing his throat. "Now," he said briskly. "As I was going to say before you got all melodramatic on us—"

"*I* got melodramatic?" Smalls cut in.

"You did." Wombat gave him a stern look. "But I forgive you," he said grandly. "Because we're going to need your list-making skills. It's time to construct Plan B. And this time, there's no Alfie to do it for us."

A twig snapped in the distance, making Smalls jump. "First, we need to get out of sight," he said quietly. Giving Wombat a nudge, he began to tiptoe his way back to the bushes.

Nearby, in the yellow cottage on the edge of the Toddles' fenced-in compound, a small, gray-haired man stood in the window. He held a steaming mug of tea between his hands and was sipping from it as he stared out into the rapidly growing darkness. In the distance, two blurry shapes moved through the shadows, one big and hulking, the other small and stout. The man frowned as he watched them. "If I didn't know better, I would say that was a bear," he said slowly. "And possibly a wombat."

The blurry shapes disappeared behind a line of bushes. "A bear at Toddle's," the man said, shaking his head. He laughed, a deep, jolly laugh that seemed as if it should come from someone much larger than him. "What will I dream up next?" Still laughing, he drew the curtains and disappeared into the cottage.

36

Silly Indeed

Bertie huddled inside the landing of the Emporium's wooden tree, breathing fast as butterflies touched down around him. He couldn't believe how careless he'd been! After the near miss in the woodshop, Bertie had returned to the Fine Woods room, eager to comb through the wooden houses again. Without Chryssy there to pester him, he'd lost track of time as he admired the tiny homes and families—and the red-haired boy that was in every one. It wasn't just the houses that featured the boy, either. He was sitting in every motorcar too, and walking the aisles of a wooden passenger train, and riding atop a brightly painted carousel. He was a part of every single carving.

As the boy's sky blue eyes stared back at Bertie again and again, he'd felt a twitch in the back of his mind, like something—he couldn't say what—was fighting to break free. He'd been so focused on it that he hadn't realized what time it was until he caught a glimpse of a passerby's watch. The store was going to close in six minutes!

What if the train had dropped Susan and Rigby off at the store while he was busy studying the wooden houses? They could be *here*, and he had less than six minutes to find them. Abandoning the wooden figurines, he'd raced through the store, calling out Susan's name as he sprinted from room to room, his eyes peeled for blond hair and white fur.

Once, he'd sworn he spotted Rigby, but it had just turned out to be a pile of toy mops. When the bell rang announcing the store's closing, Bertie had had no choice but to dive inside the tree to hide. There hadn't even been time to check on Smalls and Wombat first. He could only hope they were safely out of sight in the Stuffed Jungle. As the last of the shoppers had streamed through the store's exit, Bertie had allowed himself one quick peek. There hadn't been a blond-haired acrobat or a shaggy-furred dog among them.

Now, as Bertie squeezed his eyes shut, pleading silently not to be discovered, he heard a person clomp over to the tree, stopping dangerously close to it. "Maybe the missing hot air balloon was left in here, Margaret," the person called out in a gravelly voice. Bertie's heart took flight in his chest, flapping furiously. If a Toddle's employee looked inside the tree, it would be over: He would be caught.

But then another voice—this one higher and punctuated with a yawn—called back. "Eh, it's probably just a miscalculation. Miles did inventory today, and you know how he always makes mistakes."

"You're right," the gravelly voice replied. "We'll just blame it on Miles."

Bertie stayed frozen in place as he waited for the man to move on. Only when he heard his shoes thumping across the rubber floor did he dare move again. He sagged against the tree, his whole body tense with worry. It was nighttime, the store had closed, and Susan and Rigby still weren't there. A litany of possibilities ran through his head, one more awful than the next. *Lost, hurt, trapped . . . Claude.*

No! He couldn't let himself think like that. Harry had said it could take a few days for the train to arrive. Susan and Rigby would show up tomorrow; he had to believe that. He took a deep breath, counting slowly to ten like he used to when Claude made him angry.

By the time the employees left and he climbed out of the tree, he was feeling a little calmer. He stretched his arms over his head. The lights in the store had all been turned off, but thanks to a big solar system replica dangling from the ceiling—stars and planets and a bright, full moon—a soft glow filled the whole room. It was officially after hours; if there was ever a time to get to Tilda, it was now.

"Smalls?" he called out. "Wombat?" He walked over to the Stuffed Jungle, but no bear or wombat climbed out from the rows of stuffed animals. "Smalls?" he tried again. "Wombat?" Still nothing.

Picking up his pace, he jogged through the store, looking behind shelves and under piles. By the time he'd made his way through the whole first floor, he was positive: Smalls and Wombat weren't there. Bertie thought back to the last time he'd seen them. It had been in the Stuffed Jungle . . . but it had been several hours ago, before he went off with Chryssy.

A knot of panic climbed up his chest, settling in the back of his throat. What if they'd been discovered?

But how could he have missed that? A bear in a toy store? There would have been screaming, crying, all-around chaos. Even from upstairs he would have heard it. So where *were* they?

Snap! A noise from outside made him jump.

Snap! There it went again. This time, it was accompanied by another noise . . . Was that a grunt?

Bertie ran to the window and peeked out. There, squeezed behind a row of bushes, were Smalls and Wombat. Smalls was standing on his hind legs, and Wombat was resting in his front paws with a slingshot wrapped around him. As Wombat snorted a mile a minute, Smalls inched his paws left and right, almost as if he was trying to find a certain angle. Bertie raised his eyebrows. What were they *doing*? There was only one way to find out. Hoisting himself up on the windowsill, he jumped down into the grass.

In the small yellow cottage across the way, the gray-haired man sat hunched over his desk. "A bear and a wombat," he murmured to himself. He was whittling away at a block of wood, sending clouds of sawdust floating to the floor. "What silly things I come up with!"

As the night waned on, the man's knife continued to fly across the wood, sculpting and chiseling until a shape began to emerge from the block. Sleek curves and sharp lines, tiny etchings and scruffy texture. Narrowing his eyes in concentration, the man swept his knife over the wood one last time. "Finished," he murmured.

Holding the carving up to his desk lamp, he turned it this way and that, admiring it. Where there had once been just a square of wood, there were now two tiny figures, walking side by side: a long-tongued bear and a short, stout wombat. "Yes," he said. "Silly indeed."

37

A Flying Wombat

Smalls looked down at Wombat.

Wombat looked up at Smalls.

Bertie looked over at both of them, a wrinkle forming between his eyebrows.

"Are you sure you want to do this?" Smalls asked Wombat for the fifteenth time. He shifted uneasily, making the bushes around them rustle.

"I'm certain," Wombat replied, although the slight tremble in his voice made him sound anything but.

"It could go awry," Smalls pointed out, also for the fifteenth time. "Just like the balloon did."

"I'm aware . . ." For a second, Wombat appeared to waver. But then his gaze flickered toward the stone turret on the other side of the grounds. Night had fallen, sweeping the house in darkness. "It doesn't matter," he declared. "Tilda is in there somewhere. It is my duty as the love of her life to save her. At whatever cost to my own being." He lifted his snout above the slingshot. "Shoot me to her, Smalls!"

"Okay . . . if this is what you want."

"It is," Wombat said firmly. "Besides"—Wombat stuck his snout into the air—"if Alfie can defeat Grubs, then I can most certainly do this. It's just as he said: Little can still be mighty! Or, to put it more eloquently, minuscule can still be indomitable!"

"You're right." Smalls tightened the slingshot around Wombat. The window in the center of the turret—the one Wombat had tried to fly up to on the hot air balloon—shone with a dim beam of light. He carefully positioned himself so Wombat was aiming right at it. "If Alfie can defeat Grubs, then you can do this," he repeated, screwing up his courage. "*We* can do this."

"Easy as a karate chop," Wombat agreed.

Smalls nodded. But his paws were shaking as he slowly pulled back the slingshot.

Next to him, Bertie let out a yelp. "Stop it, Smalls! What are you doing? Are you actually going to *shoot* him? That's crazy! He could get hurt!" He grabbed onto Smalls's shoulder, squeezing tight.

Smalls froze, the slingshot stretched tight between his

paws. "Bertie's right, Wombat. It's just not safe enough. We'll have to find another way."

Wombat ignored him. With a determined grunt, he twisted around and, grabbing the slingshot in his teeth, yanked it out of Smalls's paws. "Easy as a karate chop!" he trilled. With a terrifying whoosh, Wombat launched into the air.

"No!" Smalls erupted.

"No!" Bertie cried.

Smalls's fur stood on end as he watched his friend soar through the sky. He wanted to look away, hide his head, but his eyes were glued to Wombat, his breath tangled somewhere deep in his throat.

His aim, at least, appeared to have been perfect. Wombat was catapulting in a direct trajectory toward the turret's window. Smalls dug his claws into the ground. If nothing got in his way, if no pelicans or heavy winds decided to swoop into his path, Wombat might actually have a chance at succeeding.

But once again, the animals' plan had a small but vital glitch. For, in the inky darkness of the night, neither Wombat nor Smalls could see that Chrysanthemum's window, which had stood wide open when Wombat rode up on the hot air balloon, had since been shut.

As Wombat vaulted toward the window, he opened one

eye a crack. The wind was rushing past him, ruffling his fur and slicking back his ears. Down below, the ground grew small and fuzzy, like a photograph out of focus. "I'm flying," Wombat breathed. Slowly, his muscles relaxed. His eyes opened. "It's a bird . . . It's a plane . . . It's a flying wombat!"

Wombat was just starting to look like he was truly enjoying himself when something caught his attention. He cocked his head, studying the window. The closer he got, the clearer his view became. "Window panes?" he murmured. "Window panes mean . . ." He gasped. "*Oh no!*"

Wombat flailed his paws.

He wiggled his body.

He tried to steer with his snout.

But it was pointless; he couldn't change his path.

Suddenly the window was *there*, right in front of him, glass and windowpanes and all. Behind it, Wombat caught a glimpse of a bedroom. Purple carpeting. A canopy bed. A curly-haired girl, holding a long-furred, snow-white rabbit.

"Tilda!" Wombat shouted.

Tilda's ears lifted. Her eyes darted toward the window. When she saw the animal outside, she let out an ear-piercing squeak. "Wombat!"

For a split second, the two animals locked eyes. Then

Wombat slammed into the glass with a booming, echoing *CRACK!*

"Not again," Wombat groaned—just before he went plunging toward the ground.

Inside the stone turret, Tilda leapt out of Chrysanthemum's arms. Pedaling her legs wildly, she made a beeline through the air, landing unsteadily on the edge of the windowsill. Ignoring Chrysanthemum's cries of dismay, she pressed her nose up against the glass. On the other side of the window, Wombat was spinning rapidly downward. "He really did it," Tilda said in amazement. "He came to save me."

There was a muffled thud as Wombat crashed into a thick pile of leaves, sinking out of sight. Tilda dug her nails into the windowsill as she waited for him to emerge. "Come on, Wombat," she urged.

Wombat's snout appeared first, popping out through the orange and gold leaves. Next came his head, then his back, and finally all four paws. Only when he had climbed out of the pile—limping, but whole—did Tilda breathe easily again. Wombat lifted his snout, looking longingly up at her window. "My prince of a wombat," she swooned. Rising onto her hind legs, she placed her front paws on the window, blowing Wombat a kiss.

Down on the ground, Wombat shook a few stray leaves

off his back. In the darkness, he could just make out the shape of a rabbit pressed against the turret window. "My princess in waiting," he said. He blew Tilda a kiss. "I'll be back for you soon."

38

A Newspaper Ad

Susan lay on her back in the sand, letting the waves wash over her toes. She loved the shock of the icy nighttime water, the way it sent a jolt running through her every time. Right now, she needed a jolt. It had been twenty-four hours since she'd arrived home, and still there was no sight of her parents. She fiddled with the lantern she'd brought out with her. "What am I going to do?" she murmured. She'd thought about going after her parents, but of course she had no idea how she would get to Truberg. Besides, what if she did find a way there only to discover her parents had already left?

She looked over at Rigby, who was swirling his tail through the sand, looking downright elated by the wiggly lines he was leaving behind. *He* didn't seem the least bit bothered by their predicament. Then again, Susan knew what he didn't. They were running out of food.

Earlier, while Rigby was out galloping in the yard, Susan had counted the cans left in the cupboard. *Four*. That was all. Enough for two meals each. Susan flopped over onto her stomach, reaching for the newspaper she'd been carrying around all day—the one that had told her where her parents were. She needed a distraction before she went out of her mind with worry. She knew she could get by for a day or so without food; she'd done it in the circus when they ran out of oats. But Rigby? That dog downed his meals in two seconds flat. As it was, she was worried she wasn't feeding him enough. She couldn't bear the thought of giving him nothing at all.

The lantern cast a dim glow on the paper as she flipped unseeingly through it. If only the crops were still in season. But the fields would be dry and barren by now. She could always go to the McLarens. They lived in the next house over, several miles up the road. But Susan knew they had enough trouble feeding their own six kids. She flipped furiously to the next page, barely glancing at the articles. Maybe she should check the fields anyway, she mused. There could be a few late bloomers left . . .

Rigby pressed his wet nose into her hand, drawing her out of her thoughts. She smiled, mussing up his fur. "Don't worry, Rigby, I'll figure something out."

The dog let out a whine, nosing at the paper.

"You interested in some light reading?" Susan joked.

Rigby responded by nosing the paper again. When he lifted his head, he'd left behind a wet splotch, smack in the center of an advertisement.

Susan's heart skipped a beat when she noticed two familiar green *T*'s at the top of the ad. *Visit Toddle's Toy Emporium!* it read. *Only 20 miles down Route 3!*

Susan looked over at Rigby. "Are you trying to tell me something, Rigby?"

Rigby barked, wagging his tail against the sand.

Susan ran her finger over the ad's smudged black ink. In the corner, there was a picture of a large, shiny egg. *Toddle's Golden Egg*, the ad touted. *The first of its kind!* A large building rose in the background, trimmed in white.

Susan stared at the image, transfixed. If Bertie and the others had been successful, they would be in that very building right now. She glanced toward her house, where her old bike was propped up against the back stoop. She held up the lantern to get a better look. The bike was slightly rusted and had several pairs of old ballet shoes tied to its basket, but the tires looked full. Six months ago, it had been working just fine.

Susan scratched Rigby under his ears. Whether he'd meant to or not, he'd planted a seed in her head. And as she kept staring at the bike, it began to sprout, shooting up at record speed. "Twenty miles isn't bad on a bike . . ."

Rigby barked loudly.

Susan jumped up. "You know what, Rigby? I'm thinking tomorrow might be a good day for a ride."

A Promise

Bertie raced to the pile of leaves where Wombat had landed. He'd made Smalls stay behind in the bushes, but he suddenly found himself wishing the bear was with him to calm his nerves. He'd seen Wombat climb out of the leaves, which meant he was alive, but he'd been limping pretty badly. What if he'd broken a bone? Where would Bertie find a veterinarian in a closed-up toy store?

"Wombat!" He halted to a stop in front of the animal and dropped onto his knees. Quickly, he ran a hand over Wombat's body, feeling for any bumps or cracks underneath his fur. Everything felt normal. Bertie blew out a sigh of relief. It looked like he was just bruised. He scooped Wombat up in his arms, petting his back. "You're one lucky guy, you know that? I don't know what you were thinking!" Wombat let out a snort, nudging his snout into Bertie's wrist. "You crazy wombat," Bertie said with a sigh. "I'm just glad you're okay."

He was about to head back to the bushes when he noticed Wombat lift his snout sharply, his eyes focused on something in the distance. Bertie followed his gaze up to the tall stone turret of the Toddles' house. There, pressed up against its window, was the dejected form of a long-furred rabbit. *Tilda*.

Suddenly it all made sense. That's what Smalls and Wombat had been doing. They'd been trying to get to Tilda.

Bertie hurried back to the bushes, placing Wombat down next to Smalls. "We're not giving up that easily," he told the animals. "It's my turn to try. But you both stay here." He pointed at the bushes, giving Smalls his sternest look. He wanted the animals where he knew they would be safe. "Stay," he repeated. When he was satisfied that Smalls had understood the command, he took off for the stone house. He was pumped full of energy. He'd seen Tilda with his own eyes! Now all he had to do was find a way up into that turret . . .

He was halfway across the Toddles' rolling lawn when the door to the stone house suddenly flew open. A man stepped outside, nothing more than a vague outline in the darkness. The man turned in his direction, and for a second Bertie worried he'd been spotted. But the man just lifted his head to the sky, sinking down on the front stoop.

Bertie dove behind the closest tree, trying to make himself as small as possible—Invisible Boy, just a slip of a shadow. As long as he stayed hidden, he could sneak over to the house when the man went back inside. Maybe he'd even forget to lock the door behind him!

For what felt like hours, Bertie waited there, his back pressed up against the tree, the pounding in his ears drowning out the sounds of nature. He felt like he was in one of those games: Spot What's Wrong with This Picture. Any minute now the man could come pluck him up for the win. But time crept by and the man didn't move. He just sat there staring up at the sky, as if he hoped to find an answer spelled out in the stars.

The air became colder. The moon rose higher. Crickets chirped the minutes away. And still Bertie stood there, waiting. His legs grew tired. His empty stomach protested loudly. Finally, he peeked out again. The man hadn't moved an inch. From Bertie's vantage point, he looked like a statue, turned to stone. Bertie's stomach groaned. It was clear the man wasn't leaving anytime soon, and he was starving. He'd just have to try again later. Moving as stealthily as he could, Bertie snuck back to the Emporium, stealing his way from tree to tree. "Time for a dinner break," he whispered to the animals. He lifted Wombat in through the store's window, then he and Smalls followed behind.

Bertie went to the candy room and returned with his hands full of caramel squares and peanut brittle and a jar of honey for Smalls. Just a few days ago, he would have been ecstatic at the thought of eating a dinner of candy. But he barely tasted it now as he dropped down in the Stuffed Jungle next to Smalls, blindly popping food into his mouth. His brain was too busy racing a mile a minute, rejecting ideas for saving Tilda as fast as he could come up with them.

He could—no, that wouldn't work.

Or maybe—no, much too dangerous.

How about—no, he'd get stuck for sure.

Next to him, Smalls and Wombat were snorting and grunting away, as if they too were brainstorming possibilities. Bertie looked over at Smalls with a sigh. "I've got nothing," he told him. Clearly Smalls and Wombat didn't have anything either, because the clock kept ticking the hours away, and they were no closer to Tilda than they'd been that morning. Bertie looked out the window. The man was still on the front stoop of the Toddles' house, staring up at the sky. With a sigh, Bertie rested his head on Smalls's back.

There was only one way he could think of to get to Tilda at this point, a way that didn't involve risk or danger—except to him. It was simple, really. He was going to have to knock on the Toddles' door.

"Tomorrow," he said to himself. After Chryssy helped him get back into the woodshop to see what was in that glass box, he'd march right over to the Toddles' house and beg their daughter for Tilda back. He'd do whatever it took. Maybe Susan would even be here by then, and they could go together. The thought of seeing Susan again made him feel all jumpy inside. He had so much to tell her. "Tomorrow I'm going to fix this," he told Smalls. "I promise."

Smalls let out a soft grunt, almost as if he'd understood. Before long, the bear's breathing began to deepen beneath Bertie's head, and Wombat's snorts faded into quiet snores. All around him, Bertie could hear the store whirring and settling. Already he recognized most of its sounds: the toy bird that chirped on the hour, the swish of hot air balloons as they swayed overhead, the floorboard that creaked each time the ever-looping train rolled over it. It made him feel like, in some strange way, the store belonged to him. Or like he belonged to it.

He rolled onto his side, pressing his face into Smalls's soft fur. "If only we could stay here forever," he whispered.

But, of course, they couldn't. The future was hanging over them, a big, flashing question mark. It seemed so wide and empty, the unknown. He squeezed his eyes shut tighter, willing the fear away. He still had at least one more night in the Emporium, one more night with Smalls. He wrapped his arms tightly around the bear. Soon, the sounds of the store had lulled him to sleep, like the best kind of bedtime story.

40

Damsel in Distress

"Step sixteen, final fur fluffing." Tilda gave herself an extra-rough fluff. With a sigh, she began the process all over again. "Step one, shake out fur."

"I'm off!" Chrysanthemum announced in an unusually chipper voice, interrupting Tilda's furious shaking. She pushed open the window, letting a burst of fresh morning air into the room. "There, now it's just like being outside!"

"Sure, if outside had walls and a ceiling," Tilda grumbled.

"You have the cutest squeak," Chrysanthemum declared, ruffling Tilda's fastidiously groomed fur. "You're like my real, live squeak toy!" She gave Tilda a final pat before prancing out of the room, her dress flouncing behind her.

"Why is *she* so happy?" Tilda pouted as she moved on to step two of her grooming process, picking an invisible speck of dirt out of her fur. "She's never happy! And doesn't she know this is *not* a happy day? A whole night has passed and Wombat still hasn't returned! When is he going to come save me?" She stomped her paws against the purple carpet. "If I have to spend one more day locked in this bedroom, I swear I'm going to . . . to . . . EXPLODE!"

"Tsk, tsk, sweetie. No need to yell."

Tilda jumped. Kay had landed soundlessly on the windowsill. "Stop sneaking up on me like that," she said with a scowl.

"My, my," Kay replied. "Aren't we in a funk today?"

"Maybe we are," Tilda sniffed. "But we have a right to be! Wombat was right here, Kay! He was so close! And now he's gone again." She dropped her head on her paws, looking utterly forlorn. "I'm never going to be saved."

"Well, look at that," Kay said, applauding with her wings. "Ladies and gentlemen, we've got ourselves a damsel in distress!"

Tilda glared up at Kay. "I'm not a damselfly. I'm a long-furred, snow-white Angora rabbit!"

"You're missing the point, honey." Kay paused, studying Tilda. "You know what I say? I say it's time you get off that long-furred butt of yours and save yourself."

"My long-furred *what*?" Tilda replied.

"Think about it, sweetie. Sometimes we're our own best

hero." She waved a wing at Tilda. "I'm heading off now to fly south for the winter. Maybe I'll see you when I return. Or," she added with a wink, "maybe I won't." With that, she took a swan dive off the window, flapping into the horizon.

Tilda buffed her tail against the carpet, looking bewildered. "Save myself?" she murmured. "That's impossible!" She twitched her nose, buffing faster. Minutes passed, and nothing. Then slowly a look of excitement crept onto her face. "Or maybe," she said, climbing to her paws, "it's not."

41

Super Spies to the Rescue

"Are you dead?" Bertie felt a poke in his side. He rolled over, clinging to his dream. In it, his mom was about to tell him something important about the wooden boy. *"Of course he means something to us, Bertie,"* she began. *"He's—"*

"Hell-oooo? Yoo hoo!" A finger jabbed Bertie again, and this time his eyes reluctantly fluttered open. A small boy, maybe four or five, was leaning over him, his forehead wrinkled up in concern. "You're alive!" he said breathlessly.

Bertie sat up, rubbing his bleary eyes. For a second, he couldn't remember where he was. Then, all at once, it came rushing back. Eating candy. Brainstorming ways to find Tilda. Falling asleep on Smalls. Just after dawn, he'd left Smalls and Wombat in the Stuffed Jungle and crept into the wooden tree to hide. He must have fallen back asleep—and, judging by the clamor of voices outside and the little boy staring down at him, slept right through opening.

"Do you speak?" the little boy asked. "Or are you a ghost? Is that why you're so quiet? The kids are all saying there's a dead boy in the tree, but what if they meant a dead *ghost*?" He inched away from Bertie, his face looking slightly green.

"I'm not a ghost," Bertie said groggily. His tired brain was suddenly kicked into overdrive. How many kids had seen him sleeping? How long, exactly, had he been asleep? "Do you know what time it is?" he asked the boy.

"Almost lunchtime," he replied. He beamed, revealing three missing teeth. "I can't wait, wait, wait for lunch! My mom says I can have a brownie-butter sandwich. 'Just this once,' she said, but I'll take it because once is better than never, right?"

"*Lunchtime?*" Bertie leapt to his feet, keeping his head low as he scrambled down the stairs. He was supposed to meet Chryssy at noon! If he was late, he could miss his only chance to get back into the woodshop.

"Wait!" the little boy called after him.

But Bertie didn't even pause. "Enjoy your sandwich!" he called back, jumping down from the last step. The store was only slightly less crowded than it had been yesterday. He had to squeeze through twins arguing over a doll and leap over a circle of kids rolling a chattering globe across the floor. "Alaska is America's largest state!" Bertie heard the globe announce.

He made a quick stop in the Stuffed Jungle to make sure Smalls and Wombat were safe before dashing across the main floor and up the stairs. He kept his eyes peeled for Susan as he ran, but he didn't see her anywhere. *That means nothing*, he assured himself. He planned to do a thorough search for her and Rigby after he left the woodshop. Then he'd go straight to the Toddles' house. He hadn't forgotten his promise to Smalls. He would find a way to get to Tilda today, no matter what it took.

Bertie was short of breath by the time he reached the Fine Woods room. Chryssy was leaning against a shelf of wooden houses, her arms crossed over her chest. Her poufy dress was black today, and on her feet were a pair of glittery black Mary Janes.

"It's twelve oh three," she snapped.

"Sorry, I—"

"Are you wearing the same thing as yesterday?" she interrupted. Her eyes trailed from his shirt to his pants, clearly horrified.

Bertie looked down. For the first time, he noticed the truly terrible state his clothes were in. His shirt was wrinkled and splattered with dirt, there was a chocolate stain on one of his suspenders, and his pants—too short for him as it was—were now grass-stained and sticky with marshmallow residue. "I like this outfit," he said defensively.

Chryssy wrinkled her nose. "Luckily, I brought you a change of clothes." She held out a massive pair of sweat-pants and an equally large T-shirt. Both had been sloppily painted black, so that big goops of paint were clumped all over them.

Bertie raised his eyebrows. "You want me to wear that?"

"Of course." Chryssy gave him an exasperated look. "Everyone knows that spies are supposed to wear black to blend in."

"Since when did we become spies?"

Chryssy sighed dramatically. "Bertie, Bertie, Bertie. You have so much to learn." She tossed the clothes at him. "There's a bathroom down the hall. Go change. Now!"

A hundred different retorts sprang to Bertie's tongue, but he swallowed them all back. He needed Chryssy to get him into that room. If that meant wearing black clothes, then black clothes it was. *After this, I'll never have to see her again*, he reminded himself as he pulled the outfit on over his own clothes. He had to roll the sweatpants over four times to get them to stay up. He cringed as he faced the mirror. He looked as though he'd been sent through the washing machine, and he'd come out shrunken instead of the clothes.

Gritting his teeth, he stepped back into the hall. "Here I am," he said. "All spied up and ready to go."

No one answered him.

Bertie looked around. He didn't see Chryssy anywhere. All he saw were the bewildered stares his outfit was getting. "Is that boy supposed to be a clown?" a little girl asked, making a stuffed bird swoop through the air.

"Clowns don't wear *black*, Sarie," a girl who was clearly her older sister scoffed. "He must be dressing up as a mime. Maybe he's doing a show later!"

"Don't stare, girls," their mom scolded. She lowered her voice, wrapping her arms around her daughters. "Maybe he's from another country where that's the style."

Bertie pushed past them, his face flushing red. "Hello?" he called out. He poked his head back into Fine Woods. "Chryssy?"

"Pssst."

Bertie tilted his head, listening.

"Pssst."

There it was again! And now a soft whistle accompanied it, floating out from inside an antique-looking cupboard in the hallway. He walked over to it, trying to ignore the way people's eyes kept following him as they wondered about his outfit. "Chryssy? Are you in there?"

The door to the cupboard opened a crack. Out sprung a single strand of curly hair. "Shhhh," Chryssy whispered.

Without meaning to, Bertie broke out laughing. "What are you *doing*?"

The cupboard door opened all the way. Chryssy climbed out one limb at a time. "A spy must be able to hide in any locale," she said knowingly. "I read about it in one of my dad's spy novels last night."

Bertie laughed even harder. "You did research for this?"

In response, Chryssy clasped her hands together, pointer fingers up, mimicking a weapon. "I learned this move from a film," she said, whipping her hands from side to side.

Bertie could barely breathe now, he was laughing so hard.

Chryssy aimed her pretend weapon at his forehead. "Spies don't laugh, Bertie! They prepare."

Bertie choked back another burst of laughter. Chryssy looked so *solemn*. And she was doing this for him, after all . . . He clasped his hands together, giving it a try. He grinned a little as he whipped them from side to side. "This is kind of fun," he admitted.

Chryssy smiled smugly. "Now," she said, lowering her voice. "Time for Code WW300. When I blink three times, that means to follow me."

"Wouldn't it be easier just to tell me—"

Bertie snapped his mouth shut when he saw the glower creeping onto Chryssy's face. "Three blinks," he said quickly. "Got it."

Chryssy glanced stealthily around. Then she squeezed her eyes shut three times in the most exaggerated blinks Bertie had ever seen. She took off running, keeping her back to the wall.

Bertie watched her for a second. "When in Toddle's," he murmured. He took off after her, his back to the wall as well.

They were nearly there when Chryssy made a sudden stop. "Hide!" she mouthed. An instant later, the echo of footsteps rang out in the hallway. Bertie looked frantically over his shoulder. He spotted only one door that wasn't plastered in STAY OUT! or DANGER! signs. He dove for it, Chryssy close on his heels.

They threw themselves inside at the same time. It was a supply closet, brimming with mops and brooms and cleaning supplies. Bertie yanked the door shut behind him, just as the footsteps grew closer. "We did it!" he exclaimed. He looked over at Chryssy, expecting to find her bursting with pride. If she hadn't heard those footsteps so early, they would have been caught for sure. But instead of Chryssy, he found himself face to face with a mop.

Chryssy spit several strands of mop out of her mouth. "Blech!" she shrieked.

Bertie tried not to laugh. He really did. But she just looked so funny with the mop hanging over her face, only her eyes peeking out—almost like Rigby. He couldn't help it; a laugh just slipped right out. Glaring at him, Chryssy grabbed another mop off the ground and dropped it onto his head. "There," she said. "Now we're both mop heads."

For a second, they stared out at each other through their mops. Then at the same time, they broke into peals of laughter. "Now we're really in disguise," Chryssy choked out.

"Super Spies to the rescue," Bertie wheezed. "Wherever you need cleaning!"

They were still laughing as they shook off their mops. But when Chryssy opened the door an inch to peek outside, they both fell silent. "Coast is clear," she told him in a hushed tone.

Once more, they kept their backs to the wall, hurrying the rest of the way. It took Chryssy a total of four seconds to pick the lock this time. And then they were in.

The room looked exactly as it had yesterday: bare, clean. The only change was a new note on the chalkboard: *Tod-*

dle's Staff Meeting, 1:30 p.m., Room 21R. "I'll stand watch," Chryssy said.

Bertie nodded. His eyes were already on the cabinet. Quickly, he rolled a log of wood over to it. When he climbed on top, he could just reach the key.

"What's in it?" Chryssy asked from the doorway. Her eyes were trained on the hallway, darting left and right, right and left.

"Give me a second to get in!" Bertie slid the key into the lock, and the cabinet swung open with a creak. In the center sat the small glass box. This time, Bertie had a clear view of what was inside.

It was a carved wooden boy. The boy looked like all the others: blue eyes, a smattering of freckles, a baseball cap over his painted red hair. But there was something different about him too. He'd clearly been made a long time ago, for one. He was a little faded, like a picture that had been left out in the sun too long. And there was something about the details—the curve of his hands, the swoop of his hair—that set him apart from the others.

Carefully, Bertie removed the top of the box and slid the boy into his hand. Where the wood on the others had been smooth and glossy, this one was softer, worn around the edges. Bertie turned it over, admiring the workmanship.

That's when he noticed it. On the sole of the boy's shoe, where the wooden toys were all stamped with two green *T*'s, a name was carved instead. It had faded over the years, and Bertie had to look closely to make out the letters. *ESME.*

"Esme," Bertie murmured. He turned the word over on his tongue, testing it out. It was an unusual name, but it felt familiar to him somehow, as if he'd heard it before . . . He closed his eyes, thinking hard. He could feel a memory tugging at him, like a flounder on the end of a fishing line. But no matter how hard he pulled, it refused to break through the surface.

"Bertie!" Chryssy's voice snapped him back to the present. "Code XYZ!"

"What does that mean?" he asked absently. He ran a finger slowly over the four letters.

"It means our time is up. We need to get out of here!"

"Why didn't you say so?" Bertie dropped the wooden boy back into the glass box and shoved it into the cabinet. He was just about to follow Chryssy into the hall when an idea tiptoed its way into his mind. His looked up at the note on the chalkboard. *Staff meeting, 1:30 p.m.* That meant Stan would be out of the wood shop again . . . His eyes flickered over to the desk, where a spool of tape was sitting.

"Come on!" Chryssy hissed from the hallway.

Bertie didn't have time to think it through. He quickly tore off a piece of tape. When Chryssy wasn't looking, he plastered it to the lock on the inside of the door. He had no idea if it would work; he'd never tried to jam a lock before. But he knew he had to get back into that woodshop. Down the hallway, Chryssy glared at him over her shoulder, gesturing wildly for him to follow. Bertie took one last glance at the door. Then he broke into a sprint, holding up his sweatpants as he hurried back to the store.

42

A Photograph

He'd done it! The tape Bertie had put on the door had actually worked.

After he and Chryssy had made it safely back to the Fine Woods room—and he'd stripped out of his second layer of clothing—Chryssy had taken off to have lunch with her parents. She'd told him she'd be back at the store soon, and made him promise not to go home while she was gone. He'd almost laughed at that. "Believe me, I'm not going anywhere," he'd told her. "Not if I can help it."

He'd spent the next half hour waiting anxiously for one thirty to roll around. He didn't want to draw attention to Smalls and Wombat by visiting them yet again in the Stuffed Jungle, so instead he'd walked up and down the aisles of the store, staying on constant lookout for Susan and Rigby. He'd passed a demonstration for the Ice Spinner, Toddle's newest toy, paused to admire fossils in the Prehistoric Cave, and caught author Julie Heckles reading from her latest book in the Reading Room. But even his search couldn't distract him from what he'd seen in the woodshop.

He just couldn't stop thinking about that name. *Esme.* He kept hearing it in his head, over and over, like a song lyric stuck on repeat. But still, no memories came to him. All he had were four little letters, tickling at the back of his mind like a headache.

The instant the clock struck one thirty, he'd raced back to the woodshop and found he could actually get in. Now, for the first time, he had the place to himself. He couldn't help but stand there for a moment, just looking around. Before, with Chryssy chattering and his pulse racing, he hadn't noticed the room's smell. But suddenly he couldn't *not*. He breathed in deeply. The fresh, crisp scent of wood seemed to dust every surface, lingering faintly in the air. It was a good smell, and it brought a string of pictures to his mind. A warm bed. An early morning chill. A glass bottle sitting open on a bedside table, trying to capture that very smell.

Bertie's hands tightened at his side. *Was that a memory?*

He breathed in deeper, trying to remember more. But minutes passed, and nothing else came. He blew out a long, slow breath. His chest felt twisty all of a sudden, and there was a pesky burning behind his eyes. He blinked rapidly. Sometimes a glimpse of a memory was almost worse than no memory at all. It was like someone giving him a beautifully wrapped gift, then snatching it away before he could open it.

Frustrated, Bertie sulked over to the desk. Deep down, he'd been hoping to find some kind of magic button in the woodshop, a switch to flip his memories back on. But there was no such thing as magic. If there was anyone who should know that, anyone who'd had the terrible un-magic-ness of the world shoved at him again and again, it was Bertie. He blinked back more tears. "My memories are gone," he muttered to himself. "There's no magic switch. There's no magic trigger. There's no magic."

The words were barely out of his mouth when he saw them. Two new wooden carvings, sitting unassumingly on the edge of the desk: a long-tongued sun bear and a hairy-nosed wombat. Bertie's heart squeezed. Those carvings hadn't been there earlier; he was sure of it.

He picked them up carefully. Had Stan made them? Did that mean he'd seen Smalls and Wombat? That made no sense at all. If someone had seen the animals, there would have been chaos. Screaming. Running. Sirens. Bertie had witnessed what had happened in the city. So then where had these come from?

Bertie sat down at the desk, his eyes glued to the wooden animals. They looked so much like Smalls and Wombat, perfect, tiny clones. He couldn't resist running a finger over the ridges of their fur, the lines of their faces. What would it take, he wondered, to make something so real? To start with a simple block of wood and bring it to life? Bertie glanced at an untouched chunk of wood on the other side of the desk. Next to it, a small whittling tool rested in its case.

Without stopping to think, Bertie lifted the tool. The heft of it felt good in his hand, and suddenly he was reaching for the wood too, tracing his thumb over its rough, flat surface. He couldn't resist drawing the tool to the wood, just to see how it would feel. He dug it in a little, imagining how the wood would drop away, dusting to the ground as a figure took shape before his eyes.

He'd been carving for several seconds before he even realized he was doing it. But once he'd started, he couldn't make himself stop. His fingers seemed to have a mind of their own as they flew over the block. He had no idea what he was doing, but in some strange way, he could *feel* it: where the crest of the head should be, how deep to carve for the tail, the way to twist his wrist to make curls of fur. Nothing had ever come so naturally to him before.

Soon he was completely absorbed in it, the rest of the

world slinking away until only his hand and the wood existed. He stopped hearing the tick of the clock. He stopped feeling the chair beneath him. He wasn't Bertie anymore, but a carver, pure and simple. And slowly, shapes began to emerge from the wood. Thick clouds of fur. A long, narrow snout. Four padded paws. Bertie didn't stop until the block was gone, shapes and curves and lines in its place.

He held the freshly carved figure up in front of him. It was rough around the edges and there were several chunky areas that looked more like leaves than fur, but there was no mistaking what it was: a shaggy, mop-like Komondor dog. Bertie touched the dog's fur, wondering how to make it as smooth and even as the bear's. "Maybe if I etch little lines . . ." he muttered.

He reached out to turn the desk lamp on for a better view. But he was paying more attention to the dog than the lamp, and his hand bumped clumsily into it, sending it toppling over. The noise shook him out of his reverie. The rest of the world came rushing back in. The seat underneath him. The ceiling above him. The clock ticking away on the wall.

The clock. His eyes flew to it. Two fifteen. Bertie gasped. More time had passed than he'd realized. Stan could be back any minute. Quickly, he righted the lamp. It was heavy, made of iron, and its fall had jostled open a thin drawer underneath the desk. The drawer had no handle, so Bertie hadn't even known it was there. He stood up as he went to close it. He had to get out of there before Stan returned. But as his hand landed on the drawer, a photograph inside caught his eye. In it, a woman was bent over a table, carving a block of wood. Her long, red hair tumbled over her shoulders and a smattering of freckles shone on her smiling cheeks.

Something hummed deep inside his bones. He'd recovered very few memories since his accident, but almost every one had revolved around that woman. *His mom.*

Bertie grabbed the photo, his hands trembling. A thousand thoughts slammed into each other at once, making his head spin.

Stan, Toddle's resident woodcarver, had a photo of his mom.

His mom had been a woodcarver.

Stan must have known his mom.

"Are you lost?"

At the sound of a man's voice, Bertie looked up with a yelp. Standing in the doorway was the small, gray-haired man. *Stan.* A deep wrinkle settled between Stan's eyebrows as he stared at Bertie. "This is a restricted area of the store, son," he said gently. "Do your parents know where you are?"

Bertie opened his mouth, but no sound came out.

"Hey, what are you doing with that?" Stan asked as he spotted the photo Bertie was holding.

Bertie snapped his mouth shut, looking down at the photo. In his head, he saw two flashing, neon paths. In one, he was talking. In the other, he was running.

"Son?" Stan said, his voice rising. "I don't want to have to call security."

Bertie gulped. His heart was pounding so hard it felt as though there was a herd of elephants in his chest. He opened his mouth once more, but still no words came out. He had a million questions to ask, but that word—*security*—had rendered him more speechless than ever. So he did what any sensible, terrified boy would do. He clutched the photo to his chest and he ran.

"Stop!" Stan called after him. "Bring back my photo!"

Bertie just ran faster, ignoring Stan's shouts as they rang out behind him.

43

More Questions Than Answers

Stanley Candor stood in the doorway of his woodshop, looking completely and utterly bewildered. "That boy . . ." He stared down the hallway at the spot where Bertie had disappeared around a bend. Clutched in Stan's hand was a wooden figurine with a broken arm, and he held it up now, staring at its bright red hair and freckled nose. "It's uncanny," he whispered. "The resemblance . . . it's almost as if . . ." He shook his head. "That's impossible."

With a sigh, Stan brought the wooden boy over to his desk to fix him up. But when he saw the dog Bertie had carved, the figure slipped from his grip. "So *that's* what he was doing in here," he said, plucking the dog off his desk. He turned the carving this way and that, examining every inch of it. Slowly, his eyebrows lifted and his cheeks took on a reddish sheen.

"Well, now," he murmured, admiring the arc of the dog's tail. "I haven't seen talent like this since Esme."

Meanwhile, twenty miles away, a note was pinned to the door of a small farmhouse, flapping lightly in the breeze.

Dear Mom and Dad,

Please don't worry. I'm all right. I left the circus and found my way home. I have some business to take care of at Toddle's Toy Emporium, so I'm riding my bike there. But I'll be back, I promise. I never plan on leaving again!

Love always and forever, your daughter,

Susan

P.S. The color of my room is perfect! It's like sleeping in the middle of the ocean. I hope you don't mind the new touch. My friend Rigby added it.

"I wonder if they've found my note by now," Susan panted. She wiped a stray bead of sweat off her forehead as she pedaled furiously on her bike. Rigby looked up at her from the bike's basket, two black eyes peeking out from a bundle of fur. An old, beat-up map poked out next to him.

"Grrr?" he barked.

"And I wonder if we'll find Bertie," she went on. "And I wonder if he's found Tilda . . ." She sighed. "Having more questions than answers is never a good thing, is it, Rigby?"

"Grrr," Rigby barked again, shaking the fur out of his face.

"Well, we should get some answers soon." Susan's legs were starting to ache, but she just pedaled harder. "Only a few more miles till we're there."

"Grrr!" This time Rigby's bark was unmistakably excited.

"I know, Rigby," she said softly. "I miss them too."

A Toddle

The photograph felt hot in Bertie's sweaty hands, as if it might combust at any moment. All he knew was he needed to be alone; he needed a place to think. He zigzagged through the store, making his way toward the wooden tree. When he was alone on the top landing, he would figure out what to do. He would figure out what this meant. He allowed himself another glance at the photo. His mom had a distant smile on her face, as if she were lost in her carving.

"Wait!" A hand grabbed Bertie's arm from behind, squeezing tight. For a second Bertie's heart stopped. Stan had found him. He was going to kick him out, and then he'd never see Smalls or Wombat or any of the others again. He whirled around, ready to wrench his arm out of Stan's death grip and run.

Chryssy stared back at him. "I've been looking for you

everywhere!" She pouted. "I told you not to go far! I got worried you'd left! But it's okay, I forgive you." She said it all in one breath, and she finally paused to suck in air. "Anyway," she went on, oblivious to Bertie's silence, "at least you're here now. So what should we play first?"

Before Bertie could muster up a reply, a stern voice rang out through the air. "Young lady! Where do you think you're going? You told us you were doing your homework!" A pair of parents strode toward them: a bald man with deep frown lines and a fancy silk bowtie, and a skinny woman with a pale face and watery eyes.

Immediately, Chryssy's face reddened several shades. "Mom! Dad!" she croaked. "I, uh, I am! I'm . . . writing an essay about the store!" She flashed them a bright smile.

"Then why don't you have a notepad with you? You know, I've just about had it up to here with your shenanigans lately." Chryssy's dad held a hand up to his forehead, demonstrating where, exactly, he'd had it up to. His lips tightened as he glowered down at his daughter. "Your mother might give in to your incessant shrieking, but I'm the man of the household and I . . ." He trailed off as he noticed a woman in a Toddle's uniform flagging him down. "What is it, Marie?" he asked, turning away from his daughter.

Marie rushed over, bowing her head. "I'm so sorry to

bother you, Mr. and Mrs. Toddle, but we seem to have a slight problem with the inventory."

Bertie stumbled backward. Did she say *Mr. and Mrs. Toddle?*

He stared dumbly at them. That would make them the owners of Toddle's Toy Emporium. Which would make Chryssy . . . the daughter of the owners of Toddle's Toy Emporium. Piece by piece, it all came together: how much she knew about the store, how well she knew her way around, how she could get into locked rooms. He looked at Chryssy, who suddenly seemed fascinated by her sparkly black shoes. "You're her," he said wonderingly. The girl who had Tilda.

"A life-sized sun bear?" Mr. Toddle suddenly roared. "But I never placed an order for any life-sized sun bears!"

Bertie's heart thudded as he jerked his head toward Mr. Toddle.

"Life-sized lions, yes," he continued with a frown. "And I believe we once carried a life-sized polar bear. But that would have been white . . ."

"No, no, a life-sized *black* sun bear, with a marking of a yellow horseshoe on its chest," Marie recited. "The client was very specific. She said her son saw the bear here yesterday, and now he wants it for his birthday."

Bertie gulped loudly. Any other thoughts flew out of his

mind. All he could think about was Smalls. Someone wanted to buy him.

He had to get to him. He had to help him.

"I have to go," he mumbled to Chryssy. Then once again he took off, hoping against hope that Smalls was somewhere safely out of sight.

45

A Sloppy, Gummy, Sticky Mess

Tilda stood on the floor, facing the bowl Chrysanthemum had abandoned there. It had once held the contents of a supersized ice cream sundae, but the ice cream was long gone, and all that was left now was a sloppy, gummy, sticky mess. Bright red cherry juice dribbled over chunky bits of chocolate that swirled into thick, gooey caramel and melted with dark, syrupy fudge. For a rabbit who would choose cleanliness over carrots, that bowl contained everything that was wrong with this world.

"Revolting," Tilda muttered. For a second she looked pleased by her use of one of Wombat's favorite words. But when she glanced back into the bowl, her expression turned to a grimace. She let out a loud sigh. "This is for you, Wombat," she said.

She jumped into the bowl.

A few minutes later, Petunia bustled into the room, pushing a cart with her. Usually, that cart was Tilda's cue to dive
under the bed, where she could stay out of sight until Petunia was safely gone. But today, Tilda positioned herself right
in the middle of Chrysanthemum's pile of toys. "It's time,"
she whispered. Breathing as softly as possible, she held very,
very still.

"Oh my!" Petunia exclaimed, crouching in front of Tilda.
"What did Chrysanthemum do to this poor stuffed animal?"

Tilda stared up at her, unblinking. At first glance, she
was almost unrecognizable. Where her fur had once been
glossy and smooth, it was now sticky and matted with caramel and fudge. Where it had once been white as snow, it
was now streaked red with cherry juice. And where there
had once not been a single burr or speck of dirt, there were
now chunks of chocolate peeking out between tangles. "This
one's definitely coming with me." She picked Tilda up and
dropped her into the cart. "Looks like I've got my work cut
out for me today."

Tilda sat very quietly in the cart, assuming her best toy-
like pose. Only when Petunia bent down to gather up more
toys did she allow herself a single excited tail twitch.

Her plan had worked.

● ● ●

Smalls wasn't among the furry toys in the Stuffed Jungle. He wasn't hiding behind the honey display in the candy room or jammed in between the life-sized lions that lined the stairwells. He wasn't, as far as Bertie could tell, in the store at all. And neither, for that matter, was Wombat.

Bertie's palms started to sweat. Had Smalls been found already? What if, at this very moment, he was in the backseat of someone's motorcar, all gift-wrapped and tied in bows? Bertie's eyes fell on the window he'd climbed out of yesterday. It was wide open. Maybe Smalls had sensed danger and fled on his own! It would explain why Wombat had gone missing too.

Clinging to that hope, Bertie raced to the door. The regular exit was jammed up with a family arguing over who got to ride their new rocking horse first, so he cut through the pool of colorful balls, wading past a pigtailed swimmer and ducking under a game of catch to get to the exit on the other side. It was the door that he, Smalls, and Wombat had snuck in through on their very first night at the Emporium. He couldn't believe that was only two nights ago. It was funny how you could live someplace for five years and never feel at home, and somewhere else it took only a few days to feel like you'd always been there.

Bertie scrambled out the door, emerging into the sunlight.

"Smalls?" he called out quietly, creeping along the perimeter of the store. "Wombat?" A Toddle's employee walked past, and Bertie quickly lowered his head, pretending to be searching for something. "Where is that quarter?" he asked loudly.

He might never have noticed the footprints if he hadn't been pretending so intently to look for the fake missing coin. But there they were: the faintest imprint of two paws in the grass, one small, one large. "Bingo," Bertie said.

He looked out across the vast expanse of lawn, his eyes following the trail of paws. To an untrained eye, those footprints could have belonged to a whole spectrum of animals: a rabbit and a large raccoon or a squirrel and an even larger badger. But there was no doubt in Bertie's mind. They'd been left behind by a sun bear and a hairy-nosed wombat. And he was going to follow them.

46

Four-Leaf Clovers

Petunia hummed under her breath as she rolled the cart of toys into the bathroom. "One day I'm going to make that girl clean up after herself," she muttered. She turned the bathtub on, mixing bubbly soap into the water. "We'll see how dirty she gets her toys after that!"

Tilda's eyes flickered left and right as Petunia poured more soap into the tub, her back to the cart. "It's time," Tilda said under her breath. She crouched down low, screwing up her face in determination. "I did this at the circus," she reminded herself. Sprinting forward, she took a flying hop out of the cart.

Her ears flew back as she soared through the air, executing a flawless flip–double axel–flip that landed her smack in the middle of the hallway, a solid three feet outside the bathroom. She shook out her sticky, stained fur. "I still got it," she said smugly. With a quick glance over her shoulder, she took off for the stairwell at her speediest hop. "I'm coming for you, Wombat!" she whispered.

Inside the bathroom, Petunia whirled around to face the cart. "Okay, little bunny," she said, rubbing her hands together. "I'm ready for you." She paused, frowning. Inside the cart sat a filthy dollhouse, a tarnished tiara, a splotchy paint set, a grubby I-Pee-Like-You doll, and a grimy pony. But there was no sticky, stained rabbit.

"Now, what did I do with that bunny?" Petunia scratched her head. "I could swear I put it in the cart. Sometimes I think this house is making me lose my mind." She turned on her heels. "I must have left it in the bedroom." Sighing, she headed back to Chrysanthemum's room.

Tilda, who had made it halfway down the stairwell, froze mid-hop, flattening herself against the wall. Only when Petunia had safely disappeared into Chrysanthemum's bedroom did she resume her hopping. "Only two and a half more flights to go," she said. "Then I'm free as a bird. Or," she corrected herself, "a rabbit."

"Remember to keep your head low, Smalls," Wombat preached. "A discovered sun bear is not a helpful sun bear."

Smalls resisted a groan. He knew Wombat was hurting—

and not just from his bruised leg. A few minutes ago, Smalls had caught him gazing longingly up at the turret window, a glimmer of tears in his eyes.

"There must be an open entryway *somewhere* in the vicinity," Wombat continued. They were crouched under a bush near the Toddles' house, hunting for a way for Wombat to get inside.

"Maybe around back," Smalls suggested.

Wombat eyed a rhododendron bush near the back of the house. "We'll make a dash for it," he announced. "But we must proceed with the utmost caution."

"I know," Smalls said wearily. He lifted his voice in an imitation of Wombat. "A discovered sun bear is not a helpful sun bear."

"Precisely." Wombat nodded curtly. "On three. *Un, deux,* go!"

The two animals sprinted toward the rhododendron bush, ears flapping and tails wiggling. Smalls dove under first, several branches snagging at his fur. Only when he'd managed to pull all four paws out of sight did his pulse slow. "I'll be happy when we don't have to hide anymore," he said as Wombat crawled in next to him.

Wombat was too busy scanning the back of the house to reply. "Do you see that window?" he asked excitedly. "I would venture to guess I could get in through there if you gave me a boost."

Smalls peeked out. "Which one—" he began, but he abruptly fell silent. Because for the first time, he saw what lay behind the Toddles' tall stone house. A shiver ran down his spine. "Oh," he breathed.

It was a field. But not just any field. Poking out between the blades of grass were four-leaf clovers, hundreds of them, their petals unfolding in the sun. He took a step closer, and then another, forgetting to stay concealed, forgetting about everything except the clovers. And then he was there, close enough for them to brush his fur and tickle his paws, close enough to smell their fresh, sweet scent and see their petals swaying in the breeze. He was sure Wombat was scolding him, but he didn't hear a word of it. As he crouched down, plucking several clovers with his teeth, he felt all the fears and worries that had been bouncing around inside him up for so long suddenly take flight, floating away like balloons.

"Smalls!"

Bertie's voice reached him as if from a distance. Smalls turned around just in time to see a red-faced Bertie flinging his arms around him. "You don't know how glad I am to see you, Smalls," he said breathlessly. "I was worried you were locked up in a backseat somewhere, all tied in bows . . ." He squeezed Smalls tighter. "But you're here. You're okay."

Smalls tossed his head back, flinging a mouthful of four-leaf clovers into the air. They sprinkled down around them, a shower of petals, of luck, of *home*. He gave Bertie's hand a lick. "I'm better than okay," he said.

47

Freedom

Back in Toddle's Toy Emporium, Chrysanthemum was stomping furiously along the second floor. "Everything is ruined!" she steamed, her face going beet red. "EVERYTHING!"

It had been a very bad afternoon for Chrysanthemum Toddle. "I finally, *finally* find a friend who can't choose *Lauren Nicola* over me, and my parents have to go and scare him away." She pulled several boxes of board games off a shelf, watching as they crashed down in a messy heap. "You would have thought I had the *plague* by how fast he ran away from me." She swept a hand over another shelf, sending a slew of jump ropes clattering to the ground. "Now I'm back to being friendless Chrysanthemum, who even Golden Eggs can't help!" She picked up a huge rubber snake and flung it at the wall. "It's. Not. FAIR!" With a shriek, she threw herself on top of a stack of fuzzy suitcases.

A woman in a Toddle's uniform shuffled nervously over. "Are y-you okay, Miss Toddle?" she stammered.

"Leave me alone!" Chrysanthemum howled in response.

"If you'd like," the woman replied, stumbling over her words. She hurried off, her top lip quivering.

Chrysanthemum lifted her head to spit out a mouthful of fuzz. "Stupid fuzzy suitcases," she grumbled. "Who wants a suitcase with fur all over it anyway?"

All of a sudden, she grew very quiet. She knit her eyebrows together, as if she was thinking hard about something. "Actually," she said slowly, "maybe *I* do." She jumped to her feet, bringing one of the suitcases with her. "I'm taking this," she informed the nervous employee. Without bothering to wait for a response, she stalked off, dragging the purple fuzzy suitcase behind her. "I, Chrysanthemum Toddle," she announced to no one in particular, "am running away."

Meanwhile, in the Toddles' house, Tilda descended the final step of the stairwell, looking victorious. "Now for part two," she whispered. "Or, as Wombat might say, part *deux*." She twitched her red-streaked tail. "And he thinks *he's* the one with the high IQ!"

Tilda took a deep breath. "This is it," she told herself. "If this works, I'll be free." She cocked her head, a solemn look crossing her face.

It was a strange word, *free*. To those who were, it was just four measly letters, looped together. But to those who weren't, it was more than just letters, more than just a word. It was a feeling as strong as fireworks, a feeling that sparked and boomed, setting every nerve ablaze with hope. "Free," Tilda repeated.

She looked to her left. She looked to her right. No one was coming. "Here goes nothing," she murmured. Ducking her head, she raced toward the kitchen. She was halfway there when she heard the worst possible sound a rabbit on the run could hear.

A voice.

A furious, shrieking, temper-tantrum-worthy voice, pouring in from the front of the house.

"No one wants to be friends with me here? FINE! I'll go somewhere else!"

Tilda looked frantically around. She was in the hallway, not a single piece of furniture to conceal her. With a grunt, she dove under the oriental rug.

Chrysanthemum came stomping into the hallway, dragging a fuzzy purple suitcase behind her. "I bet people at Millstone Academy will like me," she muttered angrily. "If my parents won't send me, then I'll just have to go myself!" She clomped toward the stairwell, so caught up in her misery that she didn't notice the Tilda-shaped lump in the carpet, even as she rolled her suitcase right over it.

"Tilda and I will go together," she continued. "A girl and her rabbit! It will be like my very own fairy tale." She bumped the suitcase up the stairs, her voice growing fainter. Tilda waited several more seconds before emerging from the carpet. She had two wheel tracks running through her dirty, stained fur, but she didn't bother shaking them out. Instead, she stared up the stairs, at the spot where Chrysanthemum had disappeared. Regret flashed through her eyes. "I'm sorry, Chrysanthemum," she whispered. "I think I'm actually going to miss you. But I have a wombat to find."

With that, she took off hopping toward the kitchen. She was panting a little by the time she reached her destination. She looked up at the tall metal trash can. It had a swinging door at the top to deposit trash. Or, in the rare situation, an Angora rabbit.

"Part two, here I come." Closing her eyes, Tilda sprung into the air. She crashed through the door, landing on her head inside the trash can. "Victory," she mumbled through a mouthful of paper towels. Righting herself, she settled down on a pile of orange peels. "Now, I wait."

48

Brains and Brawn

"**P**ardon me, Smalls!" Wombat called out. He was crouched beneath the rhododendron bush in the Toddles' backyard, trying to get his friend's attention. "Could you *please* return to the bush now?"

Out in the field of clovers, Smalls licked Bertie's face, oblivious to Wombat's calls.

"Ahem, I require your assistance over here, Smalls!" Wombat tried again.

Smalls pawed at a patch of four-leaf clovers, a look of pure bliss on his face.

Wombat burrowed nervously at the ground. His gaze flickered toward the tall stone house. "I'm trying, *mon amour*," he whispered.

At that second, the back door of the house flew open. Bertie yanked Smalls behind the bush just as Petunia strode outside, a bag of garbage clutched in her hand. She wrinkled up her nose as she flung the bag into a large trash can in the driveway. "Pee yew! Those chicken pot pie leftovers are stinking up a storm! Thank goodness for trash day." She dropped the lid on the can and hustled back inside.

The instant she was gone, Wombat waddled over to the door as fast as his short legs could carry him. "There must be a way to nudge this door back open . . ." he murmured, nosing at it with his snout.

"Squeak!"

Wombat froze.

"Squeak squeak squeak!"

His eyes flew to the trash can, where a series of familiar-sounding squeaks were being emitted. "Do you hear that, Smalls?" Wombat asked. "It sounds almost like . . ."

He trailed off as the lid of the trash can flew up. Out popped Tilda, a mangled scrap of garbage bag between her teeth.

Wombat's eyes widened to the size of saucers.

Smalls's eyes looked like they might pop right out of his head.

"How in the world . . . ?" Bertie murmured.

Tilda hopped down to the ground. The sun illuminated her stained and tangled fur, and bits of garbage clung to her ears. But underneath it all, she was beaming.

"Tilda," Wombat breathed. He sailed toward her as if in a trance.

"Wombat!" Tilda met him in the middle, and for a second they just gazed at each other.

Wombat's eyes filled with tears. "You are a true vision of beauty," he said.

"Who cares about beauty?" Tilda scoffed. "I escaped all on my own, Wombat! I was the brains *and* the brawn of the operation."

Wombat laughed. "Well, then I retract my previous statement. You are a true vision of brains and brawn."

Tilda nuzzled his snout. "I missed you," she whispered.

Wombat ignored the piece of orange peel that bounced off his paw as he nuzzled her back. "I missed you too, my love."

49

Bear in the Yard

While Wombat and Tilda were reuniting, Susan was busy consulting her map. "We're almost there, Rigby." She balanced her feet on either side of her bike, her cheeks pink from the exertion of the ride. "Now the question is, is the entrance to our right or our left?" She held the map up in the air, twisting it this way and that as she studied it. "I think it's to our left. No, our right. Ugh, it's impossible to tell!"

Rigby jumped out of the basket, landing steadily on the ground. Sticking his nose in the air, he took several long sniffs. "Interesting," he murmured. He took a final sniff. Wafting toward him on the breeze were four distinctly familiar smells: a Smalls smell, a Wombat smell, a Tilda smell, and a Bertie smell.

With an excited bark, he took off trotting in the direction they came from.

Susan watched him go. With a shrug, she crumpled up the map and tossed it back into the basket. "Wait for me!" she called out. She kicked off, pedaling after the dog.

A few minutes later, they came to a tall, unmarked fence. Behind it, a stone house rose into the air. Past that, a majestic green building trimmed in white soared in the distance. She recognized it immediately; it looked just like it had in the newspaper ad. *Toddle's Toy Emporium.*

Rigby pawed at the door to the fence, letting out a loud whine. Susan hopped off her bike and leaned it on the ground. Her eyes went to the green building in the distance as she walked to the door. It seemed very far away. "Is this how we get in?" she asked doubtfully. She gave the handle a little a jiggle. It was unlocked. All it would take was one pull, and the door would come swinging open. She bit down on her lip, looking nervously around. A motorcar rattled past, but otherwise the street was surprisingly quiet.

Rigby barked again, nudging at the door.

"Are you sure?" she asked.

He let out an insistent bark, thrusting his head toward the handle.

"Okay . . . " she said hesitantly. Before she could lose her nerve, she grabbed the handle and pulled.

• • •

For as long he lived, Bertie knew he would never forget that moment. One minute he was watching Tilda and Wombat nuzzle, and the next minute the back door of the Toddles' gate was swinging open, and Rigby was bounding inside. Susan followed behind him in blue pants and a yellow sweater, her hair lifting in the breeze. "Bertie!" she cried when she saw him.

Bertie couldn't move. For two days now he'd imagined running into Susan, seeing her sweep of blond hair and excited smile. So now, as he stared at her in the backyard of the Toddles' house, he wasn't sure he could believe his own eyes.

"Well don't just *stand* there!" she scolded. She walked over, giving him a hug. As her arms tightened around him, it finally hit him.

"You're real," he said.

Susan laughed. "Of course I'm real." She pulled back, studying him. "Have you been spending too much time with toys?"

"No, I just . . ." Bertie broke into a smile, the kind that crinkled up his eyes and made him feel toasty warm inside. "I'm just really glad you're here."

Meanwhile, over by the trash can, Rigby was running in excited laps around his friends, his tail wagging wildly. He stopped in front of Tilda and sniffed curiously at her dirtied fur. "What happened to *you*?"

Tilda lifted her head proudly. "I'm a true vision of brains and brawn," she informed him.

Wombat wiggled happily. "She's precisely right." He looked up at Rigby. "And you, my friend, are a sight for sore eyes."

"I'll second that." Smalls gave Rigby such an enthusiastic nudge that he sent him tumbling backward.

Rigby let out a gleeful bark. But as he scrambled back to his feet, an ear-piercing shriek made them all freeze in place.

"BERTIE!"

Chrysanthemum Toddle stood in the back doorway of her house, clutching a bulging purple suitcase. "I'm so glad you're here, Bertie! How did you find me? I know you're upset that I didn't tell you I was a Toddle, but I can explain and—wait. What is *Miss-Queen-of-the-School* doing here?" She glared suspiciously at Susan. "I thought you were off living the glamorous circus life! And who are *they*?" Her eyes darted around the yard, growing larger and larger as they bounced from Rigby to Smalls to Wombat to Tilda. "And why are they with my Angora rabbit?" She screwed up her face as she took in Tilda's tarnished state. "And what *happened* to my poor Tilda?" Her voice grew louder and higher with every word. "What is going *on?*"

Bertie never got a chance to respond.

Because the air was suddenly filled with a shriek more piercing and earth shattering than even Chrysanthemum's.

Mrs. Toddle appeared behind her daughter, her face white with fear. "Bear in the yard!" she screeched. "Someone help! There's a wild, ferocious bear in my backyard!"

50
The Truth

In the woodshop of Toddle's Toy Emporium, Stan was carving away, his hand a blur as it flew across the block. "The resemblance . . ." he murmured. He gave his tool a twist, sending tiny flecks of wood raining to the ground. "If I didn't know better, I would swear . . ."

He paused, letting the block of wood drop from his hands. Digging into his pocket, he pulled out a photo. It was slightly crumpled and covered in thumbprints, as if it had been handled many times over the years. In it, a younger version of Stan had his arms wrapped around a small, freckled boy. He touched a finger to the boy's face.

"He's gone, Stan," he reminded himself. "Just like my Esme." He stuck the photo back in his pocket, shaking his head. "Anything else is just wishful thinking."

But a few minutes later, he paused yet again. He drummed

his fingers against the desk, looking thoughtful. "Perhaps I should go search for him," he mused. "He does have my photo . . . and he did look quite lost earlier . . ." He placed his carving tool gently back in its box. "Yes, I really should go make sure he's okay," he decided. Looking resolute, he stood up and took off down the hallway where Bertie had disappeared.

Meanwhile, in the field of clovers, Mrs. Toddle was having a conniption. "A bear!" she kept screeching, fanning herself as if at any moment she might collapse in a fainting spell right there in the grass.

"What is going on, Bertie?" Chrysanthemum yelled in between her mom's shrieks.

In the field, Rigby was whimpering and Tilda was squeaking and Wombat kept repeating, "This is quite ominous, quite ominous." The cries—animal and human—filled the air, a din of voices rising to the clouds.

In the midst of all the chaos, Bertie stepped quietly forward. He looked from Susan to Rigby to Wombat to Tilda and, finally, to Smalls. He should have been scared; he should have wanted to scoop them all up in his arms and run away to safety. But instead, he felt strangely calm. *I'm with my family*, he told himself, and the thought buoyed him, made him feel as tall as a giant and as strong as a hero.

He raised a hand in the air. "I can explain," he said evenly.

The animals quieted down first, then Chrysanthemum, and finally Mrs. Toddle. Bertie glanced at Susan. She gave him an encouraging nod.

"Tell us what's going on, Bertie!" Chrysanthemum demanded.

So Bertie did just that. He told them everything: about the circus, about the escape, about how he, Smalls, and Wombat had been living inside the Emporium. By the time he was finished, Chrysanthemum's jaw was hanging open, and Mrs. Toddle kept saying, "Oh my. Oh my, my, my."

Throughout Bertie's story, no one noticed the small, gray-haired man standing off in the shadows, listening intently. Only when Mrs. Toddle stopped oh-my'ing did he step into sight. "Bertie?" he said softly.

Bertie's eyebrows shot up at the sight of Stan. But where he had once been scared, he felt only courage. He walked over to the older man, holding out the photo he'd stolen from him. "Why do you have a picture of my mom?" he asked, his voice strong and clear.

Stan didn't take his eyes off Bertie as he closed the last

bit of space between them. "I have a picture of her because she's my daughter." He put a trembling hand on Bertie's shoulder. "Bertie," he said again, his voice filled with awe. "My grandson."

51

A Menagerie

"Catch!" Smalls flicked his tongue, sending a four-leaf clover zooming toward Tilda. She rose onto her back paws, snatching it easily between her teeth. The Toddles had constructed a temporary fence around the field of clovers while they figured out what do about the animals, but Smalls wasn't bothered in the least by it. As long as he could play with his friends, he'd stay inside any fence they wanted.

"Give me a harder one than that!" Tilda insisted. "Throw one for someone with brains *and* brawn."

"Okay . . . I call this my triple-curve speed throw." Pulling back his tongue, Smalls unleashed another clover. This one shot straight into the air, twisting left and right as it rose higher and higher.

"Mine!" Tilda hollered. She sprint-hopped after it, fur

flopping and ears bouncing. She probably would have caught it too, if a familiar voice hadn't made her stop short.

"Well look at you, honey."

Tilda's eyes flew to the sky. Hovering above her was a blue-feathered bird, the silver lining of her wings flashing in the sunlight. "Kay!"

"No longer a damsel in distress, I see."

Tilda fluffed out her still-soiled fur. "I'm a damsel in control," she said solemnly. "And this," she said, hopping over to Wombat, "is my reason for escaping."

Kay fluttered her wings at Wombat. "I'd forgotten how handsome he is. Look at you, sweetie. You went and snagged yourself a hottie!"

Wombat ducked his head. "I greatly appreciate the sentiment, ma'am."

"Ma'am!" Kay hooted. "This one's a keeper."

Tilda cast a sidelong glance at Wombat. "I know," she said, almost shyly. She looked back at Kay. "What happened to flying south for the winter?"

"It's funny you should ask." By now the other animals had gathered around. Smalls settled down in the grass with Rigby leaning against him. Kay circled slowly through the air, clearly enjoying having an audience. "My flock and I had just taken off on our cross-country flight when we came across the strangest lot of animals in the woods. Normally we wouldn't let something like that distract us, but believe me when I say this was a menagerie of animals worth looking at!"

"A menagerie?" Tilda cut in.

"It's a rare or unusual collection of animals," Kay explained.

"I know what it means," Tilda sniffed. "I'm *part* of one!"

Kay paused, glancing around at the cluster of animals beneath her. "Huh, I guess you are." She cleared her throat. "Anyway, we couldn't help but slow down and stare at these animals. I mean, there were lions there! As we were flying past, I heard one of the group—a zebra—say the strangest thing. He was talking about how he hoped his 'bunny bumpkins,' Tilda, was doing okay, wherever she was. Now I thought to myself: How many bunnies named Tilda are there in this world? Chances are he's referring to *my* Tilda.

"Believe me when I tell you how badly I wanted to stop and ask him. But in a flock we make decisions together, and I was overruled. 'We have balmy weather and beaches waiting for us,' the others kept saying. 'Who cares about a zebra and some bunny?' But honey, I cared. It was eating me up inside. I had to know: Did sweet little Tilda have a fling with a *zebra?* So I turned around and I came back. I figure I can survive an extra day in fall weather for a delicious tidbit of gossip like that. So, you have to tell me, T. Do you have a steamy past with a zebra?"

Tilda let out a scandalized gasp. "Of course not! My heart has always, and will always, belong to Wombat."

"So then what?" Kay snapped her beak eagerly. "Was he some kind of secret admirer?"

"You could say that," Tilda replied.

"Minus the secret part," Rigby interjected.

Smalls pawed at the four-leaf clovers sprouting up from the ground. He never had been one for gossip, but Kay's story had sent a chill running through him. "So you saw a zebra in the woods?" he asked. "And two lions?"

"That's right," Kay confirmed. "Couldn't believe my own eyes."

"Were there any other animals with them?" Smalls asked carefully.

"Yes!" Kay squawked. "There were two little hedge-hogs lounging on the back of one of the lions, as if it was the most normal thing in the world. And you won't believe this one." She paused dramatically. "There was an elephant! A real, live, actual elephant! Right in Maplehedge Woods. The funny thing was, I could swear I heard the others call him Lord something-or-other, as if he were some kind of royalty."

Smalls went rigid. Next to him, Rigby sucked in a breath.

"Lord Jest?" Wombat asked slowly.

"That was it!" Kay did a swoop through the air. "Lord Jest, a real, live elephant, plucking acorns off the tallest tree as if it was nothing but a shrub."

"So, he was okay?" Smalls pressed. "Not injured or hurt . . . ?"

"He seemed fine to me," Kay said. "He kept trumpeting at the top of his lungs, like he thought he owned the woods."

Smalls closed his eyes, relief flooding through him. Lord Jest was okay. He had found the other Lifers—and apparently Aflie and Gem, too. They were all together, *free*. His paws felt as wobbly as jelly as he pushed himself to standing. Next to him, Rigby's tail was wagging frantically and Tilda's nose was twitching happily and Wombat's big, round eyes were filled with what he could swear were tears. "Holy horseshoe," he said, speaking for all of them. "That's good to hear."

Susan knew she had to leave Toddle's. After Bertie had told her everything—about getting kicked off the train and chased through the city and, finally, sneaking into Toddle's—she'd gone for a walk around the property, trying to convince herself to go home. But the idea of leaving Bertie and Rigby and all the others behind, just to return to a silent, shuttered house . . . it left her feeling hollow inside, like a cupboard with no food.

"It's her. It's really her."

The voice drifted over to Susan, cutting through the laughter and noise spilling out from the Emporium. She froze. She would know that voice anywhere, would recognize its soft lilt and the rise and fall of its words. She spun around, every inch of her body tingling.

There she was, standing in the exit of the Emporium. There *they* were.

"We got your note," her mom said.

"We came as fast as we could," her dad said.

They looked so *normal*, her mom with her long, blond braid, her dad with his deep, easy laugh lines, as if it hadn't been six whole months since she'd seen them last. She was racing toward them before she even realized it, a wild kind of run, arms flying, legs spinning. She threw herself at them with full force. "Mom," she whispered. "Dad." And then they were nothing but a tangle: arms and legs and hair and tears, unable to tell where one ended and the others began.

"Finally," her mom said.

And as it so often goes between mothers and daughters, it happened to be the very thing Susan was thinking too. *Finally, finally, finally.*

Home

Inside the yellow cottage, Bertie was leaning against a buttery yellow wall. He shielded his eyes from the sun as he looked out through the wide picture window. On the other side of the room, Stan was talking on the telephone, murmurs of "Uh huh" and "Mmm hmm" rising around him. A distant bark floated toward the house, punctuating an especially excited "Of course!"

Through the window, Bertie could see the fence the Toddles had put up to rein in the *wild beasts*, as Mrs. Toddle kept calling them. But the animals themselves barely seemed to notice it. Rigby was running frenzied laps around his friends; Smalls kept winging four-leaf clovers off his tongue; and Tilda was catching them happily as Wombat picked scraps of garbage out of her fur.

Bertie had never seen the animals look so relaxed. He

cringed at the thought of them being sent away to another circus or a zoo—a place where they couldn't play or run or, worse, be together. Outside, Smalls tossed his head back, flinging up several clovers. As they spiraled into the air, he glanced toward the yellow cottage. For a second, his eyes met Bertie's.

Bertie thought of a dozen things at once: a warm bed and a real meal and a soft pillow and *home*, a word that used to mean nothing—to ring empty—and now suddenly meant everything to him. Smalls let out a happy grunt, and Bertie imagined him saying, *Me too.*

"Thank you!" Stan said loudly, jolting Bertie back to the present. A smile stretched across Stan's face as he hung up the phone. "It's official," he told Bertie. "Starting next week, you'll be enrolled in Tophorn Elementary, the local public school. It was a little touch and go there for a minute, since the school year has already started, but I think our spectacular story of finding each other swayed them." He let out a deep belly laugh. Bertie was amazed that such a huge laugh could come from such a small man. "Of course, we're going to have a lot to do before then," Stan continued. "You'll need freshly sharpened pencils and new notebooks and all the books for the school year."

Bertie fidgeted with the photograph of his mom, which Stan had said he could keep. He had no memory of attending school, of learning instead of working, reading instead of shoveling manure. He wondered if there would be a cafeteria like he'd heard Susan talk about once. He wondered if he'd get to eat real, hot lunches served on freshly scrubbed trays, instead of dry oats out of dirty glasses. "That's great," he said softly.

"And then there's the matter of your bedroom," Stan went on. He put a hand on Bertie's shoulder and led him to a room at the end of the hall. It was small, but it contained a real bed and a wooden desk and a chest of drawers, and it was all his. "We'll need to get it set up to your liking. Maybe we can go shopping for some new things later today? Toddle's has a whole bedroom department. Plus, we'll pick up a few new toys." He winked at Bertie. "A perk of living on the Toddles' compound is that the toy store's never far away." Stan paused, eyeing the dirty, torn, shrunken outfit that Bertie had been wearing for days on end. "Let's add some new clothes to our shopping list too."

Bertie nodded mutely. He found he couldn't talk; his words were too heavy with emotion to lift them on his tongue. So instead, he walked around the room, imagining sleeping in *his* bed and pulling clothes out of *his* drawers. Stan came over and squeezed his hand. "Are you doing all right?" he asked softly. "I know this is a lot to take in at once."

Bertie looked up at Stan. He had spidery wrinkles around his eyes that gave him the look of being just about to smile. There was a faint smattering of freckles across his nose, and when he did smile, *really* smile, Bertie was suddenly five years old again, and for a split second he could remember: a grandfather who pulled him onto his lap and whispered silly stories into his ear. "I'm just amazed," he said finally. "I never had a real room of my own at the circus. Or even a real bed."

A look of pain settled into the peaks and valleys of Stan's face. "If I had known you were alive, Bertie, I would never have allowed Claude . . ." He trailed off, shaking his head. "But he told me you died in the motorcar crash. He was the one there; I never thought he'd lie . . ." He cleared his throat. "Things will be different now, I promise." He gave Bertie a tight hug. He smelled like wood shavings and peanut butter sandwiches and something else too, something soft and grandfatherly. "We're getting a second chance. And speaking of second chances . . ." He reached into his pocket and extracted a small wooden dog: roughly carved but unmistakably Rigby.

Bertie could feel his face heating up. "I wasn't planning on using your equipment," he explained sheepishly. "I just saw it and . . . I couldn't help myself."

Stan waved a hand dismissively through the air. "Spoken

like a true carver." He turned the dog over in his hand. "I haven't seen this kind of raw talent since Esme—your mom—was a little girl. I taught her to carve, you know. She was the one who first made the little red-haired wooden boy. She based it on you, of course. She thought she'd sell a few here or there; I don't think she could have ever guessed how popular they'd become! Soon, I was helping her carve them to keep up with all the demand. It's a special thing, working with your daughter." A hint of tears shone in his eyes and he paused, composing himself.

"How did you end up working at Toddle's?" Bertie asked.

"Mr. Toddle himself called me up." Stan smiled at the memory. "He asked if I would like to become the Emporium's resident carver. I would sell my wooden carvings exclusively through Toddle's. I didn't have to think twice about it. Before your mom died, selling at Toddle's had been her dream. Now, carving these dolls, selling them here . . . it makes me feel like, in some way, part of her is still with me."

He tossed the wooden dog to Bertie, who caught it automatically. The wood felt rough beneath his fingers, and he suddenly wanted desperately to learn how to smooth it out, to make the carving truly come to life. "Maybe now you can help me with it," Stan said.

Bertie smiled up at his grandfather. "I'd like that."

For All the Vegetables

Later that day, the Toddle family stood huddled together behind the fence. "Oh my," Mrs. Toddle kept saying. "Oh my, my, my. What in the world are we going to do with these animals?"

"I suppose we could sell them to the Howard Brothers Circus," Mr. Toddle said thoughtfully. He scratched his pointy, bald head, his ever-present frown deepening. "Or maybe we could donate them to a zoo. I bet it would earn us quite a tax write-off."

"No way!" Chrysanthemum stomped a sparkly shoed foot against the ground. "I don't want Tilda and her friends going to some zoo!"

"Please don't shriek, Chrysanthemum," Mrs. Toddle pleaded. "You can keep Tilda if you'd like, but the others . . ." Her watery eyes flickered toward the menagerie. "They're wild beasts! They have to go where wild beasts belong."

"Which is behind bars," Mr. Toddle said firmly.

As Mr. and Mrs. Toddle launched into a debate over the merits of a circus versus a zoo, a strange thing happened. One by one, people began migrating over from the Emporium—kids and parents and even a few employees—all to catch a glimpse of the incredible menagerie taking up residence behind the Toddles' house.

"Look at that, Ma!" a pigtailed girl toting a huge Toddle's bag shouted as Smalls rose onto his hind legs, juggling several clovers on his tongue.

"Believe me," Smalls said. "After fire sticks, this is nothing." Soon, there was a full-fledged crowd gathered around the fence, cheering on the animals as they cavorted and played. "This is step twelve of my sixteen-step grooming process," Tilda informed a group of squealing girls as she buffed her tail against the grass.

"As you can see, I can burrow at almost precisely the speed of light," Wombat said. He sprayed a wall of dirt behind him as he burrowed away amid a barrage of cheers.

Next to him, Rigby played peek-a-boo beneath his fur and Smalls tossed and caught clover after clover. Outside the fence, kids laughed and applauded and begged for more.

"Well, if you insist," Wombat said, starting on a second hole.

The Toddles were so busy debating what to do about the animals that they didn't even notice the crowd. But Chrysanthemum did. She narrowed her eyes, stepping closer.

"I want a sun bear just like him!" she heard a little boy beg.

"Me too, Ma," the pigtailed girl declared. "Let's go back to the store and get a sun bear stuffed animal!"

"We don't sell sun bear stuffed animals," Chrysanthemum told them automatically. She took a step back. "But maybe we should." She looked over at her parents, who were still deep in conversation. "Of course," she said excitedly. "It's perfect."

Spinning on her heels, she marched back to them. "Mom, Dad, I have a solution," she announced, cutting off her dad's detailed analysis of hard money versus a tax write-off. "We should keep the animals right here."

Mrs. Toddle shrieked. Mr. Toddle frowned. "That's not an option," he said sternly.

Chrysanthemum gestured toward the people swarming the fence. "But think of how many shoppers they'll attract! And once the kids see the animals, they'll want to go back to the store to buy their very own toy versions for themselves."

Her dad was quiet for a minute, observing the group

around the animals, which was growing larger by the minute. "Hmmm," he murmured.

"Plus," Chrysanthemum pressed, "I promise to eat every vegetable you ever give me if we can keep them. Think of how many fewer toys you'd have to take from the store!"

"Hmmm," her dad said again. His face was scrunched up in his I'm-busy-calculating look.

"Don't tell me you're considering this, dear." Mrs. Toddle winced. "Toys for her vegetables are one thing, but these are wild beasts! Just look at that bear! He can't be trusted."

At the sound of the word *bear*, Smalls swiveled around.

Chrysanthemum stomped her feet against the ground. "You told me I could have anything I want if I eat my vegetables. Well. I. Want. The. ANIMALS!" She glared at her mom, her voice rising dangerously. "This is for all the vegetables!"

"Please don't shriek," her mom said nervously, plugging up her ears. "We simply can't keep wild *beasts* on the premises, Chrysanthemum," she continued, her voice growing louder the harder she plugged her ears. "We'll be ridiculed! We'll be sued! We'll be—oh!"

She let out a gasp. While she was busy yelling, Smalls had wandered over and was now standing right in front of her, his front paws resting on top of the fence. He looked at her with his big, warm, chocolate-brown eyes. "Wild is all relative," he said. He unfurled his long tongue and gave her a lick on the cheek.

Mrs. Toddle let out another gasp. "Well . . . I never . . ."

Smalls licked her again.

"Oh my!" Her cheeks flushed bright red. "You . . . you certainly are a charmer, aren't you?"

"I do try to live by the golden rule," Smalls said modestly.

A tiny laugh suddenly escaped from Mrs. Toddle. Her hand flew to her mouth, as if she were trying to hold it in. "Those grunts! You'd think he was talking to me!"

". . . and when you add the cost of food but subtract the cost of transportation and add the cost of grooming but subtract the cost of new toys for Chrysanthemum . . ." Mr. Toddle ticked numbers off on his fingers, oblivious to the bear standing right in front of him.

"You end up with a thirty-two percent profit margin," Chrysanthemum offered.

Mr. Toddle lapsed into a stunned silence. "Th-that's correct," he stammered. "But how did you know that?"

"If you paid any attention at all, you would know I'm very good in math," Chrysanthemum said primly. "So, does thirty-two percent mean they can stay?"

Mr. Toddle looked at Mrs. Toddle.

Mrs. Toddle looked at Smalls.

Smalls stretched out his tongue, licking Mrs. Toddle smack on the nose.

"I suppose if your father thinks it's a good idea . . ." Mrs. Toddle said.

Mr. Toddle scratched his bald, pointy head. "Who can say no to a thirty-two percent profit margin?" He slung an arm around his daughter's shoulders. When he looked down at her, he was almost, nearly smiling. "As long as you do the bookkeeping."

On the other side of the fence, Smalls sat back on his haunches. The sun was warm on his back and the clovers were soft under his paws, and everywhere he looked, there were his friends, Rigby cloud watching and Wombat burrowing and Tilda grooming. And, of course, over in the yellow cottage, Bertie.

And suddenly he could see it: how one day would bleed into another and leaves would fall and grow and fall again, and all along, they'd be together. They'd be home. He closed his eyes, letting the sound of laughter and cheers wrap around him, warm him to his bones. *I'm going to like it here,* he thought.

A Different Bertie

One Month Later

Bertie dropped down at his usual table in the cafeteria, the clatter of trays and the roar of voices swirling around him. He'd been at Tophorn Elementary for one month now, and still he got a chill every time he walked into that room, with its high ceiling and blindingly orange tables. There were so many kids, talking, laughing, joking, and he was one of them—not serving them cola or cleaning up after their messes, but right there, smack in the middle of it all.

"Have I told you how lucky you are to have Miss Shandelman?" Susan lowered herself into the seat across from him, her green-brown eyes shining.

Bertie grinned at her. "Only about a thousand times."

"Well make it a thousand and one. Mrs. Tompkins is officially the bane of my existence."

Bertie pegged a grape at her. "Is she worse than Claude?"

Susan tossed the grape back, allowing herself a tiny smirk as it bounced off his forehead. "Nope," she admitted. It was their new favorite mantra. When school got hard or exhausting, or Mrs. Tompkins made Susan want to climb into one of Wombat's burrows and never come out: *Was it worse than Claude?* The answer was always, always no.

Bertie rooted around in his new green backpack. Rigby had gone nuts when he'd seen the color of it, throwing his front paws on Bertie's shoulders so he could get a better look. "I made another one," he told Susan, tossing her his latest creation.

It was a wooden carving of a sun bear, his long tongue curling up to catch a four-leaf clover. Every detail was stunningly lifelike, as if someone had taken the real Smalls and shrunk him down to toy size. Susan studied the figure, admiring its smooth finish and clean edges, the way its warm brown eyes seemed to gaze right into hers. "It's your best one yet," she declared.

"Is that Smalls?" Chrysanthemum cooed. She snatched the carving out of Susan's hands as she plopped down next to her. "So cute! You guys will not believe what Smalls did this morning on my way out of the house . . ." She trailed off as something caught her eye a few tables over. "Ah ha!" she crowed. "Don't look now, but Lauren Nicola is definitely checking out our table! I think she's totally jealous that I'm sitting with the new boy and Miss-Queen-of-the-School— *ahem*, I mean Susan," she corrected hastily.

Bertie exchanged an amused look with Susan. *Just go with it*, he mouthed.

"There are definitely some eye daggers coming from their table," Susan agreed, pressing her lips together to keep from laughing.

"I knew it!" Chrysanthemum looked triumphant as she took a bite of her broccoli-cauliflower–brussels sprout sandwich. "Oh, I meant to ask you guys. Did you see this?" She pulled a slightly crumpled sheet of newspaper out of her purple backpack. "It was in this morning's paper."

Misfit Menagerie Ignites Craze! the headline read.

Bertie's eyes widened as he stared at it. It reminded him of the first article he'd read about the Menagerie, back before he'd ever met Smalls. That felt like a different lifetime. A different Bertie. He scooted closer to his friends. As they all bent their heads in to read—Chrysanthemum giggling and Susan's blond hair brushing the table—it occurred to Bertie that maybe, in a way, it was.

Misfit Menagerie Ignites Craze!

What began as an unlikely friendship between a boy and four unusual animals has turned into a nationwide craze. Bertie Candor first met the Misfit Menagerie, as they're known, while working at the now defunct Most Magnificent Traveling Circus. Now, he and the animals—Smalls the sun bear, Rigby the Komondor dog, Tilda the Angora rabbit, and Wombat the hairy-nosed wombat—all live on the family compound outside Toddle's Toy Emporium.

"My grandfather and I just started carving the animals for fun," Bertie recounted.

"We had no idea what a frenzy they would induce," his grandfather, Toddle's resident carver, Stanley Candor, agreed. "Now we're just doing everything we can to keep up with demand!"

And what a demand it is. Every day, an estimated three to five hundred people visit the Menagerie in their home—an expansive field of four-leaf clovers. "Business has tripled since we adopted the Menagerie," Aurelius Toddle, owner of Toddle's Toy Emporium, told the *Daily Sun*. "Kids love our store more than ever!"

His daughter, Chrysanthemum, has a theory of her own. "It's the *animals* they love."

She has the sales data to back it up. Carvings of the Menagerie are flying off the shelf faster than any toy since the infamous "hotcake." It's keeping the grandfather-grandson team of Stan and Bertie busier than they could have dreamed.

"I carve in my sleep," Bertie joked to the *Daily Sun*.

But neither grandfather nor grandson seems to mind. Stanley put it best: "We're doing what we love, and we get to do it together." And judging by the lines winding out the door at Toddle's Toy Emporium, the nation is happy they are.

Acknowledgments

I've been so lucky to work with an incredible editorial team on the Menagerie series. Ben Schrank, Anne Heltzel, Gillian Levinson, and the rest of Razorbill: Thank you for being such smart, insightful, and inspiring editors. I've had so much fun working on these books with you!

Josh Adams & Adams Literary: Your faith in my writing—and in me—helped me get off the ground, and I am forever grateful for that.

Nate Resnick: Over a decade later and it keeps getting better. Thank you for being my steady ground in a thrashing world, my safety net when I fear I might fall, my gourmet chef when I would otherwise be eating cereal, my constant pep-talker and first-reader and biggest fan, and, above all, my very best friend. I'm grateful to Cornell for many things, but most of all because it gave me you.

Susan, Fred, & Lauren Greenberg: I'll say it every time. I could never have done this without you. Thank you for being behind me from the beginning, for cheering when I need cheering and commiserating when I need commiserating, for being my support system and my own personal PR team and my outlet after fifteen-hour days of writing. I hit the jackpot when it comes to families, and I know it.

Maple the dog: Such great company when I'm glued to my computer for days on end, and such great inspiration when I'm writing about the friendship between humans and animals. You deserve extra bones!

Rachel & Randy Wachtel: You've put up with my crazy schedule and been there to celebrate every step of the way. I don't know what I'd do without your excited texts while you read (Rachel) and your fingernail-spitting jokes (Randy). Thank you for surpassing everything I could have dreamed a sister and brother-in-law could be.

Tyler & Cole Wachtel: Knowing I could read these books with you one day made writing them even more special. Only a few more years!

Sid & Minna Resnick: I love that I got to share this whole process with you. Who's able to say that they actually *enjoy* their in-laws? I'm so glad I'm someone who can.

Monica, Eric, Kyla, & Daniel Allon: Your enthusiasm and your gifts and your presence have always meant so much to me. This year wouldn't have been the same without you.

Jake and Sam Greenberg: If I could have hand-picked cousins, I would have chosen you. Thank you for always being so excited and supportive, and making everything more fun.

Sean Groman: You already feel like family, but by the time this book comes out, it will be official—and I can't wait!

Popi: I can't tell you how much I value your unfailing support and constant interest in my work over the years.

The Paper Lantern Lit team (Lexa Hillyer, Lauren Oliver, Rhoda Belleza, Angela Velez, Adam Silvera!): I'm a better writer for having worked with you all. This might not be a Paper Lantern book, but your support of me and my writing has transcended *Truth or Dare*, and I hope you know how much I appreciate that.

Anne Heltzel: What would my writing world be without you?? Not just as editor, but as friend, early reader, and of course, writing date cohort. This series is as much you as it is me, and that's my favorite thing about it.

Lucy & Theresa Nguyen: You've always been there for me (even if it meant traveling to Ithaca or Manhattan!) so it didn't surprise me that you were here for this part of my life, too. But it DID make me grateful! You're those rare kind of friends—ones I can both dream with and count on—and I'm so lucky to have you.

Stacey Schor: You are the only person who wrote up a list of questions for me after reading the first Misfit Menagerie, and I will never forget that! Your enthusiasm and friendship throughout this process have been amazing.

Meryl Lozano: I can't imagine any part of my life without you, especially not this one. Thank you for reading every book, being front and center at every event, and scrounging up kids for my trivia game. You put the BFF in BFFAT.

Finally, to all my other friends: I've been so lucky to have you support me—and my books—so whole-heartedly. Caren Gradwohl, Rachel DeHaven, Ali Black, Steph Surkin, Rebecca Crawford, Alison Karmelek, Joanne Barken, Sarah Rosen, Amanda Freedman, Kim O'Hara, Lauren Benjamin, Lindsey Blumenthal, Stacy Lessen, Lauren Lower, Jocelyn Davies, Rebecca Alimena, Myra Oneglia, Maria Gomez, and all the Cornell guys (& wives!), thank you for coming out to book events and listening to all the ups and downs and reading books written for kids just because I wrote them.

See where the adventures of Smalls, Rigby, Wombat, and Tilda began in: